Praise for *Babylon 5 Dark Genesis: The Birth of the Psi Corps*

"A solid, stand-alone novel ... A fascinating spotlight on the enigmatic, deadly telepaths."
—*USA Today* (recommended reading)

"*Dark Genesis* is the kind of rare tie-in book that equals, or even bests, the franchise whose world it borrows. If you've heard the ravings of *Babylon 5* fans ... then this book is for you. You'll get a glimpse into the world they enjoy so passionately."
—*Cinescape Online*

BABYLON 5™

Book I of Legions of Fire

The Long Night of Centauri Prime

By Peter David

Based on an original outline by J. Michael Straczynski

A Del Rey® Book
THE BALLANTINE PUBLISHING GROUP • NEW YORK

A Del Rey® Book
Published by The Ballantine Publishing Group
TM & copyright © 1999 by Warner Bros.

www.randomhouse.com/delrey/

Library of Congress Catalog Card Number: 99-90991

ISBN 0-345-42718-1

Manufactured in the United States of America

First Edition: December 1999

OPM   14   13   12   11   10   9   8   7   6   5

Keep your face to the sun,
so you will not see the shadow.
—HELEN KELLER

prologue

The Drakh felt sorry for him.

Londo Mollari would have been surprised to learn that such considerations went through the Drakh's mind. Had the Drakh's sentiments been relayed to him, he would have been even more surprised to learn precisely *why* the Drakh felt sorry for him.

But he did not know, so he faced the Drakh with his jaw set, his shoulders squared, obviously doing everything within his ability to look cool and confident in the moment when his keeper would bond with him.

The Drakh, however, could already sense the accelerated heartbeats, the forced steadiness of the breathing, the general signs of rising panic, which Londo was pushing back by sheer force of will. All of this was clear, to the Drakh, for the bond upon which he and Londo would operate was already beginning to form on a subliminal level.

His name was Shiv'kala . . . and he was a hero. At least, that was how the other Drakh tended to speak of him, in whispers, or when they communed in silence, having abandoned the need for verbal speech.

Among the Drakh, there was none more brave, more diligent, more pure in his vision of what the universe should be. Nor was there any who was more sympathetic to his fellow creatures. This was what served to make Shiv'kala so effective, so pure, and so ruthless. He knew that in order to accomplish what was best for the galaxy, he had to be willing to hurt, terrify, even kill if necessary. Anything would be justified, as long as he never lost sight of the common good.

Shiv'kala loved the common man. He had the common touch . . . and yet, he had also been highly regarded by the Shadows. With equal facility and consistent equanimity, Shiv'kala was able to walk amid the mundanity and yet move among the gods. He treated the gods as mundanes and the mundanes as divine. All were equal. All were of a piece, and Shiv'kala could see all, understand all, and love all. He loved the cries of creatures at birth. And when he wrapped his hands around the throat of a creature he was sending to its death, he could glory in its scream, as well.

He was one of the most soft-spoken of the Drakh, and his mouth was pulled back in an almost perpetual smile—or at least that was how it was perceived by others.

That wasn't how Londo Mollari, imminent emperor of the great Centauri Republic, perceived him now. That much, Shiv'kala could tell even without the tentative connection that already existed between them. In all likelihood, Londo looked at that curious rictus of a smile and saw the satisfied grin of a predator about to descend on its prey. He did not know, he did not understand. But Shiv'kala understood. Understood and forgave, for such was his way.

The keeper was stirring within him. Londo would never have known it, but the keeper was fearful, too. Shiv'kala could sense that, as well. This keeper was relatively newborn, spawned from its technonest mere days before. Shiv'kala had attended to this one personally, for he knew of the great fate and responsibility that awaited it.

When the keeper had opened its single eye for the first time, blinking furiously against the light, it had been Shiv'kala's face into which it had gazed. It hadn't been able to see clearly, of course; Shiv'kala had appeared as a hazy image at first. But full vision hadn't taken long to develop.

The keeper had been born with a high degree of self-awareness, but no certainty as to what its purpose was in the broader scheme of nature. Its tendrils, mere stubs upon birth, had flickered around aimlessly, momentarily brushing against its parent. But the parent—as was always the case with keepers—was already a small, blackened husk. It had no soft thoughts to offer, no guidance to give as the offspring tried to determine just what it was doing and how it was supposed to do it.

"Calmly, little one," Shiv'kala had whispered, extending a grey and scaly finger. The keeper had tried to wrap its tendrils around the finger, and Shiv'kala had gently lifted it from its technonest. Then he had drawn aside his robe and placed the newborn keeper against his chest. Operating on instinct, the keeper had sought nourishment there—and had found it.

Shiv'kala had trembled slightly and let out a deep, fulfilled sigh as the keeper burrowed in, sucking and drawing sustenance from Shiv'kala's very essence. In doing so, the keeper had burrowed not only into Shiv'kala's soul but into the Drakh Entire. Shiv'kala would always have a special status with this particular keeper, would always be the most sensitive to its needs, wants, and knowledge. And the keeper, now that it was attuned, would be able to commune with any of the Drakh Entire at any given moment.

A magnificent creature, the keeper. It had nursed within Shiv'kala and had grown to maturity within three days. Now it was ready . . . ready to assume its most important job. Yet as prepared as it was to do so, and as much as its nature suited it for the task, when Shiv'kala opened his vest to extract it from its nourishing pouch, he was amused to discover that the keeper, likewise, was apprehensive.

What troubles you, little one? Shiv'kala inquired. Across from him, a few feet away, Londo Mollari was in the process of removing his coat and loosening the collar of his shirt.

He is very dark. He is very fearsome, the keeper replied. *What if I do not keep him properly? What if I fail in my task? Can I not stay with you, in the pouch, in the warmth?*

No, little one, Shiv'kala replied gently. *We all serve the needs of the universe. We all do our part. In that way, I am no different than you, and you are no different than he. He will not, cannot hurt you. See how he fears you, even now. Reach out. You can taste his fear.*

Yes, the keeper said after a moment. *It is there. He is afraid of me. How odd. I am so small, and he is so huge. Why should he fear me?*

Because he does not understand you. You will explain yourself to him. You will make him realize what is to be done. He thinks you will control him, always. He does not understand that we will not deprive him of free will. He does not understand that you will simply monitor our mutual interests. You will not force him toward what he must do . . . you will simply help us to guide him away from what he must not *do. He fears not being alone.*

That is strangest of all, said the keeper. *The one time I felt any fear . . . was when I was alone in my nest. Why would anyone or anything desire to be alone?*

He does not know what he desires. He has lost his way. He moved toward us, but then moved away, then toward and away again. He is without guidance. You will guide him.

But he has done terrible things, the keeper said with trepidation. *He destroyed many Shadows. Terrible. Terrible.*

Yes, very terrible. But he did so because he was ignorant. Now . . . he shall learn. And you shall help teach him, as will I. Go to him. See how he fears you. See how he needs you. Go to him, so that he may start his new life.

I will miss you, Shiv'kala.

You will not, little one. You will be with me always.

With that parting sentiment, Shiv'kala removed the keeper from its nourishment pouch. Its tendrils had grown marvelously during its sustenance period, and were now long and elegant. Moving with the grace that was customary for its species, the keeper glided across the floor and wrapped itself around Londo's legs. Shiv'kala could sense the tentativeness of the keeper. More, the keeper could sense the rising terror in Londo. Sense it, but not see it. Londo's face was a mask of unreadability, his brow furrowed, his eyes . . .

There was fury in his eyes. They bore into Shiv'kala, and had they been whips, they would have flayed the skin from his body. Shiv'kala decided that it was an improvement over fear. Fear was a relatively useless emotion. Anger, fury . . . these could be harnessed and directed against an enemy and be of great use to the Drakh. Furthermore, such emotions were far more alluring to the keeper and would make it much more comfortable with its new host.

Above all, Shiv'kala wanted to make certain that host and keeper blended smoothly, for they were a team. Yes. That was what Londo did not yet grasp: they were a team. Although the creature was called a keeper, implying a master-slave relationship, the reality of their binding went much deeper than that. It was almost . . . spiritual in its way. Yes. Spiritual. Others, including Londo's predecessor, had not understood that. He had not had enough time, or had simply been too limited in his perspectives.

But Londo . . . Londo possessed a much broader view, had much greater vision. Hopefully he would comprehend and even come to appreciate what he was undergoing.

Londo's back stiffened as the keeper crept up toward his neck. He had potential, Shiv'kala was certain of that. Perhaps the most potential any associate of the Shadows had ever shown. Perhaps even more than Morden had offered. Morden had been an excellent servant and had proven himself superb in carrying out orders. While he had been capable of actualizing the dreams of others, he had been noticeably limited. Morden had glowed brightly, but only because he had been basking in the dark light generated by the desires of Londo Mollari. Now Londo himself was in thrall to the Drakh, serving in turn the great philosophies and destinies of the Shadows, and that opened an array of new opportunities and possibilities. What was most important was the dreamer himself, and Londo was just such a dreamer. Yes, it promised to be most exciting indeed. Shiv'kala only wished that Mollari was capable of sharing in that excitement.

The keeper dug into Londo's shoulder, and Shiv'kala sensed the bonding. He smiled once more, reveling in the joy of the moment. Londo's emotions were a snarl of conflicts, fear and anger crashing into one another like waves against a reef, and he shuddered at the feel of the keeper's tendrils as they pierced his bare skin. That was all right though. He would adjust. He would learn. He would see that it was for the best. Or he would die. Those were the options, the only options, that were open to him, and Shiv'kala could only hope that he would choose wisely.

As for the keeper, Shiv'kala was pleased to sense that the creature was calming. Its initial trepidation was dissipating, as the Drakh had suspected it would. Furthermore, Londo's thoughts were coming into clearer focus, the blinders and shields falling away.

Londo stiffened slightly, as Shiv'kala eased himself into the Centauri's mind the way that he would ease his foot into a comfortable shoe. Within seconds, he inspected the nooks and crannies, studied Londo's deepest fears, viewed his sexual fantasies with morbid interest, and came to a deeper and fuller understanding of Londo's psyche than Londo himself had been able to achieve in years. Londo didn't know *how much* the Drakh had already discerned. His mind was still reeling and disoriented, and with a gentle push the Drakh steadied him, helped realign his focus.

Deciding that he would ease Londo into casual telepathy, he said out loud, "You will be all right." He spoke with his customary low, gravelly whisper, which forced people to listen closely. It was an amusing display of his power, albeit a minor one.

"No," Londo said, after a moment's consideration. "I will never be all right again."

Shiv'kala said nothing. There was no point in trying to

force a realignment of Londo's state of mind. Sooner or later he would learn and understand, and if it was later rather than sooner, well, that was fine. The Drakh Entire had great and impressive plans, long-term goals that spanned decades. The instant comprehension, understanding, and cooperation of a single Centauri—emperor or no—simply was not necessary. They could wait.

So Shiv'kala just inclined his head slightly, acknowledging Londo's remark.

Londo tried to sneak a glance at the keeper, but then looked away. Instead he started buttoning his shirt, pulling his vest and coat back on. "It . . . does not matter, in any event," he said after a moment. "Whether I am all right. It is my people that matter now. It is Centauri Prime, only Centauri Prime."

"You will rebuild. We will help," said the Drakh.

Londo laughed bitterly at that. "Unless, of course, you choose to blow millions of my people to pieces with your fusion bombs."

"If we do . . . it will be because you have chosen that path for us."

"Semantics," Londo said contemptuously. "You act as if I have free will."

"You do."

"One choice is no choice."

"The Shadows you killed when you destroyed their island . . . they had no choice in their fate," Shiv'kala said. "You do. Do not abuse it . . . lest we give you as much choice as you gave the Shadows."

Londo said nothing to that, merely glowered as he buttoned his coat. "Well," he said briskly, "we should begin this sham, eh? This sham of leadership. I, as emperor, with you guiding my every move."

"No." Shiv'kala shook his head ever so slightly. Everything he did, he did with minimal effort. "Not every move. Simply keep in mind . . . our goals."

"And your goals would be?"

"Our goals . . . are your goals. That is all you need remember. You will address the populace. They will be angry. Focus that anger . . . upon Sheridan. Upon the Alliance."

"Why? What purpose would that serve?"

Shiv'kala's skeletal smile widened ever so slightly. "The Alliance . . . is the light. Let your people look at it in anger . . . so that they will be blind to the shadows around them." As always, Shiv'kala spoke in a low, sibilant tone of voice. Then, ever so slightly, he bowed, and thought at Londo, *Good day to you . . . Emperor Mollari.*

Londo jumped slightly at that, clearly not expecting it. Reflexively he looked around, as if trying to figure out where the voice had come from, and then he looked at the Drakh. His lips drew back in anger, and he snarled, "Stay out of my head!"

But the Drakh shook his head and, with that same damnable smile, thought at Londo, *We will always be there.*

Then he extended a hand to Mollari. He did so as a symbolic gesture, for he did not truly expect Londo to take it. And Londo did not. Instead he stared at the hand as if it were dried excrement. Shiv'kala then stepped back and allowed the shadows of the early evening to swallow him up.

In a way, it felt as if he were returning home.

part i

2262-2264
Nightfall

— chapter 1 —

When Londo saw the creature emerging from the chest of the Drakh, it was all he could do not to scream.

A half dozen different ways of handling the situation tumbled through his mind. The first and foremost was to attack the Drakh, to grab a weapon—a sword, preferably—and step forward, the steel whipping through the air and striking home. In his mind's eye, he could see the monster's head tumbling free of its body, that hideous smile permanently frozen, perhaps even transformed into an expression of surprise. Then he would take the creature's head and slam it on a pole next to Morden's. He could stand side-by-side with Vir, and they would wave at them and laugh at the notion of anyone thinking that they could strong-arm or bully the leader of the great Centauri Republic.

Next he simply considered running from the room. That, in particular, seemed an attractive notion as he watched the one-eyed creature skitter across the floor toward him.

He thought of crying out for help. He thought of trying to arrange some sort of bargain. He would ask the Drakh what else he could offer beside himself—there had to be some way to appease the wrath of these beings, other than allowing that terrifying one-eyed animal to attach its parasitic self to his body.

He thought of begging, of pleading, of swearing eternal fealty to the Drakh or to the spirit of the Shadows. He thought of reminding the Drakh of all the times that he had been helpful to, and supportive of, their departed masters.

What do you want?

The question first had been posed to him by Morden, at a time that seemed eons ago. It was the question he was now tempted to hurl at the Drakh. What could he offer the Drakh that might suit them better than he himself? A terrifying array of possibilities came to him. He could offer them Sheridan or Delenn, the president and first lady of the Interstellar Alliance. Bring them to the Drakh, make them prisoners, or place keepers on them. Make them servants to the Drakh cause.

Or G'Kar! Great Maker, let them take G'Kar. Granted, he and the Narn had healed the wounds of their relationship, but there was still that vision he had had. The vision that one day G'Kar would be at his throat, primal fury boiling in his one true eye. Yes, he could turn G'Kar over to the Drakh and let *him* serve the collective Drakh will. Or . . . or . . .

He could . . . he could offer them Vir Cotto. That was a possibility. A good one. A great one, in fact. Let Vir lose his free will and independence to the Drakh—he didn't have much use for it anyway. The hard truth was, Vir was at his best when someone else was telling him what to do. So really, there wouldn't be any substantial difference from what his life had been, and it might even show marked improvement.

As quickly as all those options occurred to him, he dismissed them all. These were his friends . . . his allies . . . or at least, they had been. Though in terms of Sheridan, in particular, a deep and abiding desire for vengeance still burned brightly. It was, after all, Sheridan's Alliance that had bombed Centauri Prime back to the Stone Age, leaving the glorious world in flaming ruins. And was not Sheridan himself always quick to condemn the Centauri, in general—and Londo, in particular—for every slight, real or imagined?

But as Londo watched the one-eyed monster wrap itself around his leg and start to draw itself up his body, he came to the hideous understanding that he would not wish such a fate even on his worst enemy. That would most unquestionably *not* be Sheridan, and certainly not Delenn. No, despite their rapprochement, the title would likely still be held by G'Kar. Even on G'Kar, though, he would have no wish to see that . . . that *thing* . . . attach itself.

No one deserved that.

Including him.

It's not fair, he thought bleakly, *it's not right. I have to stop it . . . I can still pry it off me, throw it down, step on it, grind it beneath my boot . . .*

But if he did so, he knew what would happen next. The Drakh would pull out his detonator, as he had before, but this time nothing would stop his thumb from slamming home. And when he did, millions of Centauri would die, just like that. Fusion bombs hidden by the Drakh would detonate, and the victims would never even know what hit them. They would simply disappear in a massive burst of heat and flame, millions of lives terminated.

For a moment, just a moment, he considered it. After all, they would be dead and gone. Their torment would last a brief second or two at most, and then it would be over and done with. They would be placed within the safety of the grave. More accurately, their ashes would be scattered to the safety of the four winds, blowing the length and breadth of Centauri Prime. This, as opposed to Londo's living a life of continual punishment, the keeper monitoring his moves, sitting like a permanent, one-eyed pustule on his shoulder. Watching, monitoring, always there, never giving him a moment's peace . . .

Peace.

Well . . . that was what it came down to, really, wasn't it.

For when he pictured those millions of Centauri vanishing into the instant holocaust of the bombs, in his mind's eye they were battered and bewildered. Covered in soot and ash, clothes torn, looking to the sky in bewilderment and fear and wondering when the barrage would ever cease. They had no idea. No idea that Centauri Prime had been framed—made to appear warlike and aggressive. Framed by the Drakh, so that the galaxy would turn against them, and the Centauri would be left all alone in the darkness. No idea that he, Londo, was the cause for that deception.

No idea that they would still be living in peace, if it were not for Londo.

He had stretched forth his hand to lead his people back to the greatness he felt they deserved, as part of the great Centauri Republic, a term that had once prompted respect instead of snickering. Stretched forth his hand like a shepherd, but instead he had crushed his flock. His victims had cried out his name, and he had brought them to utter ruin. For if he had not desired to restore the Centauri Republic, then none of this would have happened. There would have been no Shadow involvement, there would have been no war upon the Narn. None of the heartache and grief that had permeated the last five years ever would have occurred. It was because of him, all because of him.

That's what this was, then. As the keeper poked and probed, as its tentacles swept across his bare skin and made him cringe inwardly, Londo realized that this was his punishment. A cosmic sentence of justice was being carried out. Because of who he was and the nature of what he had done, he could never be jailed. Instead, his jail would be his own mind and body. They were being taken from him, and he was going to be trapped within them while lease over them was given to the keeper. It was a prison sentence, and the sentence was life.

From where he stood, he could smell the smoking ruins of Centauri Prime. He so loved the world of his birth. All he had wanted to do was restore it to greatness. But he had made a horrible miscalculation. He hadn't realized that the very things that he so despised—the sickly peace that had permeated the society, the sense that its proudest days were behind it—that those things truly *were* great. Peace, prosperity, happiness . . . what prizes those things were, what joys they brought with them.

Perhaps he had lost sight of the truth because of those with whom he had associated. He had spent so much time walking the halls of power, rubbing elbows with emperors, plotting and planning alongside such master schemers as the late Lord Refa. He had lost sight of the fact that they had been hedonistic, scheming, and self-centered. They had cared only for pleasure, and that was usually obtained over the dead bodies of others.

Londo had forgotten that these people represented only the smallest percentage of the Centauri people. That the vast, vast majority of Centauri Prime's citizens consisted of decent, simple, hardworking people who wanted nothing more from life than to live it as simply as possible. They were not decadent; they were not power seekers. They were just decent, ordinary folk. They were the ones whom Londo had let down the most. It was their homes burning, it was their screams he fancied he could hear echoing in his head.

He closed his eyes and wished that he could clap his hands over his ears and, in so doing, shut out the cries that would not leave him.

And the keeper was there.

He felt it sinking its consciousness into his, attaching and intertwining their interests. Then he became aware of the Drakh, watching him—from without, and from within. It was as if the keeper had given the Drakh a viewport into his very soul. It was invasive, it was nauseating, it was . . .

. . . it was just what he deserved.

Despite all the turmoil that roiled through his mind, he never once allowed it to show. They could rob him of his freedom, his independence, his future, his very soul, but they could not remove from him his pride, and the way he carried himself. Whatever else happened, he was still Londo Mollari of the great Centauri Republic. That was why he had not blubbered or begged. He only sighed with inward relief that he had not given in to his momentary weakness and started offering up others to take his place, to be enslaved. For if he had done so, he didn't think he could have lived with himself.

Live with himself.

Suicide. It was an option that doubtless remained to him still. If it came down to a contest of raw will and the keeper tried to dissuade him from that course, he was reasonably sure that he could still overcome its influence at least long enough to do the deed.

But where there was life, there was hope. As long as he lived, there might still be a way of ridding himself of the damnable creature. If he was dead, he had no fallback. If he was alive . . . anything could happen.

He might still wind up waggling his fingers at the Drakh's head on a pike.

That thought led to one, and then another and another, and he couldn't understand it. It was as if every thought that he'd ever had was suddenly tumbling one over the other in his head. A veritable avalanche of notions and recollections . . .

. . . or perhaps . . . it was an overview. Perhaps the Drakh, even at this moment, was seeing . . .

With tremendous effort, Londo shoved away the intrusion, although he couldn't be sure whether it had been real or imagined. He found he could barely stand. He put one hand to his forehead and let out an unsteady sigh.

And then the Drakh said the most curious thing. He said, "You will be all right."

What an odd thing for him to have said. The Drakh were uniformly heartless, evil creatures—Londo knew this beyond a certainty. What point was there in one of their number pretending that he would be "all right."

"No," he growled, aware of the presence of the . . . the thing on his shoulder. "I will never be all right again."

The Drakh babbled some other meaningless phrases at him, and Londo barely paid attention, giving responses off the top of his head that had little meaning, that he didn't even remember moments later. All he could think about was that eye, perched so close, watching him.

The Shadows . . . the terror that they had spread had come

in the form of their vast and powerful ships. The only personal contact he'd ever had with them had been through Morden, and *he* had merely been their voice. Now, however, the enemy had a face, in the person of this Drakh who was, even as they spoke, gliding back into the shadows that had vomited him up. And the enemy had established an eternal, vigilant presence in the form of the keeper, which was settling in, part of him now until he died.

Until he died.

That was the point at which he began toying with the idea.

He held the sword, caressed it almost lovingly. It had been quite some time since he had been able to look at it. It was an elegant blade—the one he had used to kill his friend, the companion of his childhood, Urza Jaddo. Urza, who had come to Babylon 5 seeking Londo's aid in a political game that was going to leave his family name in ruins. Urza, who had obtained that aid . . . by choreographing a duel during which he had died at Londo's hands so that his—Urza's—family would henceforth be protected by the house of Mollari.

The protection of the house of Mollari. What a ghastly joke. The Mollari name had certainly afforded Londo a good deal of protection, hadn't it.

Londo's brain hadn't stopped working from the moment the keeper had become attached to him. He had picked up on the fact that the creature did not, *could* not read every thought that crossed his mind. It would report his actions to the Drakh and they, in turn, might intervene, but it had to be *actions*, actions that ran contrary to the Drakh interest. Londo had taken no action as yet, but he was strongly considering it.

Wouldn't it be appropriate. Wouldn't it be just. If the universe were really interested in the order of things, then what would be more just than for Londo to die by a thrust of the same sword that had killed Urza. Something within Londo had died that day. If he used the same sword, brought an end to the suffering that his life was to become, then perhaps he would wind up where Urza was. They would be young together, young and free, and their existence would lie ahead of them once again. They would spar, they would laugh, and it would be good.

Servants were quietly boxing up his belongings, preparing to move them to the royal suite. The sword was the only thing that he had not given over to them. Londo was simply standing there, staring at it, examining the glistening blade and wondering how it would feel sliding gently across his throat. He envisioned his blood pouring from the cut, turning crimson the white uniform of his office. A remarkable color scheme, that. Most aesthetic.

And when the Drakh found his body—somehow he knew it would be the Drakh—would the creature be smug over Londo's premature demise, feeling that the death of the Shadows had been repaid? Or would the Drakh be angry, or annoyed that Londo's usefulness had not been fully exploited? That . . . was indeed a pleasing notion. The thought of the Drakh being frustrated, knowing that he and his hideous ilk could hurt Londo no longer. Would the Drakh retaliate, by detonating the bombs and annihilating his people? No. No, probably not. The Drakh Entire didn't especially care about the people of Centauri Prime. To the Drakh, they existed merely to act as playing pieces, to keep Londo in line. If Londo were gone, the game was over. With the king fallen, what point would there be in knocking over the pawns?

It would be the coward's way out, yes. There was still so much that needed to be done, and if he killed himself, there would never be any chance to try and make good on all that he had done . . .

Make good?

The blade gleamed so brilliantly that he was able to see his reflection in it, and it reminded him of his reflection in the window of the Centauri war vessel as it had orbited the Narn Homeworld. The Centauri had smashed the Narns into near-oblivion, using the outlawed weaponry known as mass drivers.

Make good? Make reparations? Balance the scales? What

sort of nonsensical conceit was that, anyway? How could he possibly make good on what he had done? Millions . . . Great Maker . . . *billions* had died because of him. And he was supposed to set that right somehow? It was impossible, simply impossible. If he had a hundred lifetimes in which to do it, it would still be a hopeless task.

Perhaps . . . perhaps suicide wouldn't be the coward's way out at that. Perhaps suicide was simply the wise man's way of knowing when it was polite to leave. To keep his now-wretched existence going on this war-torn world, in the deluded belief that somehow he could make things better or atone for his sins . . .

Who was he fooling? In the final analysis, who was he fooling?

He became aware once more of the keeper on his shoulder. He wondered if, given enough time, he would become less aware of it. If he might become so used to it being there that he gave it no thought at all. If that circumstance did come about, he wasn't altogether sure whether it would be a good thing or a bad thing.

He placed the sword down.

It was time.

Time to see the farce through. As for the rest, well, if it came to that, there would be time enough. Or perhaps the notion would go away on its own. His emotions were too raw, and he couldn't trust himself to make a proper decision. He had to allow himself time to figure out what would be the best thing to do.

The notion, however, did not go away.

He made his speech to the Centauri people, as they huddled in their homes, cowering in the burned-out shells of buildings that represented the burned-out shells their lives had become. The mental picture of the sword remained in his head even as his own holographic image loomed in the skies of Centauri Prime. What he truly wanted to do was apologize . . . humble himself to his people, let them know that it was he, and he alone, who was responsible for this hideous pass to which they had come.

But such a speech, honest as it might have been, wouldn't be in the best interests of the Drakh. They had their own agenda, and Londo was merely required to play his part. They had made that quite clear. Do as he was told. Be a good puppet. Speak the speeches as were required, and do not for a moment anger them.

"I will walk alone to my inauguration," he announced. "Take on the burden of emperor in silence. The bells of our temple will sound all day and all night, once for each of our people killed in the bombings. We are alone. Alone in the universe. But we are united in our pain."

But that wasn't true. It was as much a sham as everything else about him. His pain was his own, and could never be shared or revealed. His pain was the creature on his shoulder. His pain took the form of nightmares that came to him in his sleep, that tormented him.

"We fought alone," he told his people, "and we will rebuild alone." But was there anyone on Centauri who was more alone than he? And the most perverse aspect of it was that he wasn't alone, not really. The keeper was there, watching him, studying him, surveying him, never allowing him a moment's peace. It served as a constant reminder of his sin. Via the keeper, the Drakh were with him as well.

And more.

There were the voices. The voices of his victims, crying out to him, protesting their fates. These were the people who had gone to their deaths screaming and sobbing and not remotely comprehending why this was happening to them. They were there, too, making their presence known.

It was entirely possible that, of everyone on Centauri Prime, Londo was the *least*-alone individual on the planet. But that didn't mitigate the circumstances of his situation at all. For there was no one, no one, whom he could tell about his predicament. To do so would have spelled death for that person, of that he was quite certain. He existed, and others maintained a presence near him, but he could allow no one to be close to him. He had to drive away those who once had known him as no others did.

The worst would be Vir. Vir, who had stood by his side every hideous step of the way, who had warned Londo against the descent he was taking into blackness. Londo hadn't listened, and Vir had been right. Perhaps that was why Londo hadn't listened: because he had known that Vir was right, and he didn't want to hear it.

And Delenn. After the speech, when they took their leave of him, Delenn stepped forward and looked at him in such a way that he flinched inwardly, wondering if somehow she was able to see the evil dropping on his shoulder. "I can no longer see the road you're on, Londo," she said. "There is a darkness around you. I can only pray that, in time, you will find your way out of it."

When she said that, the image of the sword presented itself to him once again, even more keenly than it had before. Light glinting off the blade, pure and true, calling to him. It was the way out . . . if he chose to take it.

He walked to the temple, as he had said. Alone . . . but not alone.

He took on the ornaments and responsibilities of emperor, and he could practically feel the sword across his throat now. He could almost hear the death rattle, feel the pure joy of the release. He would be free of it, free of the responsibility, free of everything. By the time he began the long walk back to the palace, the sun was starting to set. And he knew, in his hearts, that it was the last sunset he would ever see. His resolve was stronger than it had ever been, the certainty of his decision absolute.

It felt right. It felt good. He had done the best that he could, and his best had not been remotely good enough. It was time to remove himself from the game.

He sat in the throne room that night, the darkness encroaching upon him. Its opulence, with its gleaming marbled floors, lush curtains, and largely decorative—but still impressive—columns, carried whispers of Centauri Prime's past greatness. Despite the ghastly shades of times past that always hovered there, he felt strangely at peace. He felt the keeper stirring upon his shoulder. Perhaps the creature knew that something was in the offing, but wasn't entirely sure what.

The shadows around him seemed to be moving. Londo looked right and left, tried to discern whether the Drakh was standing nearby, watching him. But there was nothing. At least, he thought there was nothing. He could have been wrong . . .

"Madness," he said to no one. "I am driving myself to madness." He gave the matter a moment's blackly humorous thought. "Maybe that is their ultimate goal. An interesting thought. Reducing Centauri Prime to rubble just for the dubious purpose of sending me into insanity. Such overkill. If that was what they desired, they could just have locked me in a room with my ex-wives for a week. That would cause anyone to snap."

To his surprise, a voice responded. "Pardon, Majesty?"

He half turned in his chair and saw a man standing just inside the doorway, regarding Londo with polite curiosity. He was quite thin, with carefully cultivated hair that wasn't particularly high. That was a direct flouting of Centauri standard fashion, for usually the height of hair was meant to be indicative of the rank in society that one had achieved. There was, however, a fringe fashion element that had taken its cue from Emperor Turhan, who had publicly disdained tradition by wearing his hair shorter than the lowest of the lowborn. Some believed that Emperor Cartagia had done so as a way of showing that he wished to maintain a connection to the common man. Others felt he had just done it to annoy people. Either way, the precedent had been set, and some chose to follow it.

Though in the case of this particular Centauri, the one who had interrupted Londo's musings, it wasn't his hair that caught Londo's attention. Nor was it the starched and pressed military uniform he wore so smartly. No, it was his general attitude. He had an eagerness about him . . . but it wasn't a healthy sort of eagerness. Vir, for example, had been cloaked in eagerness from the moment he had set foot on Babylon 5. That had been an eagerness to please, one of Vir's more charming features. But this individual . . . he had the attitude of a carrion-eating bird perched on a branch, watching a dying man and mentally urging him to hurry up and get on with it.

"Durla . . . isn't it?" Londo asked after a moment.

"Yes, Majesty. Your captain of the guards, as appointed by the late regent—" He bowed slightly. "—and continuing to serve at your good humor, Majesty."

"My humor is less than good at the moment, Captain Durla. I do not appreciate interruptions into my privacy."

"With all respect, Majesty, I did not realize you were alone. I heard you speaking and thought you were deep in conversation with someone. Since your schedule does not call for you to have anyone in this room with you at this time of night . . . I thought I would make sure that you were not being subjected to any threat. I apologize most profusely if I, in some way, have intruded or made you uncomfortable."

He had all the right words and expressed them perfectly, and yet Londo, still reacting on a gut level, didn't like him. Perhaps . . . perhaps it was because, in addition to having the right words, it seemed to Londo as if Durla *knew* they were the right words. He wasn't expressing his sentiments, whatever those might be. Instead he was saying precisely what he thought Londo wanted to hear.

Another possibility, Londo had to admit, was that he was becoming so suspicious—jumping at shadows; seeing plots, plans, and duplicity everywhere—that even the most casual meeting brought sinister overtones with it. He was beginning to view the world entirely in subtext, searching out that which was not said, forsaking that which was spoken. It was no way to live.

Then again . . . that wasn't really a serious consideration for him these days, was it? Not on this, the last day of his life.

Durla hadn't moved. Apparently he was waiting for Londo to dismiss him. Londo promptly obliged him. "I won't be needing you this evening, Durla. As for your continuing to serve, well . . . we shall see how my humor transforms with the passage of time."

"Very well, Majesty. I will make certain that guards remain at all exits."

Londo was not enthused at that particular prospect. If he did decide to do himself in—as was looking more likely by the moment—the last thing he needed was for a couple of guards to hear his body thud to the floor. If they came running in to save him and somehow, against all hope, succeeded . . . the embarrassment and humiliation would be overwhelming. And what if he decided to depart the palace grounds, to commit the deed somewhere more remote?

Then again, he was the emperor.

"That will not be necessary," he said firmly. "I believe the manpower may be better deployed elsewhere."

"Better?" Durla cocked an eyebrow. "Better than maintaining the safety of our emperor? Will all respect, Majesty, I do not think so."

"I do not recall asking your opinion on the matter," Londo informed him. "They will leave, as will you."

"Majesty, with all respect—"

"Stop telling me how much you respect me!" Londo said with obvious irritation. "If I were a young virgin girl and you were endeavoring to seduce me, you might understandably offer repeated protests of how much you respect me. I feel safe in assuming that this is not your intent though, yes?"

"Yes, Your Majesty, you would be quite safe with that assumption." A hint of a smile briefly tugged at the edges of Durla's mouth. Then he grew serious again. "However, not only is your safety my primary concern, it is part of my job description. Of course, you could always release me from my job, but it would be unfortunate if I were to be fired simply because I was doing my duty. It has been my understanding that you, Emperor Mollari, are the fairest-minded individual to come into a position of power on Centauri Prime in quite a while. Is that not the case?"

Oh yes, very facile. Very good with words. Londo wasn't fooled for even a moment by his comments. Still . . .

It didn't matter. Not really. All Londo had to do was wait until he retired for the night. Then, lying in his bed, he could quietly put an end to himself. Since he would be lying flat, he wouldn't need to worry about "thumps" alerting guards.

That was it. That was all he had to do. Bid Durla good night, retire for the evening . . . and then retire permanently. That was it. Dismiss Durla and be done with it.

Durla waited expectantly.

Londo didn't like him.

He had no idea why he was operating on such a visceral level. Part of him actually rejoiced in the notion that, soon, Durla would be someone else's problem. But another part of him wondered just what Durla was up to. He was . . . a loose end. Londo hated loose ends. He particularly hated the knowledge that this loose end might unravel after he was gone.

"Would you care to take a walk?" he asked abruptly. He was surprised at the sound of his own voice.

"A walk, Majesty? Of course. Where on the grounds would—"

"No. Not on the grounds. I wish to walk into the city."

"The . . . city, sir?" Durla looked as if he hadn't quite heard Londo properly.

"Yes, Captain of the Guards. I have a desire to see it closely . . ." *One last time.*

"I do not think that would be wise, Majesty."

"Is that a fact?"

"Yes, Majesty," he said firmly. "At this time, the people are . . ." His voice trailed off. He seemed reluctant to finish the sentence.

So Londo finished it for him. "The people are my people, Durla. Am I to hide in here from them?"

"That might be prudent, at least for the time being, Majesty."

"Your opinion is duly noted." He slapped the armrests of the throne and rose. "I shall walk about the city, and I shall do it alone."

"Majesty, no!"

"No?" Londo stared at him, his thick eyebrows knitting in a carefully controlled display of imperial anger. "I do not recall asking for your approval, Durla. That is one of the benefits of being emperor: you are entitled to take actions without consulting underlings." He gave particular stress to that last word.

Durla didn't appear to take the hint, however, although he did ratchet up his obsequiousness level by several degrees. "Majesty . . . there are ways that certain things are done . . . certain protocols . . ."

"That will be the exciting aspect of my tenure in this position, Durla. I do not follow protocol. I follow the moment. Now . . . I am going for a walk. I am the emperor. I think I am entitled to make that decision, no?"

"At least"—Durla seemed most urgent in his concerns— "At *least*, Majesty, and I pray I am not overstepping my bounds here, let an escort follow you at a respectful distance. You will be alone . . . but you will not be alone. I hope that sounds clear . . ."

Something about the irony of the suggestion struck Londo as amusing. "Yes. Yes, it is quite clear. And let me guess: you will accompany these 'phantom' guards, yes?"

"I would supervise the honor guard myself, Majesty, if you wish."

"You would be amazed, Durla, how little my wishes have

to do with anything," Londo said. "Suit yourself. Exercise your free will. At least *someone* around here should be able to."

And so Londo walked out into the great capital city of Centauri Prime for what he anticipated would be the last time.

His path from the palace to the temple of inauguration had been a fairly straightforward one, earlier that day. In this case, however, he deliberately strayed from any known path. He crisscrossed the city, making arbitrary decisions and occasionally backtracking. The entire time, a small platoon of men-at-arms trailed him, with Durla keeping a close-up and somewhat wary eye upon them all.

As Londo walked, he tried to drink in every aspect of the city, every curve of every building. Even the smell of burning structures and rubble were sensations that he wanted to savor.

He had never found himself in quite this sort of mindset before; looking upon things with the attitude that he would never look upon them again. True, as he had prepared to accept the post of emperor, his life had flashed before his eyes. Each moment that had been a fond memory then was now tinged with pain. Times past and even times future . . . particularly that much-dreamed-of moment when a one-eyed G'Kar would spell his doom. Well, he was certainly going to wind up putting an end to that particular prediction. He took some small measure of comfort in that.

For so long, he had felt as if he were nothing more than the tool of fate, possessing no control over his own destiny. No matter what his intentions, he had been propelled down a dark road that he had never intended to travel. Well, at least he would confound the fates in the end. It wouldn't be G'Kar's hand that ended his wretched existence . . . it would be his own. No one could harm him at this point in his life except, of course, for he himsel—

That was when the rock bounced off his skull.

— chapter 2 —

Londo staggered from the impact. It took him a moment to understand fully what had occurred. His first, momentarily panicked impression was that he had been shot with a PPG blast. Odd that he would have been disturbed at such a notion. He was, after all, planning to do himself in before the evening was out, so it would have been almost ungrateful to be angry at someone who might have saved him the effort.

Then the very fact that he still was able to construct a coherent thought was enough to tip him to the realization that what had hit him was some sort of simple projectile. It had ricocheted off his forehead and tumbled to the ground. A rock, and easy enough to spot; it was the only one tinged with red.

Immediately the guards sprang into action. Half of them formed an impenetrable wall of bodies—a barrier against any possible encroachers. The rest bolted off in the direction from which the rock had come. Londo had the briefest glimpse of a small form darting into shadows of nearby buildings.

"Come, Majesty," said Durla, pulling at Londo's arm. "We must go . . . back to the palace . . ."

"No."

"But we—"

"No!" Londo thundered with such vehemence that the guards around him were literally caught flatfooted. That provided Londo the opportunity he needed to push impulsively through the guards and run after the group who were, in turn, pursuing his assailant.

"Majesty!" called a horrified Durla, but Londo had already obtained a decent lead.

Nevertheless, moments after the guards set out in pursuit of the emperor, they managed to draw alongside him . . . not a difficult accomplishment since they were by and large younger and in better shape. As for Londo, he found he was already starting to feel winded, and felt a grim annoyance that he had let himself get into such poor shape.

Perhaps, he thought bleakly, he should have taken a cue from Vir. Lately Vir had whipped himself into impressively good shape. "How did you do it?" he once had asked.

"Ate less, drank no alcohol, and exercised."

"Radical," Londo had responded, sniffing in disgust.

Now, as his hearts pounded and his breath rasped, he felt as if it hadn't been such a radical notion after all.

Durla, only a few steps behind, called, "Majesty! This really is most improper! There could be an ambush! It's insanity!"

"Why would it . . . be an ambush?" huffed Londo. "You said it . . . yourself . . . this is insanity . . . So who would . . . create an ambush . . . and have it hinge . . . on the target doing something . . . insane?"

The chase was slowing considerably. There was fallen rubble from shattered buildings, blocking the path. This hadn't deterred the guards, though, as they had scrambled over debris with as much alacrity as they could manage. They had dedicated themselves to corralling whoever had made such a vile attempt against their emperor.

Then they slowed and fanned out, creating a semicircle around one burned-out area. It was quite evident, even from a distance, that they had brought the assailant to heel.

Londo slowed, then stopped, and straightened his coat and vest in order to restore some measure of dignity. Durla, who drew up next to him, looked disgustingly fit and not the slightest out of breath. "Your Majesty, I really must insist," he began.

"Oh, must you," said Londo, turning on him. "On what would you insist, precisely?"

"Let me bring you back to the palace, where you'll be safe—"

That was when they heard a female voice cry out, "Let me go! Let me go, you great buffoons! And don't touch them! They had nothing to do with it!"

"That is a child's voice," Londo said, looking at Durla with open skepticism. "Are you telling me that I must be escorted by armed guards back to the palace in order that I might avoid the wrath of a little girl?"

Durla seemed about to try a response, but apparently he realized there was nothing he could say at that particular moment that was going to make him look especially good. "No, Your Majesty, of course not."

"Good. Because I certainly would not want to think you were questioning my bravery."

Quite quickly Durla responded, "I would never dream of doing such a thing, Majesty."

"Good. Then we understand each other."

"Yes, Majesty."

"Now then . . . I want to know what it is we're dealing with," he said, and he gestured toward the cluster of figures that had gathered ahead of them.

Durla nodded and moved off to get a summary of the events from the guards who had caught up with the "assailant." He listened as he was filled in on the situation, and when he returned to Londo, he clearly looked rather uncomfortable about it all. "It appears . . . you were correct, Majesty. It is a young girl, not more than fifteen."

"There are other people with her?"

"Yes, Majesty. A family . . . or at least what's left of one. They've constructed a rather crude shelter from material at hand. They claim to have taken the girl in because she was wandering the streets and they felt sorry for her."

"I see."

"Yes, and they appear somewhat . . . irate . . . that she has put them at risk by drawing the wrath of the emperor down upon them."

"Really. Let them know that my wrath is not exactly out in full bloom today, despite any untimely provocations," he said, as he gingerly fingered the cut on his head. It was already starting to become swollen. "Better yet . . . I shall tell them myself."

"It could still be a trick, Your Majesty," Durla warned. "A trap of some sort."

"Should that be the case, Durla, and they draw a PPG or some similar weapon that they plan to utilize," Londo said, clapping him on the shoulder, "I am fully confident that you will throw yourself into the path of the blast, intercept it with your own body, then die with praises for your beloved emperor upon your lips. Yes?"

Durla looked less than thrilled at the notion. "It . . . would be my honor, Majesty, to serve you in that manner."

"Let us both hope you have the opportunity," Londo told him.

Squaring his shoulders, Londo walked over to where the guards had surrounded his attacker. They hesitated to let Londo through, though, only moving when Durla gave them a silent nod. For some reason this irked Londo to no end. He was the emperor. If he couldn't even get a handful of guards to attend to his wishes without someone else validating his desires, what in the world was the point of ruling?

But move aside they did, giving Londo a clear view into the face of a wounded and hurting Centauri Prime.

There, in a makeshift lean-to, stood a Centauri family. A father, hair cut low, and a young mother. As was the style with many young women, she had a long tail of hair, which most women kept meticulously braided. In her case, however, it

simply hung loosely around her shoulders, looking unkempt
and in disarray, the entirety of it rooted squarely in the middle
of her otherwise-shaved head, so its askew nature made it
look like a follicle fountain. They also had two boys and a girl
with them, between the ages of twelve and fifteen. Even had
Londo not known which of the youngsters had decided to use
him for target practice, he would have been able to tell just by
looking at them. The boys, like their parents, were staring
toward the ground, afraid even to gaze into the face of their
emperor. The father—the *father*, of all people—was visibly
trembling. A fine testament to Centauri manhood, that.

But the girl, well . . . she was a different story, wasn't she.
She didn't avert her eyes or shrink in fear of Londo's approach. Instead she stood tall and proud, with a level and unflinching gaze. There was some redness to her scalp, which
Londo knew all too well: she had only recently taken up the
female tradition of shaving her head, indicating her ascension
into maturity. She looked quite gaunt, with high cheekbones
and a swollen lip that marred her features. The blood on her
lip was fresh. "Did someone strike you?" Londo demanded,
and then without waiting for reply, turned to his guards and
said, "Who did this?"

"I did, Majesty," one of the guards said, stepping forward.
"She was resisting, and I—"

"Get out," Londo said without hesitation. "If you cannot
rein in a single child without brutality, you have no place rep-
resenting the office of emperor. No, do not look to Durla!"
Londo continued, anger rising. "I am still the power here, not
the captain of the guards. I say you are out. Now leave."

The guard did not hesitate. Instead he bowed quickly to the
emperor and walked quickly away. Londo then turned back to
the girl and found nothing but disdain on her face. "You do
not approve of my action?" he asked.

The question had been intended as rhetorical, but she immediately shot back a reply. "You discharge a single guard

and fancy yourself the protector of the people? Don't make me laugh."

"The insolence!" raged Durla, as if he himself had been insulted. "Majesty, please permit me to—"

But Londo held up a calming hand and looked more closely at the girl. "I have seen you before, yes? Have I not?"

This time she didn't offer an immediate reply. "Answer your emperor!" Durla snapped, and Londo did not remonstrate him. Youthful insolence was one thing, and tolerance certainly could be a virtue, but if one's emperor asks a question, then Great Maker, one answers the question or suffers the consequences.

Fortunately enough, the girl at least had the good sense to recognize those things that were worth taking stands over, and those that were not. "We have . . . encountered each other one or two times before. At the palace. During official functions." When Londo continued to stare at her without full recognition, she added, "My mother was the lady Celes . . . my father, Lord Antono Refa."

The identification hit Londo like a hammer blow. Lord Refa, his one-time ally, whose political machinations had been instrumental in costing Londo everything he had held dear.

Whereas Londo had made many ill-considered decisions that had set him on a path toward darkness, Refa had dashed headlong down that same path, reveling in the lies, duplicities, and betrayals that were a part of power brokering and advancement in the great Centauri Republic. He had been a strategist and manipulator of the old school, well versed in the ways of deceit that had made the old Republic such a morass of power-hungry bastards. And he had been directly responsible for the deaths of several of those close to Londo. Londo had gained a revenge of sorts, arranging for Refa to meet a brutal and violent death at the hands of enraged Narns.

It had only been later that Londo had come to realize just how much both he and Refa had been used by the Shadows. Granted, Refa had been overzealous in embracing the power when it was presented him, but Londo had also held Refa accountable for acts that had not been his responsibility. Every so often Londo would envision what it must have been like for Refa, to die beneath the fists and bludgeons of the Narns. He had taken such pleasure in it at the time. Now the recollection only filled him with disgust and self-loathing.

Looking upon the face of the young girl, however, Londo—for the first time—actually felt guilty.

Then something about the girl's phrasing caught Londo's attention. "Your mother 'was' the Lady Celes? Then she is—?"

"Dead," the girl said tonelessly. If there was any capacity for mourning within her, it had either been burned away or buried so deeply that it could not harm her. "She was one of the first to die in the bombing."

"I . . . am sorry for your loss," Londo told her.

Durla quickly added, "However, the emperor's sympathy for your plight does not excuse your abominable assault on him."

"My assault? I hit him with a rock!" said the girl. "And what, pray tell, should excuse him for his crimes?"

"My crimes." Londo stifled a bitter laugh. "And what know you of my crimes, child?"

"I know that the emperor is supposed to protect his people. You blamed the regent for bringing us to this state, but you were the one who left the regent in place. If you had been here, attending to your people, instead of wasting your time on some far-off space station, perhaps you would have been able to prevent this.

"And where would you take us now?" she added, and she pointed at him with a quavering finger. "That whole speech about Centauri 'standing proudly alone'? What sort of . . . of prideful stupidity is that? We were the injured party here! Instead we wind up having to pay reparations that will cripple our economy beyond endurance? We lick our wounds and sulk in the darkness? We should be demanding that the Alliance help us in any way they can!"

"And what of Centauri pride?" asked Londo quietly. "What of that, *hmm*?"

"To blazes with Centauri pride!" she said with fire. "What of Centauri blood? What of Centauri bodies piled high? I've seen crying infants, looking for nourishment by pulling at the breasts of their dead mothers. Have you? I have seen people, sightless, limbless, hopeless. Have you? You claimed you wanted to walk to the temple alone to symbolize something. What excrement! You didn't want anyone around because you didn't want to have to look into their accusing eyes and feel guilty on your coronation day. You didn't want to have your personal triumph spoiled by seeing all those who suffered because of your stupidity. You didn't want to have to look upon the bodies that you crawled over to get into power."

"Silence!" Durla fairly exploded. "Majesty, truly, this is too much! The insolence, the—"

"Why do you rage, Durla?" Londo asked calmly. "She simply uses words now, not stones. It is a funny thing about words. They cannot harm you unless you allow them to . . . unlike rocks, which tend to act as they wish." He paused, and then said quietly, "You are wrong, child. Wrong about a great many things . . . but right enough about a few. Which things you are right about, I think I shall keep to myself for the time being. Think of it as imperial privilege. You are quite brave, do you know that?"

For a moment the girl seemed taken aback, and then she gathered herself. "I'm not brave. I'm just too tired and hungry and angry to care anymore."

"Perhaps they are not mutually exclusive. Perhaps bravery is simply apathy with delusions of grandeur."

"Then they are your delusions, Majesty," she said with a slight bow that was clearly intended to be ironic rather than respectful. "I have no delusions left."

"Indeed. Then perhaps . . . we should attend to that." Londo scratched his chin thoughtfully for a moment, and then said to Durla, "See that these people—this family—is fed and clothed and found a decent shelter. Take money from my discretionary funds as needed. You," and he pointed to the girl, "what is your name? I should recall it from our past encounters, but I regret I do not."

"Senna," she said. She looked slightly suspicious and uncertain of what was about to happen. That pleased Londo. Considering that she had spoken with such conviction before, and considering that all of her conviction had been tied up with the utter certainty that Londo was a heartless bastard who cared nothing for his people, it pleased him to see her a bit confused.

"Senna," repeated Londo. "Senna . . . you are going to live at the palace. With me."

"Majesty!" cried a shocked Durla.

Senna looked no less wary. "I'm not flattered. I have no interest in becoming an imperial concubine . . ."

This drew a bitter laugh from Londo. "That is quite fortunate, for if that were your career goal, I could assure you that you would not have much opportunity to pursue it on Centauri Prime."

She shook her head in puzzlement. "Then what?"

"You have a spirit to you, Senna," said Londo. "A spirit that is symbolic, I think, of not only what the Centauri Republic was, but of what it could be again. A spirit that is . . . lacking, somewhat, I think, in the palace. Too many people with their own agendas hanging about, and I do not exclude myself. You shine with the youthful light of conviction, Senna. I would have that light shining in the palace. Light tends to chase away shadows."

"Majesty . . ." For a moment she seemed overwhelmed, and then her more customary attitude of defiance came back to her. "With all respect . . ."

"You ricocheted a rock off my head, child. It's a little late to speak of respect."

"Majesty . . . those are very pretty words. But I still do not . . . I don't wish to be grateful to you."

"Nor would you have need to be. If you wish, think of it as simply something that I am doing in memory of your parents. Lord Refa was . . . an ally, for a time. I feel some degree of responsibility for his . . ."

Death. For his death.

". . . family," he continued. "His family, of which you are the only surviving member, yes?" She nodded and he concluded, "So . . . there it is."

"There what is?"

"Senna," Londo said, his patience starting to erode ever so slightly, "I am offering you a home that is a considerable step up from the streets. You will have comfort, the best teachers available to complete your education, and you will want for nothing. In that way—"

"You can purchase peace of mind?"

Londo stared at her for a moment, and then turned to Durla and said, "Come. We are wasting our time here."

Durla appeared rather relieved at this decision. "Shall we punish her, Majesty? She did assault you."

"She has lost her parents, Durla. She has been punished enough."

"But—"

"Enough." There was no mistaking the tone in his voice. A line had been drawn and Durla would cross it at his own peril. It was peril that Durla rather wisely chose not to face. Instead, he simply bowed his head in acknowledgement and acquiescence.

And so they returned to the palace, for what Londo was convinced would be his last night alive.

— chapter 3 —

Londo sat in the throne room, staring out at the rain.

It had begun within minutes after his arrival back at the palace. It had been accompanied by almost deafening blasts of thunder, lightning crackling overhead, and it seemed to Londo—who was feeling rather fanciful in what he believed to be his waning moments—that the very skies were weeping on behalf of Centauri Prime. Normally such heavy rains could be viewed as cleansing, but all Londo could envision were streams of red water washing away the blood of all those who had fallen in the bombings.

He could not get the image of Senna from his mind. Such pain, such anger on her face . . . but there was something else, too. There had been several moments there when she had seemed as if she wanted to believe in Londo. To believe that he was capable of serving the people, of operating on not only her behalf, but the behalf of everyone on Centauri Prime. In a way, it was as if Londo had embodied the entire schism between himself and his people in this one girl.

It was unfair, of course. Ridiculous, even absurd. As a symbol she represented nothing, as an individual, she meant even less. But there was something about her nevertheless. It was as if . . .

Londo remembered when he had first met G'Kar. Even before that time, Londo had dreamt of his own death, had envisioned a Narn with his hands around his throat, squeezing the life from him. When he'd actually encountered G'Kar, he had

38

recognized him instantly, had known that this was someone who was going to factor into his future in a most significant way. Most significant, indeed.

The feeling had not been quite as distinct when he'd met Senna, of course. For one thing, he had encountered her before, in passing. For another, she had never featured into a dream. Not yet, at least. Nonetheless, he couldn't help but feel that she was . . . important in some manner. That what happened to her was going to matter, to the Centauri people . . . and to him.

Then again, what did anything matter to him?

He had been drinking rather heavily that evening, as if steeling himself for what he had resolved to do. Originally he had thought that what he would have to do is slay the keeper and then—very quickly—himself, before the action of murdering the small monster could bring the Drakh down upon him. But he had noticed that, in raising his blood/alcohol level to a satisfyingly high degree, he seemed to be dulling the senses of the keeper. The creature's presence no longer seemed so . . . tangible. The keeper was so intertwined with his own neural system that he thought he could actually sense the creature snoring, in his mind.

The notion that he was capable of drinking his little companion under the table became a source of great amusement to him. It was also a relief to him. He wouldn't have to contend with the keeper or whatever unknown resources it might possess, after all. By getting drunk, he was effectively taking the monster out of the picture.

His blade hung comfortably nearby. He still remained concerned about the proximity of guards, outside the doors. But he was simply going to have to take his chances. He had considered the notion of poisoning himself, but somehow that seemed inappropriate. Poison was the tool of the assassin. He should know, having planned enough assassinations in his time, including that of his predecessor, Emperor Cartagia. Besides, the keeper might actually be able to coun-

teract poison, for all he knew. Now the blade—that was the
classic, honorable means of dispatching oneself, going all the
way back to the earliest days of the Republic.

The early days.

"I was born in the wrong century," he murmured to himself. "To have lived then . . . to have known the Centauri who
built the Republic . . . what I would give to have had that opportunity. Perhaps they would have possessed the strength to
face that which I am leaving behind. But I do not. All I have
tasted in my life is failure, and I think it is time for me to get
up from the dinner table and let others sit in my place."

"Majesty."

The voice came so utterly out of nowhere that Londo
jumped somewhat. He felt the keeper stir in its drunken
slumber, but without being roused from it.

He didn't bother to get up from his throne, but instead half
turned to see a guard enter. Thunder rumbled again. It made a
nicely dramatic underscoring to his entrance.

"Forgive me disturbing your—" began the guard.

"Yes, yes, get on with it," Londo gestured impatiently.
"What is it?"

"There is someone here to see you."

"I left specific instructions that I am not to be disturbed."

"We know that, Majesty. But it is a young girl who stated
that she was here at your direct invitation. Given that, we felt
it wisest to check with you before throwing her back into—"

Londo half rose from his chair and steadied himself on the
armrest. "A young girl?"

"Yes, Majesty."

"Would her name be Senna?"

The guard looked both surprised and a bit relieved, as if
realizing that his decision to interrupt the emperor's peaceful
evening wasn't going to rebound to his detriment. "Yes,
Majesty, I believe it is."

"Bring her in."

The guard bowed briskly and left, only to return moments

later with Senna. She was utterly waterlogged; Londo felt as if he had never seen anyone so wet. If she had had hair, it would have been plastered all over her face. As she walked in, she left a trail of water behind her, until she simply stood there with a large puddle forming at her feet. She was shivering, but trying not to show it.

"Leave us," Londo said.

"Majesty," said the guard, "for the sake of your security . . ."

"Security? Look at her," said Londo. "Where do you think she is hiding weapons, eh?" It was a true enough observation. Her clothes were sodden and clinging to her. There was nowhere on her person that she could have been concealing a weapon of any size. "Perhaps she will strangle me with her bare hands, eh? And I, of course, would be incapable of defending myself in such a circumstance."

"I meant no offense, Majesty," the guard said. He appeared about to say something else, but then thought better of it, bowed once more, and quickly absented himself from the throne room.

They remained in silence for a long moment, the only sound being the steady dripping of water from her clothes. Finally she sneezed. Londo put up a hand to hide a smile.

"I wanted to know if your offer was still open," she said after a time.

"Indeed. And why is that?"

"Because enfolded into that offer was shelter and aid for the family that helped me in my time of need. It would be . . . rude . . . of me to turn down aid on their behalf. Furthermore," and she cleared her throat, gathering confidence, "if I am here . . . then I can be a constant reminder to you of what needs to be done to help your people. It's very easy to become isolated here in the palace. You can get so caught up in the gamesmanship and machinations required in maintaining power, that you too easily forget about those in whose behalf you are supposed to be using that power. But if I am here, my presence will remind you of that. You can never turn a blind eye to it, while I'm around."

"I see. So you wish to live here, not out of any desire for comfort and warmth for yourself, but because of the benefit that your being here will render to others."

She nodded. "Yes. Yes, I . . . suppose that is right."

"Did you have any shelter for this evening, I wonder? And do not lie to me," he added sharply, his tone hardening. "You will find that I am a superb judge of such things. Lie to me at your peril."

She licked her lips and her shivering increased ever so slightly. "No," she admitted. "The family who took me in . . . threw me out. They were . . . they were angry that I had turned down your offer. They said it could have helped them. They said that in neglecting the needs of others, I was no different than you."

"Harsh words. To be no different than I—that is no way to live."

She looked to the floor. "So . . . *is* the offer still open? Or have I wasted your time and mine, and made a fool of myself for no reason?"

He considered her a moment, and then called, "Guard!"

The guard who had escorted her in made his return with all due alacrity. He skidded slightly when he entered, his foot hitting the trail of water that she had left behind, but he quickly righted himself, maintaining as much of his self-possession as possible given the circumstances. "Yes, Majesty?" he said. Clearly he was wondering if he was going to be given another opportunity to throw the interloper out.

"Prepare a chamber for young lady Senna," Londo instructed. "See to it that she is given dry clothes and warm food. She will remain in residence within the palace. Make certain, however, that hers is not a chamber near to mine. We certainly would not want the wrong impression to be given. Proximity to the imperial bedchamber might be misinterpreted by those of a more coarse bent. Is that not right, young lady?"

"It is . . . as you say, Majesty." Then she sneezed once more, and looked almost apologetic for it.

"Yes. Yes, it is. It is always as the emperor says. Why else be emperor? Go to, then. Get some rest. In the morning, we will attend to the family who took you in . . . and, as happenstance would have it, threw you out in their anger."

"They were angry. Very."

"I'm certain they were. But perhaps the more one is faced with anger, the more one should respond with forgiveness."

"That is a . . . a very interesting thought, Majesty."

"I have my moments, young lady. In the morning, then. We will talk, yes? Over breakfast?"

"I . . ." There was clear surprise on her face as she realized what he was saying. "Yes, I . . . think I would like that, Majesty. I will look forward to seeing you in the morning."

"And I you, young lady. As it happens, you see, it appears I will indeed be here in the morning. It would be rude to deprive you of a breakfast companion. And my advisors have informed me that, by morning, this storm will have passed. A new day will be dawning on Centauri Prime. No doubt we will be a part of it."

She bowed once more and then, as the guard began to escort her out, Londo called, "Guard . . . one other small matter."

"Yes, Majesty?" He turned smartly on his heel.

"Do you see that sword hanging on the wall over there?"

"Yes, Majesty. It is quite impressive."

"Yes, it is. I would like you to take it and put it into storage. I do not think I will be needing it anytime soon."

The guard didn't quite understand, but fortunately his understanding was not required. "Very well, Majesty." He bowed, removed the sword from the wall, and escorted Senna out. She paused at the door ever so briefly and glanced over her shoulder at him. Londo kept his face impassive, although he did nod to her slightly in response. Then they departed, leaving the emperor alone with his thoughts.

He sat there for some time more, listening to the rain. He took in no more drink that night, and as the time passed, he could feel the keeper slowly stirring. Lost in his own thoughts and considerations, he paid it no mind. Finally he rose to his feet and left the throne room. He made his way down the hallway, guards acknowledging his presence and majesty as he did so.

For the first time in a long time, he did not feel that he was a sham. He wondered if it was because of the girl.

He entered his private quarters and pulled off the white coat of office, removed the great seal and hung it on a nearby peg.

He'd had a work area set up at the far end of his quarters, and he turned toward it . . . and his heart skipped a beat.

The Drakh was there. How long he had stood in the shadowy section of the room, Londo had no idea. "What are you doing here?" Londo demanded.

"Studying," the Drakh said softly, his hand resting on the computer terminal. "Humans . . . interest you, I see. You have much research."

"I will thank you not to pry into my personal files," Londo said in annoyance. It was, of course, an empty expression of frustration. After all, even if he didn't like it, what was he going to do about it?

"One of our kind . . . studied Humans. Centuries ago," said the Drakh.

That stopped Londo. He made no effort to hide his surprise. "Are you saying you were on Earth?"

The Drakh nodded. "A Drakh . . . took up residence there. Few saw him. But word of him spread. Word of the dark one, the monstrous one who kept to the shadows. Who drained victims' souls . . . and ruled them thereafter," and he inclined his head toward the keeper. "They called him . . . Drak'hul. His legend lives on . . . or so I am told."

It was the single longest speech Londo had ever heard the Drakh make. As if the effort of doing so had drained him, he remained silent for some time. They simply stood there in the darkness, like two warriors, each waiting for the other to make his move.

Feeling bold, Londo said, "And what do they call you, eh? What should I call you—since we seemed to be bound in this living hell together."

The Drakh seemed to consider the question a moment. "Shiv'kala," he said at last. Then he paused a time further, and said, "The girl."

"What of her?"

"She is not needed."

"Perhaps. But that is not your concern."

"If we say it is . . . it is."

"I desire her to stay. She poses no threat to you, or to your plans."

"Not yet. She may."

"That is ridiculous," Londo said skeptically. "She is a young girl who will become a young woman and take her rightful place in Centauri society. If I left her out on the street, where her resentment could grow and fester, who knows what she might do then, eh? I am doing us a favor."

"Are you?" The Drakh did not appear convinced. Then again, with his constant but chilling smile, it was difficult for Londo to read any change at all in the Drakh's attitude. "We do not like her. We do like Durla."

"Durla? What of him?"

"He has . . . potential."

"What sort of potential?"

The Drakh did not answer directly. Instead he moved halfway across the room, seemingly gliding across the distance. "We are not . . . monsters, Mollari. No matter what you may think," he said. "We are, in many ways, no different than you."

"You are nothing like me, nor I like you," Londo replied, unable to keep the bitterness from his voice.

Shiv'kala shrugged almost imperceptibly. "We will offer

a bargain. We do not have to. But we offer it. The girl may stay . . . but Durla will become your minister of Internal Security."

"Never!" Londo said immediately. "I know Durla. I know his type. He is power hungry. And once someone who is power hungry is given power, it whets the appetite for more. The only way to deal with someone like that is to leave him famished before he develops a taste for it."

"He will be your minister of Internal Security . . . or the girl will leave."

There was a popular Human phrase that suited such occasions. Londo employed it now: "Over my dead body."

"No," the Drakh said coolly. "Over hers."

Londo's eyes narrowed. "You wouldn't."

The comment was so preposterous that the Drakh didn't even bother to reply.

"She is innocent of any wrongdoing. She deserves no harm," Londo said.

"Then see that none comes to her," said the Drakh. "For that matter . . . see that none comes to yourself . . . for her death would quickly follow."

Londo felt a chill run down his spine. "I don't know what you're talking about."

"Good," said the Drakh. "Then all will be well. Tomorrow you will inform Durla of his promotion."

Londo said nothing. There was no need. They both knew that the Drakh had him . . . had him in every way possible.

Shiv'kala glanced out the window of Londo's quarters. The rain was already beginning to taper off. "Tomorrow promises to be a fine day. Enjoy it, Mollari. It is, after all, the first of the rest of your life."

Londo went to the light switch and illuminated the interior of the room, then turned to the Drakh to offer a further protest over the promotion of Durla.

But the Drakh was gone, as if the light were anathema to him. Londo was alone.

Then he glanced at the keeper on his shoulder. It was watching him with a steady eye.

No. Never alone.

From his place of communion, hidden within the darkest shadows of the darkest area of the palace, Shiv'kala reached out and touched the darkness around him. He drew it about himself tightly, enjoying the coolness of it, the peace it brought him.

And within the darkness, the Drakh Entire was waiting for him, attending to his communication so that he could impart to them the progress on Centauri Prime. To his surprise, there appeared to be a bit of annoyance on the part of the Entire. They did not scold him or reprimand him, of course. Shiv'kala's reputation was too great, his status too elevated, for him to be treated in an offhand or condescending manner. Nevertheless, there was . . . concern . . . and a desire to find out why certain actions had been taken, actions the Drakh Entire could not quite comprehend.

At what game do you play, Shiv'kala? You told him your name.

"He asked. It makes no difference."

Why do you bargain with Mollari? Why do you not simply tell him what must be done?

"For what purpose? To show him that we are the stronger?"

Yes. He must know who is the master.

"He knows. He knows. He is, however, unwilling to accept. He resists our hold upon him. He contemplated taking his own life."

Are you certain?

"Yes. I am certain. He thought to hide it from me, but he can hide nothing. He merely thinks he can. And if he cannot live under the stewardship of the keeper, we will lose him."

If we lose him, then we lose him. He is simply another tool. A pawn. Nothing more.

"No," said Shiv'kala sharply. The sternness of his tone drew the Entire up short. "He is more. He is much more. He is not interchangeable, and although he is of course expendable, he is not to be so lightly tossed aside as the others. He is a visionary. We can help that which he envisions to come true. But our task becomes that much easier when our vision becomes his, as well."

What do you propose?

"Nothing except that caution be displayed, as much as possible. That we allow events to play out, rather than force hands. That Mollari be guided in our path rather than be forced. Particularly because if he believes certain things to be inevitable, or that certain ideas are his own, it facilitates our making use of him. It will bring matters to fruition that much more quickly and efficiently."

It does not matter how subtly you wish to influence him. He will never willingly accommodate certain aspects of our plan. His spirit must be broken, not treated gently.

"What will he refuse to accommodate?" asked Shiv'kala skeptically. "This is an individual who aided in the massacre of entire races. From what will he shrink?"

Sheridan. He will never assent to the death of Sheridan. Nor will he willingly stand by while the entire Human race is obliterated. Not unless he is made to realize that he has no choice.

"Do not underestimate the lack of love he feels for the Alliance, and for Sheridan in particular. As for the Humans . . . he had no difficulty in allowing the entire race to stand, by itself, at the edge of oblivion during the Earth-Minbari War. Now, when the personal stakes are so much higher, he will be even less likely to intervene.

"No, my brothers . . . trust me in this. Londo Mollari is at his most effective when he feels that he has some measure of control . . . even though that control is merely an illusion that we permit. One such as he will not be broken immediately. His spirit must be winnowed down. It must be carefully shaped. We must understand his weaknesses and his strengths, and work with both to our best advantage."

Shiv'kala . . . there are moments when it seems as if you actually like *this creature.*

"I feel he has great potential . . . and I would not see that potential wasted through mishandling. That, my brothers, is all."

Very well, Shiv'kala. You have earned our trust and our respect. We leave it to you to attend to Centauri Prime, and to Londo Mollari, in whatever manner you see fit.

"Thank you, my brothers."

But in the end, of course . . . it must turn out the only way that it can.

"With Londo's humiliation and death, and the final destruction of Centauri Prime?" Shiv'kala smiled mirthlessly. "I assure you, my brothers . . . I would not have it any other way."

With that, he felt the presence of the Drakh Entire slip away from him, like a shadow dissolving in light. And Shiv'kala was left alone, with his own thoughts and own agenda.

No. Never alone.

In the bowels of Babylon 5, the sleeper slept.

He did not know what he was, or who he was. He thought of himself merely as a vagabond, one who had found—if not a home—at least a place that was less hostile than other places in the universe. Down Below had a stench, but it was a familiar stench. The doctors were there every now and then, to deal with the most scabrous. Work could be had, if one wasn't looking to question the legality of it too closely.

Not much of a life . . . but it was a life, and he was content.

He did not know that all his memories were false.

He did not know that his recollections of how he came to reside on B5 were erroneous.

He thought he had a fairly good eye on his world, and understood the ins and outs. He didn't realize that he understood nothing.

But he would. He would. The only problem was, at the point where he understood . . . that was when it would be far, far too late.

— chapter 4 —

Senna lay back on the greensward, gazing toward the skies and the clouds.

"What do you see?" came the question from nearby. Telis Elaris lay there.

It was how they always tended to conclude their study sessions, Senna and Telis. Telis explained that it gave him an idea of just how much he had managed to expand her mind in that particular day's lessons. Senna, however, had come to look at it as simply an excuse for creative woolgathering.

As opposed to Senna, who always lay flat upon the grass, Telis had a decorative mat upon which he always reclined. "I am not as young as you," Telis would say to her, which always struck her as something of an odd excuse, because in truth Telis was only a little more than twice as old as she. He was, however, fond of claiming that he was far older than she in experience.

Senna had been assigned a number of teachers since she had first come to live in the palace, eight months ago. She remembered that night as if it were a distant dream. Indeed, she had trouble associating the girl she was then with the young woman that she was now.

The emperor had extended a hand of friendship to a girl who had ricocheted a rock off his skull, and she had had the temerity to slap that hand away. When she had come crawling back to him that night, she had been convinced he was going to throw her out, chortling with amusement over the pathetic young woman who had thought that she was somehow entitled to anything more than contempt.

Instead she had been given everything she could have wanted.

"Why?" she had asked him the next day over breakfast. She had not felt the need to go any further into the question than that. The one word spoke volumes.

And Londo had understood. "Because," he replied, "if I cannot attend to the body and soul of one woman . . . what hope have I in doing the same for Centauri Prime?"

"So I am to be a living symbol?"

"Do you have a problem with that?"

She considered it a moment, and then said, "No, Majesty." And that had seemed to settle it.

What had become more hotly debated was her choice of teachers. Londo had not hesitated to assemble a list of all the very best tutors, scholars, and lecturers to address Senna's education. This, however, had not gone over particularly well with Durla, the captain of the guards whom Londo—for reasons that remained inexplicable to Senna—had appointed to the key position of minister of Internal Security. The main reason Senna wasn't able to understand it was that she was certain—absolutely, one hundred percent certain—that Londo did not trust the man. And if one did not trust the minister of Internal Security, what could possibly be the point in having him in that position?

She remembered one day when she had heard particularly loud discussions coming from within the throne room. Londo and Durla had been disagreeing about something at extremely high volume. Once upon a time, Durla would have backed down immediately, but such was no longer the case. Durla no longer hesitated to tell the emperor precisely what was on his mind, and precisely why the emperor would be a fool not to attend to it.

On that particular day, she had heard several names being bandied about, and she recognized all of them as having been on Senna's own list of desired teachers. One name had been mentioned at particularly high volume, and that was the name of Telis Elaris.

That hadn't been surprising . . . all things considered.

Senna rolled over, and Telis looked at her quizzically. "Well?" he said in that no-nonsense air he had. Telis was another one of those who openly flouted convention; his black hair was long, but instead of wearing it upswept, he allowed it to run down over his shoulders. The style was abhorred by most older men and adored by most younger women, with the latter phenomenon leading to even greater ire among those members of the former faction.

"Well, what?" she replied.

"Well, what do you see in the clouds?"

"Great Maker take the clouds," she answered in annoyance. Telis had been her historical philosophy tutor for some months now, ever since Londo had first sent for him and hired him at Senna's request. She had been reading treatises of Telis' opinions ever since she was a child, and once had watched as her angered father had tossed one into the trash. She had recovered it from the rubbish, and Elaris had been her guilty, secret pleasure ever since. Historical philosophy specifically covered the various schools of thought that had served to shape much of the Republic's early years, examining how those philosophies interacted with politics. The topic was of particular interest to Senna. "Why must we stare at the useless clouds, when so much of great importance is occurring, right here under our noses?"

With that, Senna gestured toward a section of the capital city that had already been heavily rebuilt. The entire section had been blocked off as being too badly damaged to be safe for the citizenry, so the populace had been relocated and reconstruction had progressed quickly. In some ways, it was breathtaking.

"Why? Because it means nothing," said Telis.

She looked at him in surprise. "How can you say it means nothing?"

"Because that which we build ourselves, by definition, has no permanence. The clouds, on the other hand . . ."

"Have even less," Senna countered. "Look. Even now the wind wafts them away. By morning they will be a memory, but the buildings will still be there."

Telis smiled lopsidedly. "I have taught you too well. Countering your teacher in that way . . . whatever shall I do with you?" Then his face took on a more serious countenance. "I refer to more than those particular clouds, Senna. I refer to nature . . . to beauty . . . to the light. Those things will continue long after you and I are gone . . . long after all memory of the Centauri Republic is washed away, lost in the mists of time."

"That will never happen," Senna said confidently. "We have far more of a destiny to fulfill."

"That—" he pointed at her "—is the emperor talking. Not you."

"Why? Because it's believing in something for once?" She stretched out again, the back of her head cupped in her hands. "You are exhausting sometimes, Telis. Everything, everything is always being questioned. Nothing taken for granted. Everything must be debated, analyzed, debated and analyzed more . . ."

"What is your point, Senna?"

"Doesn't it sadden you? Having nothing that you truly believe in?"

"Is that what you think?"

He actually sounded stricken. She glanced over at him and was surprised to see that he appeared seriously upset at the remark. "Is that what you think?" he asked again. "Because if it is, then in all these months as my pupil, you've learned nothing."

She wasn't happy that she had upset him, for truth to tell, Telis Elaris was her favorite teacher, and she would not have wanted to hurt him for all the world. But having taken a stand, she felt constrained to defend it. "Well, what else am I to think? You dispute every conclusion I make. Even the most fundamental aspects of our life, when I bring them up, you disagree with them. Sometimes I think you'd dispute the existence of the Great Maker himself."

"I would."

Senna visibly blanched at that. "You're not serious."

"I am."

"But why?"

"To make you think, of course," Telis told her. "To make you question, to encourage you to probe. You must accept *nothing* at face value, Senna."

"You're telling me that I should never have faith in anything."

"Am I?"

She thumped the ground in frustration. "There! You're doing it again! Answering questions with a question."

"That should be welcome in a free-thinking society." He looked away from her and said softly, "And I am concerned . . . that it will not be welcome . . . by all."

She noticed that he was looking in the direction of the palace, off on a hill. "Telis," she said firmly, "you can't be speaking of the emperor. He fought to have you assigned as my teacher."

"Yes. He fought. He fought because there are others who prefer not to allow freedom of speech . . . freedom of thought. They don't desire it because it serves neither them nor their purposes. They require you to accept that which is presented you, and for you to question further is anathema to them.

"If, as you say, the emperor fights for freedom, well, that is to be applauded. But, my dear Senna . . . emperors come and go. It is the society that continues . . . at least for a time. And oftentimes those who shape the society . . . prefer to do so from hiding."

"*You* don't. Right there . . ." and she pointed. At the outer edge of the city there was a small building, rather unimpressive. The fact that it was still standing, considering the bombardment that the planet had taken, was impressive in and of itself. "Right there are your publishing offices. Everyone knows it. From there, you publish your papers and articles, challenging *everything* we do on Centauri Prime. You let everyone know that you believe in nothing . . . and yet you fault me when I point it out?"

He shook his head sadly. "And here I thought you were one of my best pupils.

"First, my dear, I do not attempt to shape society. I would not presume to impose my will upon it. I do not even guide. I simply attempt to get society to think for itself—about that which it has not previously considered—and to shape itself. As for what I believe in, Senna . . . what I believe in . . . is believing in nothing."

"You can't believe in believing in nothing."

"Of course you can," said Telis easily. "Child, it's not enough to open yourself to new ideas. Anyone can do that. The problem with that mindset is that usually there is a limit on the amount of 'openness' a person will accept. Sooner or later, the door to the mind swings closed once again. Most will accept just so much, and no more. The truly wise person, however, empties him- or herself of all knowledge . . . and remains that way. Only in that way can you remain open to all new things, all the time. Only in that way can you truly accept the endless varieties and opportunities that the world will present you."

"Those are fine words, Telis," replied Senna. "But words you can easily offer up with impunity, since you are not a leader. Leaders cannot remain open to all things, all the time. Leaders have to lead. They have to make decisions."

"And you believe the leaders are presently making good decisions?"

"Don't you?"

"A question answered with a question," he smiled. "Perhaps there *is* hope for you."

Suddenly Senna felt extremely impatient with what she perceived as constant verbal fencing. Her time with Telis frequently seemed to devolve into such matches. "Tell me. Tell me what you think," she demanded.

"I asked you first," he responded calmly.

"All right." She nodded, feeling that it was a fair enough point. "I think the answer speaks for itself. Look. See the industry that is underway? And the people . . . they have been through so much. Suffered through the bombings, seen their homes destroyed, their livelihoods shattered. There was a time when the emperor's walking among them posed a great security risk because there was so much anger directed toward him. But now, now they are focused on things other than anger. They are focused on re-creating Centauri Prime, achieving the greatness it once knew. The emperor has put forward a vision and they share it. Certainly this is better than anger, or hostility. Better than a sense of hopelessness. The outlook of the people is far better than any would have credited possible."

"And is that of consequence to you?" he asked.

"Of course it is! Why would you ask such a thing?"

"Because in referring to the people, you refer to 'they' . . . and not to 'we.' "

She opened her mouth to respond, then closed it.

"Would you have spoken in that manner six months ago, I wonder?" he continued. "A year ago? Who knows . . . perhaps you would have, back when your parents were people of rank and privilege. It could well be, Senna, that you have the snobbery of privilege so deeply ingrained within you that all it takes is the most gentle of stirrings to bring it bobbing to the surface."

"You think I don't know you, Telis," Senna said. "Well, I don't think you know me very well. Not very well at all."

"Perhaps. I am open to that possibility."

She swung her legs around and curled them up under her

chin, pointedly keeping her back to him. "I answered you. I apologize if my answer wasn't up to your usual demanding standards. You, however, have not answered me."

There was a long pause. Then he said, "Why?"

She looked back at him, angling her head slightly, which indicated her puzzlement. "Why what?"

"That should be the first question you ask yourself about everything . . . and once you have the answer . . . keep asking it. Why is there this drive to rebuild Centauri Prime?"

"To reattain our greatness," she said in confusion. The answer seemed self-evident.

"Why?"

"Telis, this is silly. It's like talking with a child. 'Why, why, why?' "

"Children are the greatest philosophers in existence. The purpose of the adult is to beat that drive out of children, because it threatens the status quo as created by the adult. Very well, though . . . I shall answer the questions myself, since it seems too tiresome for you."

"It's not a matter of tires—"

But Telis was already moving forward with his train of thought, ticking off the elements on his fingers as he went on. "There is a drive to rebuild Centauri Prime to make it what it once was. Why? To focus the people. Why? Because people of one mind become easier to manage. Why? Because then you can direct them where you want them to go. Why? Because you have someplace specific in mind for them. Why? Because you have a goal for yourself. Why?" He paused and then said, quite slowly, "Because you have decided that the return to the old ways necessitates a return to the expansionism that typified the old Centauri Republic. Because you have decided that no lessons are to be learned from the destruction that befell this planet except that one must be stronger and more focused than one's opponent if one is to win. Because what you truly seek is a return to a time when the Centauri Republic was the preeminent force in the galaxy, master of all it surveyed. Because you realize that times have changed, and that the Alliance now stands in the way. To overcome the Alliance requires new resolve, new weapons, new and even more fearsome allies, and a rededication and rebuilding that presages a new time of war. It's all in the histories, Senna. The so-called Age of Rationality of the Gaim that led to their Great Conquest March, a campaign that left four worlds burning in their wake before it ended. The rebuilding of Germany on Earth after their first World War, which set the stage for an even more calamitous second World War."

She stared at him, wide-eyed. "You're wrong," she said, her voice hushed.

"I spoke to you of allowing yourself to be empty, in order that you might become filled with knowledge. Beware those, Senna, who sense their own emptiness . . . and fill it with ignorance."

"You're wrong," she said again, shaking her head far more vehemently. "And I will tell you why. Because let us look at the history, indeed. In the circumstances you've mentioned, the sort of conversation we are having would never be allowed to happen. Particularly, it would not be allowed to happen between a teacher and a ward of the emperor himself. Such regimes as you describe are the antithesis of thought. Free will is not only discouraged, it is forbidden. Dissidents, intellectuals, writers . . . anyone who can ask the eternal 'why' such as you do, is silenced. And that is not the case here."

"Are you sure?"

"Of course I'm sure! I—"

And then, to her astonishment, Telis reached forward and grabbed her by the forearm. There was an intensity—even a bit of fear—that she had never seen in his eyes before. "You are still a member of the privileged elite, Senna. If it *were* happening, would you truly know until it was too late? I see others, persons such as myself, others who have questioned or probed . . . and suddenly they have changed their opinions. Suddenly they have accepted that which is presented . . ."

"Perhaps they have simply realized the rightness of—"

". . . or else they have disappeared," continued Telis.

Senna became silent for a moment. "Disappeared? What do you mean?"

"They move into outlying lands. Or simply drop off the face of the planet. Oh, it's all done very privately. Very efficiently. When they come for me . . ." he said thoughtfully, as if speculating about the fate of someone else entirely, "I imagine I shall be one of the ones who just drops off. For they know they cannot silence me any other way. I am publishing a paper at the end of this week that questions the true motives of those who are running the great machine that is our government. It will not earn me any friends and will garner me enemies even more formidable than I presently have."

Senna could see that this was no longer one of his mind-twisting journeys of curious logic. She took his hand firmly and squeezed it, and said, "Nothing will happen to you. You are my teacher. You are favored by the emperor. You are protected, and your thoughts are valued. Say what you will. No ill will befall you."

"Is that a promise to me?" He seemed genuinely amused by her fervency.

"That is my conviction and belief in our system, in our society . . . and in our emperor. I believe in all three."

He couldn't help but smile. "Why?" he asked.

She was annoyed, but still couldn't help but laugh at the insouciance with which he said it. "Because I do."

"That is circular logic," he said reprovingly.

"Perhaps. But the nice thing about circular logic is that you can't break through the circle."

To her surprise, Telis Elaris then reached over and hugged her tightly. And he whispered into her ear, "Don't ever change . . ." And then he paused and added, ". . . unless it's for the better."

* * *

When Senna returned to the palace, Durla was waiting for her.

She wasn't quite certain that he was actually waiting for her specifically, but as she approached her chambers, he seemed to materialize from around a corner. "Young lady Senna," he said with a slight bow. The informal title by which Londo had referred to her had come into common usage around the palace. It seemed almost a term of endearment when spoken by the right individuals . . . one of whom Durla most certainly was not.

Once again she found herself wondering just what it was that the emperor saw in him. She could only assume that he was extremely efficient in his job. For some reason, however, that thought chilled her even more.

"Minister Durla," she replied, attending to the response as courtesy demanded.

"I hope your lessons today were appropriately stimulating to the intellect," he said.

"Yes, they were. Thank you for your consideration." She started to head toward her chambers, and Durla stepped ever so slightly to one side. It was just enough to block her without coming across as threatening. She stopped in her tracks, folded her arms and regarded him with a raised eyebrow. "Is there something else, Minister?"

"We would be most appreciative if your lessons with Telis Elaris were held within the palace from this day forward," Durla said.

"Would you?" She was not enamored of the notion, as was painfully clear in her body language and dubious expression. "And why would that be? Pray tell?"

"It is a matter of security."

"And being minister of Internal Security, that would naturally be important to you. Your concern is noted, Minister, but Telis and I find the fresh air of the outdoors to be more . . .

what was the phrase you used? More 'intellectually stimulating' than the walls of the palace."

"Nor would I wish to hamper your educational growth. These are, however, dangerous times."

"Indeed. How so?"

"Agents and allies of the Alliance lurk everywhere."

Senna let out an overdramatic gasp and quickly looked around, as if she were concerned that enemies might spring out from the very walls around them.

Durla, for his part, was clearly not amused. "You can afford to take such things lightly, young lady, for your youth gives you a very limited sense of your own mortality. And since you see no enemy, you do not fear one."

"Actually, it is my understanding that something which you cannot see can be the most dangerous."

For a moment, Durla actually appeared startled. Senna couldn't quite figure out why he reacted the way he did, but then he smoothly composed himself, doing it so quickly that Senna wondered if she had perhaps imagined it all. "Quite so, and since you understand that, I take it that you will acquiesce to our request."

"You keep saying 'we' and 'our,' Durla. Is this your initiative, or the emperor's?"

"It is my recommendation. The emperor is in accord with it."

"I see. And if I ask him, he will verify it?"

"Absolutely. Although I will be hurt if you doubt my word in such an obvious manner."

Senna considered the situation. She had a feeling that Durla wasn't lying. That the emperor would indeed back up his minister of Internal Security. Then again, she was a ward of the emperor. He should care about her concerns as well. "You have also said this is a recommendation. Are you prepared to have the emperor order me to confine Telis and myself to the palace?"

To her surprise, Durla said quite soothingly, "Of course

not, young lady. No one has any desire to make you feel a prisoner, or constrict your movements beyond that which you are prepared to allow. We . . . I . . . am concerned only about your safety."

"Look at it this way, Durla," she said. "I became orphaned during a time when death rained from the heavens. At a time when so many died that the corpses were piled up as far as the eye could see. And I survived all that, without your help. So I think I'm more than capable of attending to my own safety."

"As you wish, young lady. But do be careful. If something were to happen to you, I know the emperor would be most upset. And I doubt that he would be overly enthused by my presenting, as an excuse, the notion that you simply wished to continue taking the air while learning at the feet of Telis Elaris."

"Your job is not without risks, Minister Durla. Certainly you must have known that before assuming the position."

"All of life is risk, young lady Senna." He bowed and began to walk away.

And then Senna—somewhat to her surprise—stopped him as she asked, "Minister . . . have you noticed a reduction in the number of writers, artists . . . creative individuals . . . in residence on Centauri Prime?"

"No more so than usual, young lady."

"Than usual?" She found the phrasing rather odd.

"Why yes. Such types are notoriously undependable and prone to difficulties. They starve for their art and so are lost . . . or they require dangerous drugs or drink in order to achieve their 'creative vision,' and come to harm through improper dosage.

"And then, of course, there are those of a radical bent. A thoroughly pugnacious and bellicose type, given to unfortunate accidents through altercations with others who possess opposing viewpoints. A rather sordid crowd, truly," he sighed. "Oh, I suppose that handsome, loquacious types such as Elaris make them seem . . . romantic. But as a group, they are quite unstable. If you do research, I think you'll find that many of them tend to come to rather bad ends. Let us hope that Elaris is not among those."

Something in his last statement chilled Senna slightly. "What do you mean by that, Minister?"

"Why, nothing, young lady. Nothing at all. Enjoy your . . . outdoor chats." He bowed and then went on down the hall.

Senna considered his words—and then went straight to the room that was usually used for her assorted lessons. She went over the room as meticulously as she could, searching for some sign of a listening device, to see if her lessons and conversations were being monitored. But she found nothing. Finally, exhausted from looking, she flopped down in a chair and sat there, wondering what Telis would say when she told him of the exchange she had just had with Durla.

— *chapter 5* —

She only caught the flash of light from the corner of her eye.

It was several days later and Senna was seated upon the hillside, wondering when Telis Elaris would show up. She was becoming somewhat apprehensive, for Telis was never late. In fact, he was so punctual that it bordered on the annoying.

She realized that they had never finished their "game" of seeing images in the clouds. Fortunately, this day was as nicely cloudy as the other had been, and so she let her mind wander as she gazed upon the billowing fluff high overhead.

She decided that one of them had taken on the shape of a giant spider. And another, with the odd crest to it and the curious convergence of shapes, looked like the emperor's face, only scowling. Scowling at the giant spider. She found that amusing for some reason.

So absorbed was she in her game that she barely noticed the light flash coming from the direction of the city. However, notice it she did, and she sat up quickly. It was then that she heard the explosion that had accompanied the flash. She could tell from the sound of the explosion that something large had gone up, though, and naturally her first thought was that Centauri Prime was once again under attack by the Alliance.

She scanned the heavens, preparing herself for some follow-up blast, but all remained silent. Then there was a second, even louder explosion, and by that point a column of thick black smoke had begun rising from the source.

Now Senna was on her feet, shading her eyes with one hand as she tried to make out precisely where the explosion had come from. Her breath caught in her throat, and she staggered slightly. Even from where she was, she could make out that the explosion had originated in the building that housed the home and office of Telis Elaris.

She didn't even remember starting to run. She was halfway there, her legs moving like pistons, and it was only when she realized that she was cutting her feet to ribbons on assorted stones and such that she remembered she was still holding her shoes. She stopped for a few seconds, never taking her eyes off the column of smoke, almost stumbling but recovering quickly. Then she continued to run, her breath ragged in her chest, gasping for air but never slowing down.

She came to an incline, tripped, fell, and tumbled heels over head the rest of the way. The incline butted up against the street and she slid down it in a most undignified fashion. However, so many people were running around, pointing and calling to each other, than no one took any notice of her. She scrambled to her feet and staggered toward the place where the explosion had occurred.

There had been some residual fire, but fortunately most of it had been contained by the time she got there. The building was already something that had become all too common on Centauri Prime: a burned-out shell. The last of the smoke was wafting heavenward, and people were pointing and speculating in hushed tones.

Rescue workers were emerging with several bodies of persons who were obviously beyond rescue. Senna scanned their remains desperately, hoping and praying that she would not see what she most feared would be there. Her hopes and prayers went unanswered, however—the third body brought out from the ruins was clearly the charred remains of Telis

Elaris. Half his face was gone, but there was enough left to recognize him.

She turned away, her hand to her mouth, trying to stifle both her urge to scream and her urge to vomit, all at the same time.

Then she heard one of the rescuers say, "We found this, Minister." She forced herself to look back, and there was Durla, taking what appeared to be some sort of heavy box from one of the rescue workers. It was scorched but otherwise undamaged, and Durla bowed slightly upon receiving it.

Something within Senna snapped.

"Murderer!" she howled, and she launched herself straight at Durla. Thanks to her dishevelled appearance, he clearly did not recognize her at first as she charged him, fists balled, her face a mask of pure rage. She got to within five feet of him, and then two guards were there, intercepting her and lifting her off her feet. She kicked furiously, arms outstretched, fingers clawing spasmodically, and she shouted, "You did this! You're behind this! You murdering bastard!"

It was then that Durla realized who it was shouting at him. "Young lady!" he said in obvious surprise.

"Don't call me that! Don't you *ever* call me that! You did this! You killed him!"

"Such ludicrous accusations. The girl is distraught. Take her back to the palace," said Durla unflappably as he tucked the box firmly under one arm. "We shall sort this mess out later."

"You killed him because he was a free thinker! Because he challenged! Because he made other people think! You'll pay for this, Durla! I'll make you pay!"

He shook his head sadly as Senna, still kicking and screaming, was carted away to the palace.

"Have you completely lost your senses?!"

The emperor stood over her, body trembling with indignation and perhaps even a sense of personal humiliation.

Cleaned up and wearing fresh clothing, Senna sat in a chair, hands folded, looking down. Nearby, Durla stood and observed the confrontation impassively.

"You accuse my minister of murder, in front of a crowd of people!" continued Londo. "A tragic circumstance, transformed by you into a suspicion of my government! What were you thinking? Well? That was not a rhetorical question—what were you thinking?"

"I said what I was thinking," Senna said quietly. "I believe that's why you're chastising me, Majesty."

"Outrage! It was an outrage!"

Annoyingly to Senna, it was Durla who spoke up in her defense. "I beg you, Majesty, do not be harsh with the girl. She was upset, obviously distraught. Considering the circumstances, I would say it was most understandable. She did not know the truth of the matter . . ."

"The truth of the matter?" She repeated the words with no inflection. "What are you talking about . . . 'the truth of the matter'?"

Durla sighed heavily, as if he were about to release a great burden. "I would have given anything if you were not to find out this way, young la—Senna. Do you remember that box the rescue worker removed from the rubble? Well . . . the evidence found therein was—shall we say—rather damning."

"What evidence. What sort of nonsense . . ."

"The truth is," and he addressed his comments to the both of them, "that it appears Telis Elaris was, in fact, a sympathizer with the Alliance."

"What? Are you sure?" asked Londo. "Have you any real proof?"

"Positive, Majesty. The box we found contained detailed logs, correspondence . . . communications with several key member races of the Alliance who still feel that the assault on Centauri Prime should continue. Races who will not be satisfied until every last one of us, no matter how young and pretty," he said pointedly to Senna, "is wiped from existence. Nothing less than wholesale genocide will suit them."

"This is utterly preposterous," Senna said. "Telis Elaris loved his fellow Centauri. It was only because he cared for them that he tried to expand their minds, to—"

"What he cared about, Senna, was undermining and undercutting the current regime. It wasn't entirely his fault," said Durla. "I believe he himself was being manipulated by the Alliance, who found in him a convenient patsy. Be that as it may, we have also uncovered the reason for the explosion: apparently Telis Elaris was experimenting with the construction of an incendiary device. His ultimate use for it, we do not know, although we can speculate based upon his communiqués. We believe—although I emphasize, there is no proof—that he intended to assassinate you, Majesty. Blow up the palace."

"This is insane!" shouted Senna.

"Is it?" Durla asked, never coming close to losing his patience. "It was he who suggested you take your lessons out of doors, was it not? We believe he intended to detonate the bomb during one of your sessions, so that there would be no chance of you coming to harm. Apparently he felt quite affectionately toward you. In any event, while he was certainly of quite high quality as a thinker, he was a bit deficient in the category of terrorism. The device went off prematurely, and . . ." He shrugged.

Senna turned to Londo. "Majesty, surely you can't believe this. You know Telis. You know the kind of man he is . . . was. Do not let this . . . this . . ." she waggled a finger at Durla, "this *person* . . . besmirch the good name of Telis Elaris. It's bad enough that he assassinated the man. Now will he be allowed to assassinate the man's character as well?"

"Senna . . . you have become very dear to me," Londo said slowly, "but I warn you, do not overstep yourself, for it—"

"Overstep myself! Majesty, we stand in the presence of a murderer and liar! Murder and lying are not in the job de-

scription of the minister of Internal Security! Who has over-
stepped whose bounds?"

"We do not know that," Londo said, "and if there is proof—"

"Proof that he could easily have manufactured!"

"Interrupt me again at your own peril, Senna!"

Senna, who had risen from her chair when confronting
Londo, took a step back as she realized that he meant it. She
had never seen him as angry as he was at that very moment.

With a distinct effort, Londo composed himself, then said
tightly, "I will inspect the evidence myself. If the findings are
as Minister Durla says, well . . ." He paused, considering the
matter a moment. "As a matter of internal security, I see no
reason at this time to inform the populace that there may have
been a traitor in their midst. Why stir matters up more than
they are, or contribute more fuel to the fire of paranoia. They
need peace of mind. If at the end of his life, Telis Elaris har-
bored traitorous alliances, that does not negate the good he
accomplished through his teachings. We can always attribute
the explosion to something routine—a furnace or some such.
You can come up with something, I trust, Durla?"

"Yes, Majesty," Durla replied dutifully.

"Good."

"So it would seem," Durla commented to Senna, "that
sometimes lying *is* part of my job description."

Senna said nothing. For some moments, in fact, no one
said anything. Then Londo told her, "Since you are so concerned, Senna, about the public perception of a man who is
already dead . . . do you not think you owe Minister Durla an
apology for your public assault on his character, particularly
considering that he is still alive to hear whatever criticism
may arise from your actions?"

"If you are indeed asking me, Majesty . . . no. No, I don't
believe I owe him that at all."

She looked at Londo with her chin slightly upthrust and as
much moderate defiance as she dared display.

"Majesty," Durla said, coming to her rescue once more, "it is not necessary. Truly."

"Very well," Londo nodded. "Senna, you may go."

She walked out of the room, and it was only when she was a safe distance that she allowed the tears to flow.

Durla handed the box of evidence to Londo and bowed. "Return it whenever you are done, Majesty. I expect that you will find everything as I've said."

"Oh, I expect I will," Londo told him.

Durla turned to leave. He started toward the door, and then he heard quick footsteps behind him. Before he could turn, he suddenly felt one powerful hand on the back of his neck, and another grabbing him by the back of his coat. The slim minister was propelled forward and slammed face first against the wall. The impact knocked the breath out of him, and then Londo's mouth was right up against his ear, whispering to him in a sort of perversely intimate moment.

"Understand, Durla . . . if I learn that this evidence has indeed been falsified . . . that you were responsible for the death of Elaris . . . your head will wind up next to that of a fellow named Morden who was, I assure you, far better connected and far more dangerous than you. And I further assure you that I personally will attend to the task of decapitating you, with Senna there to catch your head and stick it on the pole with her own eager hands. Is that clear?"

"Majesty, I—"

"Is. That. Clear?"

"Yes, Majesty."

He released Durla then. The minister did not turn around. Instead he straightened his coat, smoothed some ruffled strands of his hair, and walked out of the throne room.

The moment he was gone was when the pain hit Londo.

White hot, stabbing, exploding through his brain and offering him no place to run. He staggered across the throne room, trying to locate the source, and then he realized. The keeper, the keeper on his shoulder was doing this.

He tried to reach around, to rip the monstrosity off him once and for all, but all such efforts only increased the agony, and that was when he heard a voice in his head saying, *I would not do that if I were you.*

He staggered to his throne, clutching the arms, gasping as the pain finally started to recede. But a sense of it still remained, like a great beast lurking in the high grass, ready to come at him once again if he so much as made the slightest wrong move. Even in his head, he recognized the voice of the Drakh Entire or at least the Drakh emissary who seemed to haunt the palace like an omnipresent specter of death.

"How . . . how did—"

No questions. Sit. In the throne. Hands on the armrests.

Londo did as he was instructed. He had no choice—he realized that.

You abused Durla. The voice sounded almost disappointed. *He is chosen by us. You are not to do such a thing ever again.*

"Chosen by you. Then he has a keeper, too?" growled Londo, taking at least some measure of joy in picturing what it must have been for Durla to watch one of those abominations crawling across the floor at him.

So he was disappointed to hear in reply, *No. He does not require one. He already believes—that the Republic has become vulnerable because of its decadence, that you have lost the fire of your early years. He believes in discipline, order, and total obedience. He does not need to know of our existence, does not require a keeper. His pure enthusiasm and rightness of spirit will make him far more effective than any keeper could.*

"I'm so happy for you. Then may I ask why you need me?"

We don't.

Well . . . there it was, wasn't it. The Drakh could be accused of many things, but prevarication was not one of them.

Sounding almost regretful, the Drakh voice said to him, *We take no pleasure in this, Londo. No joy. The work you have done thus far for Centauri Prime is laudable. You have focused them, directed them, uplifted them, brought them far from their fallen state in just a few short months. Left to your own devices, you might indeed be a worthwhile emperor. But you are our device, not your own. You will attend to our wishes and remember that you can pretend to serve the people, but you truly serve us. To help you in remembering . . . you will sit silently in your throne now.*

"But—"

For just a moment, the pain welled up, like a threatening tidal wave.

Silent . . . ly.

Then Londo sat perfectly upright, staring straight ahead, looking neither left nor right.

You will remain that way . . . until we tell you otherwise. You will hear the noises, the conversations, the normal life of the palace outside . . . but you will not participate. All audiences will be refused. You will be alone for hours . . . or days . . . however long we feel it necessary in order to make our point.

You spoke of Centauri Prime being alone? You have no grasp of the concept. But you will. You will, for the greatest loneliness of all is to be alone among others. Do not move, Londo. Do not speak. Dwell on what you have done, and what will be required of you . . . and what will happen to you if you do not live up to those requirements.

Then the voice in his head ceased, but Londo—wisely—did not move. He continued to stare resolutely ahead, lest the voices and the pain return.

I am in hell, thought Londo.

And a voice replied, *Yes. You are.*

He tried not to think after that.

* * *

It was a brisk day, the wind whipping sharply over the hills. Senna went to their place and sat upon the grass. She stared off into the distance toward the ruined building, which was already in the process of being torn down, now part of the emperor's renovation program. Considering the speed and efficiency with which the workers had been moving, a new structure would probably replace it within a week.

She had been checking through libraries, through data bases. The writings of Telis Elaris were quietly being removed, disappearing one by one.

She lay back on the grass, looked up at the clouds. She tried to conjure up images . . . and nothing suggested itself. They were just white collections of mist and vapors, and would soon go away, just as everything went away.

Tears began to roll down her face, even though she made no noise.

"Why?" she whispered.

No answers came.

The sleeper began to stir.

He did not fully realize what was happening, not on any conscious level. He simply developed the oddest feeling that everything around him was . . . incidental. That it would soon cease to have any true relevance to his life.

He went about his business, trying to ignore the faint buzzing that was becoming more pronounced in his head. When he could ignore it no longer, he went to the medical people, but their rather cursory examination found nothing. He didn't fault them for it, not really. He was having trouble explaining to them just what it was that he was feeling, so how could they know what to look for? He didn't even understand it himself.

So he pushed himself to go on with his life and not dwell on that which he did not understand. And when word trickled down that the president of the Interstellar Alliance was going to be doing a walk-through of Down Below . . . that he was, in fact, endeavoring to develop a program that would be of help to everyone there, why . . . that all sounded fine. Excellent, in fact. Down Below could use all the help it could get.

He did not realize yet that he would be assassinating President Sheridan. Assassination was the furthest thing from his mind. He was just a normal guy, trying to get on with his normal life. Thoughts of murder and mayhem were far, far away.

He didn't understand that they were going to draw quite close.

— chapter 6 —

Vir hadn't known what to expect when he arrived back on Centauri Prime.

When he had departed, right after the inauguration, it had been under less-than-ideal circumstances. Cities had been reduced to smoldering ruins, and Londo had delivered a bizarre speech that sounded as if it was designed to fan the flames of hostility and rage against the Interstellar Alliance. *What good could possibly come from getting the Centauri people even more worked up?* Vir had wondered, mystified. They had to understand that it was a time of reconciliation. Of redemption.

Yes . . . that was what was required, Vir thought as the transport ship that carried him the final leg to his destination drew within reach of the Centauri Prime main spaceport. *Redemption.* The Centauri had much for which they had to redeem themselves.

The truth was that they had done great evil. They had attacked the Narns, they had provided aid to the most evil of evil races, the Shadows. As a race they had sinned mightily, and as a race they were being called upon to repent. Repenting for their sins, however, was not going to be easy if their ire was stirred and they were made to feel as if they—the poor, put-upon citizens of Centauri Prime—were the victims. Yes, there had been misunderstandings. Yes, there seemed to have been deliberate plots to vilify Centauri Prime in the eyes of other races. But wasn't the truth that they, the Centauri people, had left themselves open for precisely that sort of under-the-table assault?

If they had had a reputation for being peaceful, gentle, un-aggressive . . . certainly no one could have manipulated them into a position where they were considered to be a threat. But the Centauri had, through their own actions and with their own blood-covered hands, made certain that everyone knew they were a dread force to be reckoned with.

Well, the reckoning had come, hadn't it. And look at what the result had been. Just look.

"Just look to your right," the pilot's voice came over the speaker system of the transport, "and you'll see the restoration of the entire north quarter of our glorious capital city. Work is continuing on the city's other sections, under the building-relief programs created and overseen by our glorious emperor. In the meantime, increased Centauri industry has bolstered our economy, supporting not only our rebuilding efforts, but also paying off—oftentimes in trade—the reparations that we have so generously agreed to pay the members of the ungrateful Interstellar Alliance."

Vir gulped. He did not like the sound of that at all. Further-more, he had the feeling that the pilot was reading from a pre-pared text. He wondered just who had prepared it. He glanced around the shuttle at his fellow passengers. Everyone else in the shuttle was Centauri. He was curious to see that all of them were nodding their heads in unison over the comments about the emperor's great works . . . and unsettled to note that they were shaking their heads together and scowling when there was mention of the Alliance.

No, not good at all. He was definitely going to have to talk to Londo about it. The problem was, he had absolutely no idea what he was going to say.

He had endeavored to remain in touch with Londo, as was his mandate while he served as the Centauri ambassador to Babylon 5. He hadn't anticipated that it would become a problem. If nothing else, he had figured that the normally gregarious Londo would retain his interest in his associates back on the station. That he would be anxious to check in with Vir as often as possible, to learn who was up to what, catch up on all the latest gossip. Such had not been the case, however. Weeks, even months would go by without Vir being able to communicate with Londo at all. Instead he found more and more of his conversations being held with Durla, the minister of Internal Security. The last time that he had encountered someone that chilling it had been the notorious Mr. Morden, and there had certainly been no love lost in *that* relationship. Lives and heads lost, yes, but no love.

"I will relay your concerns to the emperor. The emperor is busy at the moment. The emperor appreciates your communiqués." These and a litany of stock phrases had tripped off Durla's lips so often that Vir knew them by hearts. And on those occasions when Vir somehow, miraculously, did get through to Londo, the emperor had always spoken with such care and judiciousness that Vir couldn't help but get the feeling that all their conversations were being monitored somehow. The thought itself should have been absurd. Londo was, after all, the most powerful person on Centauri Prime. Theoretically, there should be no one and nothing who would have the temerity and the power to oversee his interests and activities. Who did Londo have to fear?

Then Vir considered the fate of previous Centauri emperors, and filled in the answer to that: Everyone.

But Londo wasn't like other emperors. Certainly he was nothing like Cartagia, the madman. And he was nothing like the regent, who had brought their world to the brink of ruin. Londo was a good man, a decent man. That had to count for something, didn't it?

Didn't it?

Unfortunately, even in his own mind, he could not divine an answer for that.

Fortunately for everyone aboard the transport, Vir's concentration wasn't necessary for the transport to land safely. So his thoughts were able to ramble about all manner of concerns while the craft settled safely onto its landing spot in the main spaceport.

*   *   *

"Ambassador Vir!"

Vir's first impulse was still to look over his shoulder, to see if someone else was being hailed. Hearing the designation "ambassador" in front of his name was still something of a jolt to him, and he always felt slightly guilty—as if he were an imposter. Or perhaps a mistake had simply been made and another Vir was being summoned . . .

In this instance, however, he managed to fight the impulse and look instead toward whomever it was that was endeavoring to get his attention.

There was a rather tall individual standing there. He was somewhat pale in complexion, with sunken eyes and a voice that seemed to originate from somewhere around his ankles. When he walked it was with a slight hunch, as if he perpetually had to lean forward to hear what you had to say. His medium-high hair was quite light, as pale in its way as his skin tone. Standing next to him was a young boy who couldn't have been more than thirteen. Curiously, although the tall man was dressed in the sort of finery that Vir had come to associate with the imperial court, the boy was sporting some sort of uniform, such as Vir had never seen before. It was mostly black, which gave Vir eerie flashbacks to the Psi Corps, but it was broken up by a bloodred sash draped across his chest.

"Ambassador Vir," said the tall man. "I am Castig Lione, chancellor of Development, attached to Minister Durla's office. It is an honor to meet you. Throk, take the gentleman's bags."

"Oh, that's quite all right," Vir started to say, but he spoke too slowly. The teen, Throk, was already at his side and was gripping firmly the bags that Vir held in either hand. Vir took one look into the boy's eyes, and promptly released the bags. The boy wielded them easily . . . actually, with a great deal more ease than Vir had carried them. Vir told himself that it was just because he was tired from the trip. "I . . . wasn't expecting anyone to pick me up, actually. I just figured I'd make my way to the palace on my own. I didn't mean to put anyone out."

Lione smiled. When he did so, however, it looked as if he

were in some sort of vague pain. Just as quickly as it appeared, the smile vanished. "You are everything that I have heard. Humble and self-effacing, as if you still do not appreciate your importance."

"Well . . . once upon a time, you have to understand . . . being ambassador to Babylon 5 not only wasn't especially important . . . it was actually sort of a . . . well . . ." He lowered his voice as if he was concerned about offending Londo, who was nowhere in sight. ". . . a joke. A position that no one took particularly seriously."

"Times change," said Lione.

"Yes, they certainly do. And who is this young man? Throk, I believe you said his name was?" Vir smiled broadly at him and was greeted with an unflinching, sullen face, and eyes that somehow gave him a free-floating sense of anxiety. "Is there some significance to the uniform?"

"Throk is one of the first members of the Centauri youth group. We call them the Prime Candidates. And indeed, they are excellent candidates to be the next generation of leaders of our world."

"Oh, a play on words! That's very cute," said Vir.

Throk gave him a look that, Vir realized, could have brought on a new ice age if there were a way to harness it. "We are not cute," he said succinctly.

"Throk . . ." chided Lione warningly.

"Sir," amended Throk stiffly. "We are not cute, sir."

"I . . . stand corrected," said Vir, who was already feeling more and more creepy about the entire business.

"Chapters of the Prime Candidates are opening across Centauri Prime. The young are the hope of the future, Ambassador, as is always the case. So it was felt that one of the best things that could be done for the morale and spirit of our citizenry was for them to see the energies and enthusiasm of our youth harnessed in a positive manner."

"And what do the Prime Candidates do, exactly?" Vir asked Throk.

Throk did not hesitate. "Whatever Chancellor Lione tells us to."

"Oh."

"They do public works, public services. Clean-up campaigns, running public information offices . . . that sort of thing," Lione explained.

"That all sounds wonderful. And this was the emperor's idea?"

"Minister Durla's, actually, but the emperor embraced it immediately. I was then brought in by Minister Durla to oversee the program . . . and also explore other means of lifting morale throughout Centauri Prime."

They climbed into a waiting transport that immediately hurtled in the direction of the palace.

"You know . . . I have a thought on that."

"On what, Ambassador?"

"On boosting morale. There's this remarkable Earth game I was introduced to on Babylon 5 by Capt—by President Sheridan. If we could organize teams to play it, that might do wonders."

"Indeed." Castig Lione once again made that slightly winced smile. Throk sat in the seat just ahead of them and stared resolutely forward. "What might that be?"

"It's called 'baseball.' "

"Indeed," Lione said once more. "How is it played?"

"Well," said Vir, warming to the topic, "you have nine men on each side. And one man, he stands in the middle of the field, on an elevated pile of dirt, and he has a ball, about this big." He shaped the imaginary spheroid in his hands. "And there's a man from the other team, and he stands a distance away holding a stick."

"A stick."

"Well, a large stick. And the man on the dirt throws the ball at the man with the stick."

"Endeavoring to injure or kill him?" Castig Lione's interest seemed piqued.

"Oh, no. No, he tries to throw it past him. And the man with the stick tries to hit it. If he misses it, he gets two more attempts to try and hit it. If he hits it, he runs to a base—"

"A military base?"

"No, it's a square, about so big. He tries to run to the base before one of the other men on the field gets the ball there ahead of him."

"And . . . if he accomplishes this . . . what happens?" Lione didn't seem to be quite as intrigued as he had been when he had thought the object was to concuss the man with the stick.

"If he doesn't make it, he's out."

"Of the game?"

"Oh, no, no he can try later when it's his turn again. But if he does make it to the base, then he has a chance to try and get to another base."

"That seems rather pointless. Why doesn't he just stay on the one he's on?"

"Because if he gets to a second base, then he gets to try for . . ."

"A third base?" Lione's interest was definitely flagging. "Is there a point to all this somewhere?"

"Oh, yes! After he gets to the third base, he gets to try to go home."

"Home? You mean he leaves the game?"

"No, it's called home base. If he gets to home base, then his team scores a run. And they do this back and forth, getting runs or outs, until there's three outs from each side, and that's called an 'inning.' And the game goes until nine innings, unless it's tied in which case it can go on forever, or it rains or everyone just gets sick of it."

Castig Lione stared at Vir, then asked, "And this is a popular game on Earth?"

"Humans love it," said Vir.

And Throk said dourly, "No wonder the Minbari tried to wipe them out."

—— chapter 7 ——

"Vir! *Viiiiir!*"

Londo's greeting of him was big and boisterous and not at all what Vir had expected. Then again, there was a large party going on, and in that sort of environment Londo was most definitely in his element.

It was all quite exciting for Vir. Certainly he had attended enough parties, particularly in Londo's presence. The Londo of old was something of a magnet for such festivities. Many were the revelries that he was able to recall on Babylon 5, although admittedly his memory of some of them was recalled through a bit of a haze. A pleasant haze, but a haze nonetheless.

But this . . . this was a party in the court!

For all that Vir had been through—for all of the secret plots, and his own hideous involvement in such dire schemes as assassinations—he had never truly left behind the relatively innocent individual that he once had been. And that individual was the fool of the Cotto clan, the embarrassment, the one who was never going to amount to anything. When he had been shunted away to Babylon 5, to serve as aide to the equally despised Londo Mollari, it had simply been the latest insult in a life laden with insults.

To be part of the court, to rub elbows with the movers and shakers of Centauri rank and society . . . inwardly he still felt a sort of disbelief over how everything had turned out. This was not how it was supposed to go for Vir Cotto. He was

83

supposed to eke out an existence, and try not to get into anyone's way. That had been the entirety of his aspirations.

So to be arriving in court, to be able to hold his head high . . . he still felt as if he had to pinch himself to make certain that he wasn't dreaming it all. That was how he felt, even though he knew that the dream had its dark, nightmarish side. Yes, he knew that all too well.

The grand reception hall was alive with activity. There was song and dance and merriment. A scantily clad dancing girl bumped up against Vir and smiled at him . . . at *him* . . . in a most sultry manner before pirouetting off, thin veils trailing from her hands. Waiters bearing an assortment of gourmet tidbits converged on him from all sides, almost stumbling over one another to serve him. People were dressed in the most glorious finery, chatting and laughing and acting as if they had not a care in the world.

"Vir!" Londo shouted once more and began to make his way through the crowd. When one is the emperor, such an action is far less taxing than it would be for others. The crowd magically melted before him to make way, closing itself behind him as he passed. It gave him the appearance of being a great ship moving through the ocean. *The ship of state,* Vir told himself.

Londo was holding a drink. He passed one nobleman and, without hesitation, plucked the drink from the man's hand and bore it toward Vir. It took a moment for it to register on the nobleman, but when he realized who it was who had absconded with his drink, he simply gestured toward one of the wandering waiters and signaled that another would be required.

"Vir! I must tell you a riddle!" Londo said as he thrust the glass into Vir's hand.

Several things were tumbling about in Vir's head: to thank Londo for the drink; to tell him he didn't need it; to tell Londo that he, Londo, was looking quite well; to tell him that he was pleased that he had been invited to this get-together. All of this occurred to him, but was promptly washed away by the unexpected declaration. "A . . . riddle?"

"Yes! Yes, it is quite clever. Senna told it to me. Clever girl, our young lady."

"Yes, you've told me about her. Tragic thing, the loss of her teach—"

"Do you want to hear this riddle or not?" Londo demanded.

"Oh . . . absolutely, yes." Vir bobbed his head.

Londo draped an arm around Vir's shoulders, bringing his face closer. The smell of alcohol was even more pungent than usual. "What is greater than the Great Maker . . . more frightening than a Shadow ship . . . the poor have it . . . the rich need it . . . and if you eat it, you die."

Vir silently mouthed the elements of the riddle, then shook his head. "I give up."

"You give up!" Londo sounded almost outraged. "You give up? That is your problem, Vir. That has always been your problem. You give up, far too quickly. You have to give things thought, Vir. Even if you do not succeed, you have to at least *try!*"

"All . . . all right. Let me think. Greater than the Great Ma—"

His thought process was promptly interrupted when a voice from at his elbow said, "Ambassador. What a pleasure it is to see you."

Vir turned and saw Durla standing there.

He had seen the man before in passing, but not since Durla had been promoted to the ministry. Durla had never really registered on Vir, back when he was captain of the guards. But now that he was seeing him, really seeing him for the first time, he sensed that this was a man to watch out for.

"And I, you, Minister," Vir replied easily.

"How nice that you were able to get away from Babylon 5 to attend this little celebration. I'm sure you've been very busy there."

Vir watched Londo's gaze flicker from Durla to Vir and

back. He seemed curiously content to watch the two of them converse. It was as if Londo had something very specific he wanted to see accomplished, but Vir could not for the life of him imagine what that might be. The last thing that Vir was interested in doing was getting into some sort of verbal sparring match with Durla just because it might suit Londo's purposes, whatever those might be. Nevertheless, there was something in Durla's tone and attitude that Vir couldn't help but consider off-putting. It wasn't in the words so much, but in the condescending voice attached to it.

"Oh, yes . . . yes, I've been very busy," Vir said.

"I'm sure. Although," Durla continued, "the true future of the Centauri Republic would lay, I think, with what is developing on Centauri Prime, rather than on a hunk of metal light-years away. A place that is the base of operations for an Alliance that is dedicated to wiping the Centauri off the face of creation, eh?"

"Minister," Vir said carefully, "with all respect, if the Interstellar Alliance were 'dedicated' to it, I doubt we'd be all standing here right now, in an intact palace, enjoying this quite wonderful wine. Excuse me!" he called to a passing waiter, indicating with a gesture that he could use a refill. Vir normally wasn't a drinker, but in recent years he had driven his tolerance level up, just through practice. A lengthy association with Londo Mollari tended to do that.

As the waiter scurried off to fulfill Vir's request, he added, "Keep in mind, Minister, that I'm posted on Babylon 5. I've known the president of the Alliance for a great many years. I wouldn't presume to comment on what I've heard goes on here, so you might want to consider carefully your own sentiments when speaking about the Alliance."

"And what have you heard 'goes on' here?" Durla asked with one eyebrow slightly raised in curiosity.

Vir looked down and saw that the next drink was in his hand, as if it had materialized there by magic. He downed half of it in one gulp. He had a feeling that this evening, he was going to need it. "Oh, crazy rumors. People disappearing. Our more moderate politicians losing face, losing power . . . losing lives. And all of them being replaced by associates of yours."

"You overestimate me, Mr. Ambassador," Durla said, sounding quite sincerely modest. "Granted, I tend to recommend to the emperor people whom I know to be trustworthy. But since Internal Security is within my purview, naturally it would make sense to bring in those who I know will be loyal to the Republic."

"Don't you mean, to you?"

"I say what I mean, Ambassador," Durla replied, unperturbed. "In point of fact, it is the emperor who is the living incarnation of the spirit of the Centauri Republic. If I am to be concerned about loyalties to anyone in particular, it should be to him."

"How very gracious of you, Minister," Londo finally spoke up. "These are, after all, dangerous times. It is difficult to know whom we can trust."

"Absolutely true," Durla said. He clapped Vir on the shoulder. "I believe that I may have given you the wrong impression, Ambassador. May my tongue snap off if I say something that gives you a moment's concern."

"Now that's something I'd pay to see," Vir said.

Apparently missing the sarcasm, Durla continued, "Ultimately, we all want the same thing. A restoration of Centauri Republic to the arena of interstellar greatness we once enjoyed."

"We do?"

"Of course, Ambassador!" Durla said, as if he were stating a given. "At this point in time, to many, we are nothing but a joke. A beaten, fallen foe. Entire systems are allied against us and would keep us down. Once . . . once they quivered in fear at the very mention of our name. Now . . . they quiver with laughter."

"Terrible," intoned Londo, as if he'd had the conversation a thousand times before. Vir couldn't help but notice that Londo was putting away liquor at somewhere around triple the rate that Vir was maintaining. Indeed, faster than anyone in the place, it seemed. "A terrible thing."

"And even now, as we rebuild, as we break our backs to settle the 'reparations' while we try to restore our own pride . . . they watch over us. They treat us as we once treated the Narns. Now what would you call that?"

"Poetic justice?" ventured Vir.

As if Vir had not spoken—indeed, Durla probably hadn't even heard him—Durla answered his own question. "Insults! Insult piled upon insult! The potential for greatness still lives within Centauri Prime, still burns like a fever within the bodies of our people."

"Aren't fevers generally considered a bad thing?" Vir asked. "You know . . . sometimes you die from them . . ."

"And sometimes they bring greater clarity of vision," said Durla.

"I usually just get headaches."

"We walked among the stars," Durla said forcefully. "When you have had the stars, how are you supposed to content your-self with the dirt beneath your feet? Do you know what I want for my people, Ambassador? Do you want to know the truth? I want my people to reclaim their rightful place in the galaxy. I want to see the Centauri stretch forth their hand again and command the stars. I want a rebirth of glory. I want us to be what we used to be. Does that seem too much to ask, Ambassador?"

It was Londo who replied, swirling a drink around in his glass and staring down at it. "No," he said softly. "No . . . it does not seem too much to ask at all."

Durla was about to continue, but someone called his name from over on the other side of the room. Apparently some sort of friendly dispute was going on, and Durla was being asked to come and settle it. He bowed quickly and graciously to Vir and Londo, and headed off.

Several more officials came toward Londo, clamoring for

his attention, but Londo waved them away. Instead he placed a hand on the small of Vir's back and said, "Come, walk with me, Vir. Catch me up on all the latest developments."

"Well, here's a late development: I do not like him, Londo. This Durla. Not one bit." Vir was speaking in a whisper, albeit an angry one.

"Durla? What is wrong with Durla?" Londo sounded almost shocked.

"Look, don't take this wrong, but . . . in some ways, he reminds me of you. That is, the way you used to be."

"He doesn't remind me of me at all."

"Are you kidding? All those things he was saying about what he wants us to be? Doesn't that sound like something you might have said once?"

"No. I never would have said any such thing."

Vir rolled his eyes in annoyance as Londo guided him down one of the large corridors. "Where are we going?" he asked.

"On a tour. Much work has been done on the palace since you were last here." He glanced at Vir. His vision appeared a bit bleary. "So let me understand this: you say that Durla reminds you of me, and on that basis you don't like him. I suppose I should be insulted, no?"

"When I first met you, back then you . . . well, you were somewhat intimidating, Londo. And you had these visions for what the Centauri should be. And you . . ."

"Fulfilled them," Londo said softly.

"Yes. And millions died because of it."

"Such harsh words. Do you judge me, Vir? You dare judge the emperor?" There was challenge in the words, but in the tone there was only interest.

"I know you, Londo. Sometimes I think I know you better than anyone alive . . . or at least, anyone who's left alive. He shares your dream, Londo. And look what became of it. Look at all the death, destruction, and tragedy that arose from it."

"The road to one's destiny is never a smooth one, Vir. There are always bumps along the way . . ."

"Bumps! Londo, we slaughtered the Narns! We spread a reign of terror! And that sin came back to revisit us a hundredfold! Those actions came solely because of the kind of thinking that Durla is standing there spouting! When are we going to learn, Londo? What's it going to take! The annihilation of every Centauri in the galaxy?"

"Why are you asking me?" inquired Londo. "Do you know who you should ask? Rem Lanas."

"I'm sorry . . . what?" Vir felt as if the conversation had abruptly veered off at another angle completely. "Rem Lanas? Who is—"

"He is on Babylon 5, as I recall. Has been for some time. Very wise individual. Do you know why you are here, Vir?"

Vir was having trouble following the thread of whatever it was they were supposed to be talking about. "Well, I . . . well, no, Londo, to be honest. I'm pleased that this party is being held, just because it's nice to see our people celebrating something—anything—even if it's just a group pat on the back to enjoy the reconstruction plans. But I'm not sure why you asked me specifically to come."

"What are you insinuating, Vir?"

"Insinuating? I . . ." He sighed. "Londo . . . perhaps, well . . . you may have had a little too much to drink. Because to be honest, you're not talking very sensibl—"

"Could you possibly be implying," continued Londo, "that I couldn't speak to you via standard communications means if I desired to? That I'm worried about being unable to find a secure channel? That everything I say could be monitored by others? You're not saying that, are you, Vir?"

Mr. Garibaldi had once used an expression that Vir had found most curious: he had spoken of "the dime dropping," as a means of indicating that someone had just realized something. It wasn't a term Vir completely understood, particularly because he had no idea what a dime was, or where it might drop that would inspire in any way a moment of clarity.

However, at that moment, as Vir listened—really listened—to what Londo was saying, he suddenly got a vague inkling as to what a dime dropping might mean to him personally.

"No," Vir said very carefully. "I didn't intend to imply that at all." But he said it with such a careful tone of voice that he hoped to make it clear to Londo that he had grasped the subtext.

The mists of emptiness that had clouded Londo's eyes up until that moment seemed to part, ever so briefly. He nodded wordlessly. Then he opened his mouth to speak once again . . .

. . . and he staggered.

"Londo?"

Londo passed his face in front of his hands as if trying to brush away cobwebs, and when he lowered his hand there was an expression that seemed a combination of anger and resignation. "Building up your tolerance to alcohol, I see," he muttered.

"Somewhat, yes," Vir said.

"I wasn't talking to you."

"But—"

Londo suddenly switched his mood, sounding rather jovial again. "We have a superb gallery that is a tribute to previous emperors. We took existing statues and paintings, gathered them in one place—come, Vir! You should see it!"

"*Uhm* . . . all right . . ."

Chatting with what seemed excessive cheer, Londo guided Vir to the end of the corridor, hung a sharp right, then a left, and led him into a very sizeable room. Just as Londo had boasted, the walls were lined with a most impressive array of paintings and sculptures, the latter ensconced on carefully crafted shelves inset into the walls.

The first painting that naturally caught Vir's eye was

Cartagia. Londo saw where Vir was looking, and echoed Vir's thoughts aloud: "Why is he here, eh?"

Vir nodded. "He was insane, Londo. An ugly part of our history. He shouldn't be here with the others."

"He has to be, Vir, *because* he is a part of history. If we do not recall that which we have done wrong, how can we be guided toward that which is right?"

"Apparently not everyone can agree on what is right and wrong," Vir said ruefully, glancing over his shoulder as if worried that Durla was going to be standing right behind him.

"You wouldn't be referring to Durla, would you? Calm yourself, Vir. His is not the only opinion out there."

"One wouldn't know it to look at the people in that room. They—"

"Vir . . . it doesn't matter. Look at these paintings. Are they not lovely?"

Vir was beginning to lose all patience with his emperor. "Yes, they're very lovely, but that's not the point—"

"Emperor Turhan . . ." Londo indicated one painting. "A great man."

"A great man," sniffed Vir. "With his dying words, he urged us to attack the Narn. You should know, you were the one he whispered them . . . to . . ." Vir's voice trailed off as he saw the expression on Londo's face. Once more, a dime dropped as he realized the awful secret Londo was hinting at . . . that Turhan's last words were *not* words of war. "Londo . . ."

"He died wanting peace with the Narn . . . and said that we and Refa were damned. A wise man, that." He said it without any hint of anger. If anything, he sounded amused.

But Vir was horrified. He took a step back, the blood draining from his face. "Londo . . . Great Maker, Londo . . . how could . . . how could you—"

Londo shrugged.

"That's it? That's all the answer I get? A shrug? Londo, how . . . how could you?"

"I have heard that question a great many times in my life, Vir, and interestingly, the answer is always the same: Easily."

Vir had absolutely no idea what to say. He had never before been rendered utterly speechless by Londo. Londo, for his part, seemed utterly unperturbed by Vir's clear discomfiture. Instead he simply said, "We do what we must, Vir. We always do. All of us. Take Emperor Kran. Do you remember him, Vir? Do you recall what happened?"

Vir's head was still spinning, as he tried to pull together all the fragments of what Londo had been saying. "Emperor Kran . . . vaguely, yes. But that was before I was born, it—"

Londo had stopped in front of a bust of Kran. It was easily the smallest one in the room, as if its inclusion had almost been an afterthought. "Such a short-lived reign he had . . . barely a footnote in our illustrious history. Ruler during a period of great transition. At the time, the Centauri houses were more fractured than ever before. The previous emperor, Turis, had been quite weak-willed, and with his passing, all the houses had commenced fighting for power. It threatened to be a bloodbath. Poor Kran . . . do you recall what happened to him?"

"Yes, I think so. But—"

"Sometimes it is possible to agree on what is right and wrong. And we would not want the wrong things to happen again. Not to anyone. Not to *anyone*, Vir. Do you hear me?" Londo's voice was rising with unexpected vehemence. "Do you hear me, Vir? Are you attending to the words coming out of my mouth?"

"Yes, yes, of course." Vir felt more lost than ever. "Every word."

"Good. I am glad we had this talk. It will be best for all of us. Come . . . the party is progressing without us. We wouldn't want them to think that fun can be had without us in the room, eh?

"Do you know what, Vir? And I want you to remember this: Everything around here, all that we have rebuilt, all the power at my command . . . it makes me think of what I truly have. Not only that, but what we will all, within less than a week's time, all have."

"And what would that be?"

"Ah," grinned Londo. "That's all part of the great riddle of life, isn't it."

And with that utterly cryptic remark, he headed out of the room, leaving a completely perplexed Vir behind, to scratch his head and wonder what in the world had just occurred there.

When Vir entered his quarters for the evening, he was astounded to find the nubile dancing girl he'd been ogling earlier. She was wearing considerably less than she had been before. To be specific, she was clad in his bedsheet, which was wrapped around her on the bed. Vir stood there a moment, and then realized that since his mouth was moving, it would probably be at least good form to have syllables emerging in conjunction with the movement. "Uh . . . uh . . . uh . . . hello . . ."

"Hello," she purred.

"I'm . . . sorry to disturb you. I thought these were my assigned quarters. I'll just be out of your way . . ." Then Vir saw his suitcase over in the corner, and realized that he was exactly where he was supposed to be. So, apparently, was she.

"Would you care to join me?"

"Why? Are you coming apart?" Vir then forced laughter at his rather feeble attempt at humor. He saw no change in the small smile on the woman's face, and so he composed himself. "Uh . . . look . . . perhaps there's been some mistake . . ."

"You are Vir Cotto?" She repositioned herself, sweeping the blanket around her. Vir suddenly felt rather sweaty. He also felt some stray movement in the area of his chest and willed himself to calm down.

"Yes. But . . . may I ask how . . . that is to say . . ."

"Minister Durla felt that he might have offended you . . .

and out of respect to your long history with the emperor, he asked me to make sure that there would be no hard feelings."

At the mention of Durla's name, even the most preliminary stirrings of interest promptly evaporated. "Durla. I see. Well . . ." Vir cleared his throat forcibly. "Here's a thought. I'll turn around and avert my eyes, and you can go get dressed and tell him everything's fine, and I appreciate the thought. All right?"

Disappointment flickered across her face. "Are you sure?"

"Miss . . . believe me when I tell you, decisions aren't always my strongest thing. I kind of go back and forth. But about this, yes, I'm absolutely sure." He turned his back to her and waited. He heard the rustling of the sheets as she slid out of bed, the whisper of cloth against her body as she dressed.

Moments later her hand trailed across his back as she cooed, "Good night then, Ambassador."

"Good night," Vir said in a strangled voice.

He waited long moments after the door hissed closed before he dared to trust himself to turn around. Then he let out a sigh of relief when he saw that she was, indeed, gone.

Durla. Durla had sent her. The very thought was horrifying. Furthermore, when he'd turned his back to her, he'd watched the shadow she cast quite carefully, to make sure she didn't come at him with a knife while his back was turned. That, rather than generosity, would be much more in character with Durla's way of doing things.

"Now I remember why I don't spend a lot of time on Centauri Prime. I hate it here."

He made sure his door was locked and changed quickly for bed. But sleep did not come. Instead he lay on his back, staring up at the ceiling, thinking about what Londo had said. It seemed so random, so confusing, as if Londo was unable to hold a coherent thought in his head.

Who was Rem Lanas? And all that conversation about Emperor Kran? And . . .

That riddle. About what was greater than the Great Maker?

What did that riddle have anything to do with anything? The truth was, it seemed completely unrelated to anything that had gone on.

What was greater than the Great Maker? The rest of the riddle made no sense, couldn't progress any further, because the truth was that, quite simply, nothing was greater than the Great Maker. Oh, certainly it was impossible to understand why he had allowed the Republic to slip into such disarray, why he had stood silently by and allowed the bombings and . . .

Suddenly Vir sat up, his eyes wide, and he felt a momentary sense of glee, almost childlike in its exuberance.

"Nothing," he said out loud. "The answer is nothing."

It made perfect sense. Nothing was greater than the Great Maker. Nothing was more frightening than the Shadow ships . . . to that, Vir would personally attest. The poor have nothing. The rich need nothing. And if you eat nothing . . . then you die.

A good riddle. A thought provoker.

But then Vir thought of something else Londo had said. Something about . . .

What had Londo's exact words been?

"Everything around here, all that we have rebuilt, all the power at my command . . . it makes me think of what I truly have. Not only that, but what we will all, within less than a week's time, all have." And he had referred to it as being part of the great riddle of life.

Nothing. Londo was telling him that he felt he had nothing. As if he wanted to make sure Vir was aware that he was truly unhappy with his situation. But why? Why not just come out and say so? And why was he so unhappy anyway, if he was being given the opportunity to rebuild Centauri Prime in his own image. Where was the tragedy, the sadness in that?

And . . . they would all have nothing? Within a week's time?

It made no sense.

Or perhaps it did, and Vir was simply unwilling or unable to put it all together.

The next morning he went straight to the throne room, but guards blocked the door. "I need to see the emperor," he said.

The guards simply stared at him as if he hadn't spoken.

"It's urgent."

"I'm afraid that the emperor is seeing no one today." The voice came from behind. It was Durla, strolling calmly down the corridor and looking so at home that it seemed to Vir as if Durla thought he owned the place.

"And why is that?"

Durla shrugged. "I do not question my emperor's orders, Ambassador. I simply obey them. I would suggest that you do likewise."

"How do I know that those are his orders?" Vir demanded. "How do I know he's even still alive?"

Durla appeared startled at the very suggestion. "I am shocked that you would insinuate some sort of plot against the emperor, Ambassador. I assure you he's in his throne room. He simply desires seclusion."

"Look," Vir said hotly. "Unless I—"

The door to the throne room suddenly opened.

Vir turned and peered through and, sure enough, there was Londo on his throne. He sat there, resolutely, staring straight ahead, not so much as an inch of his body twitching or giving any indication that he was alive. And then, ever so slightly, Londo turned his head and looked in Vir's direction. He nodded once as if to say, *It's all right. Go.* Then he went back to staring straight ahead, not speaking, not even giving any indication that he was aware Vir was still in the doorway.

Vir stepped back and the doors closed. He turned to Durla, who simply smiled and said, "Have a safe journey back to Babylon 5. Do visit us again . . . very soon." And with that he headed off down the corridor.

The sleeper approached wakefulness. One of the dark ones was nearing. He sensed its approach and prepared to come to full consciousness. He had remained hidden in the darkness, waiting for his chance, preparing for the opportunity to serve the dark ones.

It was a confusing time for him. He felt as if his mind were splitting in two, and yet merging for the first time. As if he were about to encounter a long-lost twin from whom he had been separated moments after being spit from his mother's womb.

He found himself staring at shadows for long periods of time. There was quite an abundance of them in Down Below. Each of them seemed to cloak its own mysterious secrets. Once, like most people, the sleeper had feared shadows. But now he found himself embracing them, feeling the coolness of them.

Then the shadows began to call him . . . one in particular. He felt himself drawn to it, to one particular corner. There was no one else around. Step by unsteady step he drew closer and closer to it, sensing that for the first time, his life was going to make some degree of sense. Indeed, of late he had been filled with a curious emptiness.

He remembered his parents, his mother holding him close, his father schooling him in his first lessons. He remembered them . . . but only as if from a distance, as if his mind embraced them, but they were absent from his heart.

He remembered the first woman he had made love to, the

*press of her flesh against his, the warmth of her kiss. He re-
membered her . . . but he could not actually feel her. He knew
that he had been intertwined with her, but could not feel the
sensation of it.*

*It was as if the entirety of his life had been some sort of
video, observed but not actually experienced firsthand.*

*He wondered if this was a commonplace feeling. If other
people felt the same way about their memories.*

*Meantime, deep within him, something not quite biologi-
cal, not quite technical, stirred and moved in response to the
summons from the shadowy area.*

*He moved toward the corner, and there was something
there . . . something grey, with a hand outstretched, summon-
ing him . . .*

. . . no . . . not him . . . it . . .

— *chapter 8* —

Zack Allan, the security head of Babylon 5, was staring at Vir, one brow arched, his piercing eyes filled with open curiosity. "Rem Lanas? You want to find out about a Rem Lanas?"

Vir, sitting in Zack's office, kept his hands neatly folded in his lap. "If it wouldn't be too much trouble."

"Is he one of yours? I mean a Centauri?"

"That's right. Normally, we could find one of our own people, of course, but thanks to the bombings, our records are a mess. We think he's here, but we're not sure."

"Important in some way?"

Vir shifted uncomfortably in his seat. "Is there any reason you're asking me so many questions, Mr. Allan? Not that," he added quickly, "I mind answering them. I don't. I wouldn't mind answering your questions all day. I really didn't have anything else blocked out on my schedule. So if you want to keep—"

Zack put up a hand to still the torrent of words spilling from Vir. "I just wanted to know," Zack said slowly, "if he presents any sort of a security risk and if I should be worried."

"A security risk! Oh . . . oh, no. That's funny." Vir quickly laughed, a sort of high-pitched blurt. "That's really funny. A Centauri, presenting a security risk. No," he said, suddenly serious. "No, none of our people present any sort of a risk, security or otherwise. We, that is, I, wouldn't want anyone to think that the Centauri in any way are threatening. Because, you know, as soon as that happens come the ships, and the booming, and the shooting, and, well . . . it's a mess. We don't want that. No one wants that. I know I don't, you don't . . ."

"Rem Lanas."

"I'm sure he doesn't, either."

"I mean," Zack said patiently, "who is he? Why do you need to find him?"

"Well . . ." Vir *harrumph*ed to buy himself a few seconds, and then said, "Money."

"Money? What about it?"

"Rem Lanas has come into a sizeable amount of it. His father died. And Lanas has come into a sizeable inheritance, so his parents want to get in touch with him, let him know . . ."

" 'Parents.' You just said his father was dead."

"Yes, that's . . . right. That is, his adoptive parents. His father gave him up for adoption when he was quite young, and when his father was dying, he felt so guilty that he left everything to his son. It's a tragic story. Very unexpected death. His father was an opera singer, you see, and he was performing an outdoor concert, and his mouth was wide open as he was trying to jump an octave, and suddenly this low-flying bird—"

"Okay, okay, okay," said Zack quickly, clearly not wanting to hear the climax of the story. "Let me see if we've got any record of a Rem Lanas coming through here."

As Zack checked through the computers, Vir's mind was racing. Lying simply was not his strong suit. He felt tremendously uncomfortable and very exposed whenever he was trying to do it. One would have thought that, working with Londo for as long as he had, he would have acquired a knack for it. The one thing he had going for him was that he tended to babble to the point where people would accept whatever he was saying, just to shut him up. With one lie, he was ineffective. With an avalanche of lies, he could squeak by.

The thing was, he wasn't sure who Rem Lanas was, or what significance he held. But out of nowhere, Londo had made mention of him.

Vir remembered that day on Centauri Prime, that day when Londo had made his address to the Centauri people, an address that had reeked of anger and had seemed more an urging for revenge than reconciliation. When Sheridan, Delenn, and G'Kar had expressed their reservations about such a curious direction for his speech, Vir had loyally assured them that Londo must have had his reasons. He had believed it at the time, and he believed it still. Londo always had reasons for what he did. Some of them were truly horrific, but they were reasons nonetheless.

So when Londo had spoken of this Rem Lanas fellow, Vir—after fighting through his initial confusion—had resolved that somehow, for some reason, Londo was trying to tell him something. For that reason, he had gone straight to Zack's office as soon as he had returned to the station. He wasn't sure why he was there, or what he was trying to find out, or what he would do with the knowledge once he did find it, but he couldn't think that far down the line. He had to operate one step at a time.

"Got him," Zack said.

Zack's declaration brought Vir out of his reverie. "You do? Where?"

"I don't mean that we actually have him in custody . . . why? Should we?"

Vir laughed nervously. "Of course not. Why would you?"

"According to this," continued Zack, looking over the records, "he arrived on the station about six months ago." He paused, studied the computer screen for a few more moments, and then said, "This could be a problem."

"What? What's a problem?"

"Well," said Zack, scratching his chin thoughtfully, "there's no record of him leasing any rooms here. No job employment record. If I had to guess, he's probably in Down Below."

"Down Below? Are you sure?"

"No, I'm not sure. For instance, if he'd somehow managed

to sneak off the station without our knowing it, he'd be gone. Or he might have gotten a room or job using faked ID."

"But that doesn't make a lot of sense. If he had fake ID, why would he use it for one thing, but not the other?" Vir said.

Zack grinned. "Very good, Mr. Cotto. You might have a future in the exciting field of security."

"Really? You think so? Or you are kidding?"

"I'm kidding."

"Oh." Vir felt slightly crestfallen.

"But you're right. There's no reason for him to come in under his real name and then fake his presence elsewhere. Which brings me back to my original guess: he's Down Below. Residences down there are pretty much catch-as-catch-can; set up a tent and you're a resident. Run money for one of the shady types down there, and you're employed. Do you want me to send some people down to find him?"

"No," Vir said quickly. "I'll handle it. I'm, well . . . I'm a friend of the family. I promised I'd do it. It's kind of . . . an honor thing."

"Oh. An honor thing."

"That's right. Well, thank you for all your help. If you could forward a copy of his photograph and records to my quarters, I'd be most appreciative." Vir stood, pumped Zack's hand with such ferocity that he threatened to snap it off at the wrist, and then left Zack's office as fast as he could.

When he got to his door, he stood there, slightly out of breath, composing his thoughts. His hearts were racing and he didn't even fully grasp why that would be the case. All he knew was that he was beginning to sense that something was happening . . . something that Londo actually had the answers to. But Londo would not tell him more than he already had, would not give him anything more than dribs and drabs . . .

Would not? Or . . . could not?

Was it possible that Londo had simply told him as much as

he could, somehow? Even that made no sense, though. There
had been no one except Londo and himself there in the por-
trait gallery. Was Londo that concerned that he was being
watched, listened to wherever he went in the palace? But they
could have gone outside, then, or found a place—some place,
any place—that could be shielded from prying eyes and ears.
Londo would certainly have been clever enough to come up
with somewhere that was secure.

But . . . what if there was no place left that was secure?

The notion was utterly horrifying to Vir. Could that be possible? Could it be that someone was capable of monitoring
Londo, no matter where he went? Perhaps they had managed
to implant some sort of tracking or listening device upon him.
But . . . why would he stand still for something like that? Why
would he submit to it? He was the emperor. The emperor of
the Centauri Republic! Much of the Republic might be in
ruins, but it still was what it was. One had to respect the office, if not the man holding it.

*Then again, I assassinated Londo's predecessor, so who
am I to talk . . .*

If that were the case . . . if Londo was somehow wearing
some sort of bugging device, or if—at the very least—there
was someone whose presence was so pervasive that even
Londo was wary of it, then that was a situation that had to be
addressed. But who could be responsible for such a state of
affairs?

Durla. That had to be the answer.

Perhaps, Vir reasoned, Durla was blackmailing him somehow. Perhaps he had gotten his hands on some sort of dire
truth about Londo, and was trading upon silence in exchange
for power. And while he was at it, he was keeping Londo on a
tight leash . . .

It made Vir wonder—what could Durla possibly know that
would cause Londo to submit to that . . . that slimy little
man's will, rather than allow it to be made public? After all,
Londo's greatest and most awful actions weren't secrets, they

were part of the résumé that had obtained him the rank of emperor in the first place. What could Londo possibly have done that would be considered so repellant?

No matter what it was, the whole business made Vir extremely edgy. It made him wonder just how paranoid he himself was becoming, and how paranoid he should be. Durla definitely knew Vir's background, and Vir had the uneasy feeling that he, too, might be targeted somehow. It depended, of course, on just how seriously Durla perceived him as a threat, and whether Vir stood in the way—intentionally or not—of whatever it was that Durla saw as his goal.

Vir's mind was spinning, and as he finally opened the door to enter his quarters, he jumped nearly a foot in the air when a voice said, "Hi there."

Vir sagged against the wall, clutching his major heart. "Mr. Garibaldi," he managed to gasp. "What are you doing here? How did you get in here?"

"When you've had a job like security chief," Michael Garibaldi said, rising from the chair in which he had apparently made himself quite comfortable, "you pick up a few things. And you hang on to them, even when you move upstairs to become the head of security for the president of the Alliance. Speaking of which . . . he'd like to see you."

"He would?"

"Yes. What? Does that make you nervous?"

"Nervous?" laughed Vir. "Why would you say that?"

"Well, when you're nervous about something, you tend to flap your hands about a bit . . . kind of like you're doing right now."

"What? Oh, this. No, no . . . I'm just having some minor circulation problems, so I'm trying to get the blood flowing." He flailed his hands for a moment, then said, "Well, that seems to have done it," and folded his arms tightly across his chest. "What does he want to see me about?"

"Beats me. You know how it goes . . . 'ours is not to question why, ours is but to' . . . well, you know."

"Yes, of course I do. I do? I mean . . . actually, I don't. Ours is but to . . . what?"

"Do or die."

"Ah. What a wonderful saying," Vir said with a marked lack of enthusiasm.

"It's from a poem, actually. 'The Charge of the Light Brigade.' "

"Oh. It's about a brigade that charges at faster than light speeds?"

Garibaldi let out a sigh, then smiled gamely and gestured toward the door. "I'll explain on the way," he said.

They stepped out and headed down the hallway. Vir's mind was in even more turmoil. Garibaldi, as always, wasn't giving any indication as to what was on his mind. What did he know? How *much* did he know? For that matter, how much did Vir himself know? He felt as if he had no grounding at all, as if he were about to float away.

Garibaldi was chatting away about something of absolutely no consequence. Vir continued to smile and nod and give every indication he was listening, which he really wasn't. He rubbed the corner of his eye . . . and saw . . . something.

It was just there, just for a moment, but when Vir turned his gaze to look head on, it was gone. He blinked, rubbed his eye again, and tried to spot whatever it was, without truly knowing what it was he was endeavoring to see.

"Vir, are you all right?" asked Garibaldi, actually sounding a touch concerned.

Vir tried to recreate for himself the mental impression that had been left upon him. He thought he had spotted someone, someone cloaked, watching him with what appeared to be a wry smile. But now he was gone, and Vir was wondering whether or not he was completely losing it from the stress.

Yes, that was it—stress. More stress than he had ever really known. And the killing aspect of it was that he still had no clear idea of just what it was he was stressed over.

With more honesty than was probably wise for him at

that particular point in time, Vir answered, "No, Mr. Garibaldi. No, I'm not all right. And you know what? You know what the absolute worst part of it is?" Garibaldi shook his head. "The worst part," continued Vir, "is that if I *were* all right . . . the feeling would be so unfamiliar to me, that I'd probably be totally terrified of it and wouldn't know what to do. Do you know what I'm saying?"

"Yeah. Yeah, I think I do. Basically, you're afraid to let your guard down."

But Vir shook his head. "No. That's not quite it at all. It's not that I'm afraid to do so. It's that I've forgotten how."

"Vir," Garibaldi said slowly, "considering the things that have gone on here . . . and the things that continue to go on back on Centauri Prime . . . maybe that's a blessing in disguise."

"Then it's a very cunning disguise," said Vir.

John Sheridan rose from behind his desk when Vir entered. Dressed in his customary dark suit, he stroked his neatly trimmed, slightly greying beard and looked at Vir pensively. Vir tried to get a read off Sheridan's face that might indicate exactly what the problem was, but Sheridan was far too old a hand to let the slightest hint slip through. Sheridan had been president for nearly a year, and in the four years that Vir had known him, he had never seen the man tip his hand until he was ready. "Vir, it's good to see you," he said, extending his hand. "Your trip to and from Centauri Prime went without incident, I trust?"

"Oh yes. The best kind of space travel. The uneventful kind."

He shook Sheridan's hand firmly. It was just one of the many Human traditions to which he'd had to become accustomed. He recalled very clearly when he'd first arrived on Babylon 5—he had been so nervous that his hands had been incredibly clammy.

Vir had never forgotten the expression on then-Captain

Sinclair's face, or the way he had fought to maintain a polite demeanor while subtly trying to wipe his drenched hand on his trouser leg. As for Londo, well, Londo had just been too stunned to say or do anything other than to get Vir the hell out of there.

He'd come a long way in the succeeding years. Yet, in many ways, he felt just as disconcerted as ever.

"That's good. That's good." Sheridan rapped his knuckles briskly on the desk. "Well . . . I'm sure you're quite busy . . ."

"Actually, no. I just got back, so my schedule is wide open."

Vir was just trying to be helpful, but he could tell from Sheridan's expression that that wasn't what he had wanted to hear. He realized belatedly that it was simply a conversational gambit, a means of jumping briskly to the point. "But if anyone's busy, it's you, Mr. President," Vir added quickly, "and I appreciate your taking the time to discuss . . . well, whatever it is we have to discuss. So . . . why don't we get right to it, then."

"Yes, I . . . suppose we should." He paused for a moment. "This is in regard to the tour of Down Below that's scheduled for tomorrow."

"The tour," Vir echoed, his face a perfect blank.

"Yes. There's a movement among various members of the Alliance to attend to the conditions in Down Below. They feel it represents, well . . . something they're not comfortable with. Some of the races don't like to be reminded that their cultures have any 'have-nots,' and Down Below is most definitely a haven for the unfortunate."

"So they want to get rid of a haven?"

"Not exactly. There's a sort of reclamation project in the works. Various races are pooling their resources, trying to convince many of the expatriots who have fled to Down Below to return to their Homeworlds. Plus, there are corporate sponsors who are interested in becoming involved in Down Below. Cleaning it up."

"It's hard to believe that would be possible."

"I know. Taking the dark underbelly of Babylon 5 and making it over into something approachable—I swear, some sponsors actually believe they can transform Down Below into a place so friendly that people would take their families down there, on holiday. It's a pipe dream, I think, but . . ." He shrugged. Vir mirrored the gesture. "In any event, representatives from the various sponsors and member races are gathering for this tour. It's been fairly well publicized, actually. If you ask me, it's more an exercise in politics than anything else. A chance to stage a media event in order for the representatives to look good to the folks back home. Oldest political maneuvering in the book. And, as you know, an invitation went out to you, asking you to be a part of the tour. Since you are the Centauri representative to Babylon 5, it only seemed right."

"Yes, of course. And don't think I didn't appreciate it," said Vir.

In point of fact, he didn't remember receiving the invitation. Vir's appointment as ambassador was still relatively recent. He didn't even have an assistant—one had not been assigned him. His personal finances were extremely tight, particularly after the bombings had left his family's holdings in disarray, and he still hadn't had any sort of concrete budget established by the home office. He had hoped to discuss that problem with Londo, but somehow the opportunity had never presented itself.

As a result, Vir often felt a bit overwhelmed. Fortunately he had a great many organizational skills of his own, what with having been Londo's aide for all those years. But while it was one thing simply to be the aide to the ambassador, to juggle both positions was proving something of a strain.

Still, he saw absolutely no reason to admit as much to Sheridan. So instead he nodded and smiled and maintained the fiction that he was perfectly clear on just what it was that Sheridan was getting at.

"The problem is . . . I find myself in a bit of an uncomfort-able situation," Sheridan admitted. "The simple fact is that several members of the Alliance looked over the list of in-vited attendees, saw that your name was on it, and became rather . . . incensed."

"Incensed?"

"Understand, Vir, it's nothing personal," Sheridan said quickly. "I know you to be a fine, upstanding, and highly moral individual. But the others, they don't know you, and just assume you to be a . . ."

"Typical Centauri?" He saw Sheridan's discomfiture and sighed sadly. "It's all right, you can say it. I know my people's conduct hasn't won us a large number of allies. We've raped what we've sown; isn't that how you Humans would put it?"

"Actually, we'd say 'reaped,' but considering what was done to some worlds by the Centauri . . ." Then he shook it off. "No. No reason for rehashing the past. The bottom line, Vir, is that several key members' races have stated that they don't want you—that is to say, any representative of Centauri Prime—along on the tour. There's still a good deal of anger and bruised feelings, not only over the Republic's past ac-tions, but in response to the current attitude that's being dis-played on Centauri Prime—toward the Alliance. Everything from Londo's speech to the publication of *Verity*, the new Centauri official newspaper."

"Oh yes. *Verity.*" Now that was indeed something with which Vir was quite familiar. Since the restoration had begun, the various independent publications available on Centauri Prime had dwindled very nearly to nonexistence. But then, out of nowhere, *Verity* had appeared, billing itself as the "Voice of the Centauri People."

It purported to be an utterly independent publication, but the rumor was that it was simply the mouthpiece of certain government factions. Now that Vir had been back to Centauri Prime, he would have bet that Minister Durla's hand was somewhere deep into *Verity*'s pockets, controlling everything that went on with the publication. There was no way to prove it, though, and there was certainly no reason to raise the issue with Sheridan. It wasn't as if he could do anything, or should even if he could.

Verity took every opportunity to besmirch the name, honor, and intentions of the Interstellar Alliance. The publication advocated a return to Centauri greatness . . . although Vir couldn't help but notice that precisely how they might return to greatness was always left rather vague. It was as if the publication was content to stir nationalistic fires among the readership without actually giving them a tangible goal. Or at least, not just yet.

"So you're saying that you don't want me to attend," Vir said.

"No. No, I'm not saying that at all. The Alliance has to understand that the best way to work toward a future is to do so with as many allies as possible. And that includes the Centauri. I'm letting you know about the hostility, though, because it's very likely that there will be some who will do everything they can to make you feel uncomfortable. Rest assured, though, that I will do everything within my power . . ."

"That . . . won't be necessary," said Vir quietly. "I have no desire to put you in a difficult position."

"Vir—" Sheridan had to laugh. "—I'm president of the Interstellar Alliance. Being in difficult positions comes with the job description."

"Yes, I know that. Nevertheless, that doesn't mean that I have to make the job any more difficult than it already is, right? The simple truth, Mr. President, is that I don't want to be somewhere that I'm not especially wanted. Trust me on this: I've had a lot of experience with not being wanted in various places. So I've got a fairly thick skin when it comes to this kind of thing."

"Vir—"

Vir got to his feet. "I very much appreciate the opportunity to have this talk, Mr. President. I'm glad we did. I'm glad I know where I . . . where we, that is to say, the Centauri Republic . . . stand."

"Vir, didn't you hear what I said?" Sheridan said, in obvious exasperation. "I'm not about to let the Alliance push me around. I was just giving you a sort of 'heads up' over a potentially difficult situation, but that doesn't mean . . ."

"Actually, Mr. President . . . it does. It does mean . . . precisely what you think it does. I have to go now."

Vir headed for the door. Sheridan came around his desk, looking rather concerned. "Vir . . ." he started to say.

Vir turned to face him, squared his shoulders and said, "I think . . . I think it'd be better if you called me 'Ambassador Cotto' for the time being." And with that, he walked out of Sheridan's office.

— *chapter 9* —

Everything seemed so clear to Durla, although rarely more so than when he was sleeping.

When he was awake, he knew what it was that he wanted for Centauri Prime. But there was so much to deal with, so many details to attend to. People clamoring for his attention, this chancellor wanting something, that minister requiring five minutes of his time. It was always five minutes, at least in theory. Naturally, once he was in any given meeting, five minutes became fifteen, or twenty, or half an hour, and the next thing he knew his entire schedule was simply shot. It was just so easy to get distracted by everything.

But when he was asleep, why, there was when he saw the future—his future—with glorious clarity.

He saw himself standing hundreds of feet tall in the air, a giant holographic projection that could be seen for miles. That, indeed, could be seen all over the world. He saw himself addressing the people, leading them, rallying them, and they were shouting his name over and over, praising him, begging him to let them share in his glorious and great vision.

He spoke to them of the magnificence that was Centauri Prime's destiny, of all that the great republic was going to accomplish under his leadership. Once more they shouted his name, and over and over again. It was quite exhilarating, really.

He had always aspired to greatness, ever since he had

been told that it was something he would never be able to accomplish.

His father was a military man, and very demanding. He had produced two sons, within a year of each other, and it had taken very little time in their development to realize who was the favored son. It wasn't Durla. No, it was his older brother, Solla.

It had been difficult for Durla to hate Solla. In addition to being a great scholar and a brilliant soldier, Solla had also possessed a kind heart. As fearsome as he could be in times of combat, he was equally compassionate when dealing with his younger brother. Only a year separated them, true, but it might as well have been a chasm. Durla had had to work for everything that he achieved, whereas for Solla it seemed to come easily. He made it all appear effortless. He rarely seemed to study, and yet he scored higher grades than Durla. Durla never saw him practicing, and yet Solla's blade was easily the deadliest in the city.

Everyone knew that Solla was going far.

That was why Durla had to kill him.

The final straw had been Solla's woman. She had been incredibly beautiful, amazingly exotic, the daughter of a highborn noble. And young Durla, just turning his twentieth year, had seen her during one of their infrequent trips to the emperor's court. Unfortunately for Durla, the woman had seen Solla, and become instantly smitten with him. Solla was likewise taken with her, and who could blame him? Luminous eyes, a long, red, plaited braid that hung alluringly off the side of her head, a body so firm and sculpted that when she walked the sinew of her muscle played gloriously just beneath her bronzed skin. Every time Durla saw her, his body ached for her.

As it turned out, he wasn't alone. There was another Centauri as well, who served in the imperial troops alongside Durla and Solla. His name was Riva, and his passion for the woman—Mariel—was so great that he and Solla came to blows over her. A vicious battle it had been, and Solla had won because, well, Solla always won. Riva, however, had loudly vowed vengeance, declaring that his conflict with Solla was not over by a longshot.

This was all the opening that Durla had needed. Smitten with the woman, resentful over his brother's greatness and the way that his parents had always treated Solla with the respect and idolization Durla had felt he was entitled to, Durla had required no further incentive. He had poisoned Solla . . . and himself.

That had been the trickiest aspect of it. He had ingested the same poison that he had placed in Solla's food. It was the most effective means of avoiding suspicion. What he'd had to do was be certain to eat enough to show genuine signs of illness, but too little to prove fatal to him. He had succeeded, and no sooner had Solla breathed his last, the venomous poison having consumed his body, than Riva had been accused of perpetrating the deed. Riva's fellow squad mates had gone to arrest him. Unfortunately—or fortunately, depending upon one's point of view—Riva hadn't surrendered quietly. Ultimately, he didn't surrender at all, but instead resisted arrest, which was always a foolish notion when those who are trying to arrest you, *a*, outnumber you and, *b*, are already incensed with you because they believe—however mistakenly—that you are responsible for the death of their friend.

As a result, by the end of the arrest, pieces of Riva wound up littering the immediate area.

This had all been tremendously beneficial for Durla, as was to be expected. His grief-stricken parents had lavished their attention on him, partly out of guilt, but mostly because he was their only remaining son and they knew that he was their only chance for vicarious success.

As for the girl . . .

Durla had gone to her with his medals on his breast and his heart on his sleeve. He had gone to her and, while acting the tragedy-struck younger brother, also made it clear to her that he adored her, and hopefully no longer from afar.

She had looked at him with a mixture of amusement and pity. "Pathetic boy," she had said archly, although it was a curious choice of words since she was, in fact, several years younger than he. "My house has greater plans for me than being tied to you. Your brother was going places: Places of strength. Places of power. But you . . . you will only see such places from a distance. At least, that is what my father says, and he is usually quite intuitive when it comes to such things. He thought highly of Solla as husband potential . . . Riva slightly less so, but viable. You, though? You will always be the younger brother of the noble Solla, who was cut down in his prime. You, I am afraid, don't matter very much at all."

Then she had laughed and walked away, with a sway of slender hips under a stunningly sheer fabric. "Mariel!" he called after her. "Mariel, wait! Wait, I love you! If you only had any idea of what I did to be with you—"

She didn't, of course. That was likely fortunate, for if she had known, Durla would have wound up in prison . . . if his father and mother hadn't killed him first. Instead, Mariel was shortly thereafter linked with the House Mollari. Her hand in marriage had been given . . .

To him.

To Londo Mollari.

Durla had been present at their bonding. He had no idea why he had subjected himself to it . . . no. No, he did have an idea. It was more like a fantasy, actually. He fantasized that Mariel would suddenly come to her senses at the last moment. That she would throw over Mollari for him. That she would run from Mollari, realizing the hideous mistake that she was about to make, and call to Durla to rescue her.

And then . . . then there would be a glorious battle. He would fight his way out, Mariel at his side singing his praises. He would battle through the crowd, and then he and Mariel would run and keep running, leaving it all behind to start a new life.

It was a very nice fantasy. Unfortunately it had no relation whatsoever to reality. The bonding ceremony had proceeded without interruption, and Mariel hadn't so much as glanced in Durla's direction.

He stood in the back of the room, trembling with suppressed rage as the sight, the very thought, of Mollari sent him into barely contained spasms of fury. Mollari was an appalling specimen of Centauri manhood. He was too old for Mariel, he was too ugly for Mariel. Mollari was a respected house, true, but Londo wasn't an especially promising member of that house. A third-level bottom feeder at best, that was Durla's assessment of him. Everything about Londo had grated on Durla. The way he wore his hair, the scowl lines in his forehead, his deep, pronounced northern province accent, his tendency to declaim as if, even in casual conversation, he was speaking to people from a balcony. A thoroughly deplorable and unlikeable individual, that was Londo Mollari.

And yet it would be his lips upon Mariel's. It would be his hands caressing her, his tentacles that—

It was all that Durla could do to remain there and see the ceremony through to its end. But he did, and when the crowds of well-wishers surrounded Londo and Mariel as they prepared to depart, Durla had made certain to hang far back. He kept waiting for Mariel, at the very least, to look around and see if she could spot him. She did not. Instead she never took her eyes from Londo. She seemed happy to be married to him, content with her lot in life.

Inside, Durla was screaming.

That had been many years earlier, of course. His interest in Mariel had been a blistering hot obsession forged in the fires of youthful interest, and nothing more. That was what he told himself. He was over her; she was part of his past . . . indeed, truth to tell, she had never really been a part of his life at all. Merely a fantasy.

And yet, he had never married. Never even seriously pursued a romantic relationship.

Instead he had focused all his energies upon his career. If he could not please himself, at least he could work on pleasing his parents, in general, and his father, in particular. In that regard, he attained a measure of success.

To his father, it was Solla who remained the true jewel in the family crown. Even in death, Solla was thought of more highly. However Durla managed to work his way through the ranks by dint of sheer determination and hard work, and that sort of dedication had to count for something.

In the meantime, he had kept tabs on Londo Mollari. It hadn't been difficult. People generally spoke of him in very derisive tones, making no secret of their opinions. Mollari would talk longingly of times past and how he wanted the Centauri Republic to be what it once was. But anyone could speak of such things; it took a man of action and vision to actually bring them to fruition. Mollari was neither.

If he had kept his mouth shut, it wouldn't have been such a problem, but Mollari was renowned for getting himself liquored up and shouting at the top of his lungs about what the Republic could be and should be. When he had received the assignment of ambassador to Babylon 5, the word around the court was that, at last, Mollari would be sent someplace where even his bellowing tones would not be heard.

Durla had loved it. He wanted nothing but to see Mollari spiral into hopeless disgrace.

And who knew? Perhaps he would become so bored and fed up with his lot in life that he would do the honorable thing, throw himself on his sword and put an end to it all. Once that happened, Mariel would be available to him once again. And if Mollari waited to dispose of himself, giving Durla enough time to work himself up to a position of sufficient importance, why . . . perhaps Mariel might see him in a very different light.

Some nights as he lay on his spartan, military cot, Durla

would envision the shade of Mollari, screaming from the afterlife in helpless frustration as Durla bedded his widow in far greater fashion, and with greater potency, than Londo ever could have achieved.

There might well have been people in the court who were more surprised than Durla, when word of Londo Mollari's growing power base began to trickle back to the Homeworld. But no one could have been more horrified than he. The last thing he needed—or desired—was for Londo Mollari to make a success of himself, to turn his career around. Unfortunately, to Durla's horror, that was precisely what happened.

His horror turned to delight when Mollari unceremoniously tossed Mariel aside, divorcing her along with one of his other wives, Daggair. He had chosen to keep as his wife a diminutive, brittle shrew named Timov, and that decision had mystified a number of people who were familiar with all three wives, and who would have wagered their life's fortunes that—if Mollari were to keep only one wife—it would be the stunningly beautiful Mariel. Ultimately, that had left the way clear for Durla once more, but his luck still had not improved.

His calls to Mariel went unanswered. Gifts he sent her remained unacknowledged. The silence was an obvious response: he had not sufficiently acquitted himself in the grand scheme of things to have placed himself on Mariel's horizon.

And with Mollari maneuvering himself, positioning himself to be the next emperor, Durla became certain he had to build his own power base within the government. Such a power base would have to consist of friends and allies who were his and his alone. But Durla, as yet only the captain of the guards, had no power of his own, no means of bringing in his people. Once Mollari became emperor, naturally he would bring in his own flunkies, and Durla would be frozen out.

As much as it galled him to do so, Durla had embarked upon the only strategy he could devise: he decided he would be the *perfect* captain of the guards. He would get as close to

Londo as possible, with an eye toward obtaining a position of power and, once he had done that, building from there. He figured the entire process would take a number of years, and hoped that nothing would dramatically change Mariel's marital status in the meantime.

To Durla's astonishment, however, his timetable was thrown completely out of whack when Londo—defying all predictions of the court pundits—promoted him to the key position of minister of Internal Security. Mollari had proven himself a bizarre study in contradictions. For Durla had had the distinct and unshakeable impression that the emperor really couldn't stand him. That somehow Mollari had sensed, on a very basic level, that Durla despised him, hungered for power, and wouldn't rest until he himself was wearing the white.

But for reasons that surpassed understanding—call it stupidity, call it a death wish, call it whatever one desired— Mollari had not only entrusted Durla with formidable responsibility, but offered no resistance whatever to Durla's placing loyal associates in key positions of power.

Durla didn't know why Mollari was doing it. He had theories. One he found the most plausible was that Mollari was, for some reason, experiencing massive guilt over the war he had engineered, and so was setting himself up to fail. It not only made the most sense, it was just about the only one that made any sense at all.

On this particular evening, he had been dwelling on the curious chain of events that had brought him to his present state when he had fallen asleep. Probably because everything was so fresh on his mind, faces flittered past him as his consciousness hovered in the grey area between sleep and wakefulness. His parents, his brother, other soldiers, Mollari, and looming above them all, Mariel, with her perfect teeth and her eyes sparkling . . .

"Durla," she whispered to him.

She was holding out her hand, and the dream was most curious, for it didn't seem as insubstantial as dreams normally are. "Durla." She called him once more, and this time she beckoned to him. A miasma of color was swirling about her.

Durla saw himself through his mind's eye, stepping toward her. He took her hand. *No,* he mused, *this is definitely not like other dreams.* Usually dreams simply provide a feast for the visual memory. But when he took her hand, it felt firm and warm and alive.

"Come," she said, and she tugged on his hand slightly, but just to test the situation Durla resisted. Instead of moving, he pulled her toward him, gripped her shoulders, and kissed her roughly. She didn't resist; her body seemed to melt against his. Warmth flooded over him, and then she was no longer in his arms, but instead a few feet away, gesturing coquettishly for him to follow. "Time enough for that later, my love," she said teasingly.

He followed her then, unreality swirling around them. Clouds of red and purple seemed to pulse with an energy all their own, and Durla realized they were in hyperspace, moving effortlessly through that light-speed bridge. They didn't appear to need a space vessel; they were above such petty needs, beyond them, outside them.

"Where are we going?" he asked.

"You'll see," she replied.

Hyperspace dissolved around them, and a world materialized far below Durla's feet. Then there was a sudden flash of light, and Durla found Mariel and himself standing on the planet's surface. The sky hung in an orangy haze, and the dirt beneath their feet was kicking up in clouds of dust.

"Where are we?" Durla asked. "What is this place?"

"A fringe world. It's designated K0643," Mariel said. She squeezed his hand affectionately and added, "Walk with me."

He did so. And as they walked, he realized he had never known such happiness, such bliss. He was afraid to speak anymore for fear of shattering the moment and sending himself spiraling back to wakefulness.

"The Centauri Republic must expand," she said.

"I know. We must show the allied worlds that we are to be feared, to be—"

But Mariel shook her head. She didn't seem the least annoyed with him; indeed, her evident fondness for him only appeared to be growing. "You speak of conquest. That is not your immediate concern."

"It's not?"

"No, my love."

He thought he was going to cry out with joy, and was barely able to contain his euphoria. *My love! She called me "My love!"*

"You must look for that which no one else knows about. There are other worlds, worlds in which the Alliance has no interest. Remote worlds such as this one. You must mount archaeological investigations. You must dig. You must locate. While you do this, the Interstellar Alliance will laugh at you. They will sneer and say, 'Look at the once-great Centauri Republic, rooting around on barren worlds and scraping about in the dirt like the basest of creatures.' Let them say these things. Let them lull themselves into a false sense of security.

"It will not last, and they will discover the error of their ways . . . but by then, it will be too late. Look outside Centauri Prime, Durla. There, and only there, will you find your true greatness."

"And you? If I do these things, I will have you?"

She laughed, and nodded, but then added warningly, "Do not seek me out. As tempted as you may be, do not do so. If you chase me, I will find you contemptible. I must come to you. You must know that by now. I must be drawn to you, and only then will you truly be able to call me your own."

"And this planet offers the way?"

"This, and others like it. You have the resources. Organize the diggers. Organize the crews. Assign the manpower. You can do it, Durla. I believe in you. And you can believe in me."

She gripped both of his hands, kissed him gently on the knuckles, and then released him. They did not drop to his sides but remained there, in midair, and he looked at them as if they were appendages belonging to someone else. She backed away, gliding, almost floating. He tried to move toward her, but she easily kept the same distance between them, even as her arms stretched out toward him in mute pleading.

Durla twisted in his bed, his arms flailing about in the real world as he tried to touch Mariel in the dream sphere.

And then he stopped thrashing, as a small, spidery creature descended from his right temple and scuttled across the floor. The last few feet to its destination, it did not even bother to walk, but instead vaulted the distance. The dreamweaver landed on Shiv'kala's abdomen and nestled there securely.

"Well done," Shiv'kala said softly.

He will not take action due to this one vision, warned the dreamweaver, a special offshoot breed of the keeper.

"Yes. I know. It will take several instances of this 'recurring dream' for him to truly embrace it. But once he does . . ."

He did not need to finish the sentence.

He heard footfalls. Durla had cried out once or twice during the session, and apparently night guards were coming by to ascertain whether or not he was all right.

The guards opened the door and peered in, but Durla had calmed. He was sound asleep, his chest rising and falling steadily. They performed a scan of the room that was so subtle Durla didn't even stir. The scan accomplished nothing.

And so they moved off, never seeing the Drakh as he stood quietly in the shadows and planned.

The sleeper was completely awake. Within him resided the will and the means to accomplish that which he had been designed to accomplish.

The procession was moving toward him, and the sleeper moved himself into position . . . and waited . . .

Soon . . . soon the reason for his existence would be carried out. Soon, very soon . . . Sheridan would be dead. It was only a matter of moments.

—— *chapter 10* ——

Vir sat in his quarters, staring at the wall and wondering whether there was any point in his continuing to remain at Babylon 5. He had spent a sleepless night pondering the question and was no closer to an answer now than he'd been before.

As an ambassador, he felt his talents were questionable at best. And even if he were the greatest, most skilled diplomat in the history of the galaxy . . . what good would it do if no one was interested in speaking with him?

He felt it more and more, every time he would walk around the station. The eyes upon him that seemed to regard him with barely concealed contempt. Or scorn. Or anger.

Once upon a time, Babylon 5 had seemed a very intimidating place to him. Secrets lurked behind every corner, and he had always felt as if he were watching helplessly while Londo descended into darkness. At the time that it was happening, he would have thought it insane if someone suggested to him that he would become nostalgic for those days.

But indeed, that was exactly the case. As complex as his life was, as terrifying as that slow downward spiral into war and even murder had been . . . those were, in fact, the good old days. At least people had liked him then. He had had friends.

Garibaldi had certainly liked him well enough, because obviously he had never considered Vir any sort of threat to B5 security. Now, however, the Centauri were considered a

perpetual problem, a race not to be trusted, not to be left to
their own devices. A race who would leave you with a dagger
quivering in your back if you let down your guard. And
Garibaldi, whose responsibilities included anticipating and
neutralizing any potential security problems for the entirety
of the Interstellar Alliance, had come to regard Vir with suspicion at all times.

Sheridan . . .

He had considered Sheridan a friend. A bit distant, what
with all his responsibilities as captain of Babylon 5, but a
friend nonetheless. Someone to whom he could unburden
himself. But the truth now was that Sheridan didn't dare be
friendly with him. It might cause too many negative ramifica-
tions for him with the rest of the Alliance. Not that Sheridan
would admit to such a thing; he was too much the individu-
alist to let public sentiment sway him from following a particular path. Vir, though, couldn't find it within himself to risk
putting Sheridan into that position. The stakes were too high,
the Alliance too important in the long run, to risk upsetting
member races just because Vir felt lonely.

Lennier . . . of all of them, he missed Lennier the most.
When they had both been mere attachés serving their respec-
tive diplomatic leaders/mentors, they had met regularly to
unburden themselves to one another. Of all of them, Lennier
had probably best understood what it was that Vir was going
through at any given time.

But Lennier had joined the Rangers, for reasons Vir had to
admit eluded him completely. Lennier was deeply religious,
thoughtful, a pacifist. What business did he have traipsing
about the galaxy as a man-at-arms? When Vir had mused out
loud to Londo about that, Londo had looked thoughtful for a
time. He seemed to be running through his mind everything
he knew about Lennier, reaching some conclusions. Then he
had said to Vir, "There is an old Earth organization—very
much romanticized—whose history might provide you with

some answers, if what I suspect is correct. Read up on the French Foreign Legion."

Vir had done so, but had come away from it understanding no more than he had when he'd begun. Soldiers who joined a demanding, even cruel organization in order to forget their past? A past usually haunted by beautiful but unattainable women who'd broken their hearts . . . at least according to the "romanticized" literature Londo had recommended. Vir had absolutely no idea how that could possibly apply to Lennier, and had said so. Londo had simply shrugged and said, "What do I know of such things?" and dropped the subject.

Londo.

He missed Londo. He missed the way things had been. Even when they were bad . . . at least Vir had had an idea of what was going on. Now here he was, in a position that supposedly offered him more power and authority, and yet feeling more confused and helpless than ever before. There he had been, speaking to Londo of the mysterious Rem Lanas and Emperor Kran, and he had no idea whatsoever what any of it had to do with anything.

Rem Lanas, a homeless Centauri who hid in Down Below. No criminal record, no nothing. The thought of roaming around Down Below under any circumstance wasn't an attractive one to Vir, and he had delayed the prospect for as long as possible, while trying to determine if there was any particular reason he should seek out this individual. Londo had seemed of the opinion that he should, but really, who knew what was going through Londo's head anymore? He seemed so erratic, so inwardly torn. Not for the first time, Vir found himself wondering if Londo hadn't genuinely had some sort of mental collapse. It wasn't a pleasant thought, but it certainly seemed to be a valid explanation.

And Emperor Kran? What was the point in discussing rulers long gone?

"Emperor Kran," Vir said out loud.

Why had Londo been speaking of him? What was it that Londo had said, again?

Sometimes it is possible to agree on what is right and wrong. And we would not want the wrong things to happen again. Not to anyone. Not to anyone, Vir. Do you hear me?

Just what had happened to Emperor Kran? Vir realized that he couldn't recall all the details. He'd been killed, that much he remembered. Assassinated. Then again, so had a number of Centauri emperors, so on that basis alone he hadn't really stood out.

Vir moved to his computer terminal and started checking records, pulling up history files. The difference between Kran and the others who had been assassinated, as Vir started to remember, was that unlike others—such as Cartagia—Kran hadn't really been that bad. He'd had a good heart, good ideas, and a determination to try and bring the feuding houses of the Republic together. His interest hadn't been self-aggrandizement or personal enrichment, but the betterment of all Centauri Prime.

After skimming some of the highlights of Kran's life, Vir started reading over the details of Kran's death.

It had been so stupid. A waste, a tragic waste. Kran had grown impatient with the noble houses of Centauri Prime, because he felt they had lost touch with the common people. The houses, after all, basically consisted of people of rank, of status, of title. A relatively small percentage of the planet's population had held a staggeringly large percentage of the money and access to the world's resources. Kran felt that the best way to remind the houses of where their obligations lay was to bring them down to the common folk and "reintroduce" them.

Centauri Prime was like any other world: it had its seedier side. There were places where the poor went when they had nowhere else to go. Where people in need scraped together meager livings with whatever they could get their hands upon. And, as was always the case, those above knew where those below resided. But those above simply found a way to turn off that part of their mind that would have caused them to feel pity or empathy for those with nothing. "They got themselves into it," was the most frequently heard comment, or "Let someone else handle it," or similar sentiments.

Kran wasn't about to stand for it. His intention was to realign the thinking of the houses' heads in the same way that one trains an offending pet not to relieve himself inside the house. In the case of the pet, you are to shove the creature's nose into his own waste product. It was Kran's notion to do the same—metaphorically speaking—with the houses' heads.

He amassed a "Great Expedition," as it was dubbed. He brought together all the houses' heads for a guided tour through the seamier side of Centauri Prime. His intention was twofold: to remind the household heads that there were those in desperate need of help, and to provide, by his physical presence, a symbol of hope to all those who were too indigent to share in the planet's wealth.

His long-term goal had been to build a sort of global sense of patriotism. He sought to cause all of Centauri Prime to pull together as one, the great and the small, with the ultimate aim being a return to the greatness that had once marked the Republic. "One cannot build a palace on a foundation of mud," he had written. "The mud must be treated, crafted into a foundation upon which greatness can be created."

He had sought unity. He sought—ironically enough—an alliance. Vir couldn't help but smile to himself in a sort of sad way. In some ways, Kran reminded him of Sheridan in that regard.

So there Kran had been, planning for magnificence, thinking about ways of elevating the whole of Centauri society. According to the history text Vir was reading, the procession of the Great Expedition had wended its way into the dark quarters of Centauri Prime, and had been quite a sight to see. All the richest Centauri, dressed in their finery, looking and

probably feeling completely out of place as they gazed—
many of them for the first time—upon the faces of need and
want, of hunger and frustration. Their ignorance of the conditions of the poorer Centauri had led them to apathy, and
Londo had once told Vir that ignorance and apathy were a
lethal combination. Ignorance can be cured by education,
apathy attended to by finding something, somehow that can
stir the blood and move the soul to take action. But ignorance
and apathy, entwined inseparably around each other, form a
wall that is nearly insurmountable.

Kran had taken it upon himself to crack through that wall
and, by all accounts, the initial moments of the Great Expedition began to do just that. The heads of the households were
transfixed, unable to turn away from the sight of such need. It
was said that some of them were even moved to tears.

That was when it had all fallen apart.

The man's name was Tuk Maroth. He had been born poor,
raised poor, and had viewed the nobility and the greatness of
the Centauri upper echelon only from a distance his entire
life. He sat in the gutter, watched the approaching procession
through eyes filled with hate and envy. He told people later
that all he could see was the sun glinting off the gilt and trim-
ming of the greatcoats of the nobility. And the emperor . . .
"He seemed to shine, to glow," Maroth had said, "as if pow-
ered by all the souls of those who had died with nothing, so
that he might have everything." Apparently the thing that had
sent Maroth completely over the edge was the shining imperial crest which hung around Kran's neck.

Maroth later claimed it had been a purely spontaneous act,
and that he had no idea what came over him. This was widely
thought to be some sort of appeal for leniency, as if a tempo-
rary madness that drove him to regicide was somehow more
acceptable.

Kran never even saw the shot coming. One moment he was
smiling, waving, nodding. There was a great deal of noise
from the crowd; he probably didn't hear the shot. But the next

thing he knew, he was looking down in astonishment at the vast stain of red that was spreading across his chest. His legs sagged and his dumbfounded guards, who had not been expecting any such assault during such a well-meaning and philanthropic mission, caught him. Maroth turned and fled, disappearing into the back alleys of the district. Kran was rushed directly to the hospital, but it was far too late. He was dead by the time he got there. Indeed, there were some who said that he was dead before the guards even caught him.

The incident touched off waves of recriminations, including one particularly massive riot in which the nobles sent the military to storm the poorest quarters of the city, demanding the assassin, demanding justice, and generally taking the opportunity to vilify the poor in their own minds by condemning them all for the actions of one. By doing that, they basically absolved themselves from any sense of responsibility for helping the needy. An entire section of the city went up in flames before Maroth was turned in, by his grief-stricken mother as it turned out. The poor woman subsequently took her own life by stabbing herself, cutting out the womb that had once housed the child who had grown up to commit such a heinous act.

However it was the power brokers of Centauri who got to write the history. The power brokers who had stormed the poor and later sought to excuse their actions. So when history referred to Kran in later years, it portrayed him as a fool who had misplaced his priorities. The poor, it was decided, had brought their lack of fortune upon themselves, deserved whatever happened to them; and any ruler who felt any sympathy for them likewise had coming to him whatever tragedy should occur.

Vir set aside the reading material and shook his head in dismay. Poor Londo. Obviously what he'd been telling Vir was that he, Londo, was doomed to fail. That history was going to judge him a fool.

Or worse, Londo was concerned that he was going to die at the hands of some demented assassin. Or . . .

Or . . .

*"I'm an **idiot**!"* Vir shouted as he leaped to his feet so violently that he slammed his knee on the underside of the table.

He didn't take time to note the pain. His mind raced, trying to figure out what to do. Then quickly he went to his closet and found old clothes. It wasn't difficult. Vir had lost a considerable amount of weight in the past months, but he had kept the clothes that no longer fit him properly because he wasn't the type to waste anything. To say nothing of the fact that, should he wind up gaining the weight back, as had happened to him from time to time, he wanted to have something he could fit into.

He hauled out one of his old suits, a mismatched shirt, vest, and pants and threw them on. The unfortunate combination and the fact that they hung loosely on him combined for a generally satisfactory air of shabbiness.

He returned to his terminal and hastily printed out a photo. Then he hauled out his cloak. He rarely wore it; it had been a going-away gift from his mother, which he had never quite understood. It was a hooded, all-weather garment, which made no sense as a gift for going to Babylon 5—how much weather variation was there going to be on a space station? It wasn't as if there were days he needed to bundle up because it looked cloudy with a chance of rain.

But he drew it about himself now as if a major thunderhead were rolling in, and drew the hood up over his head to conceal his features. Thus outfitted, he made his way to Down Below, and prayed he would be in time.

Perhaps the prospect of descending to Down Below had been anathema to Vir, but he knew he had no choice. Again he weighed all the options, and this seemed unfortunately to be the only viable one.

It was the smell that hit him first. The atmospheric filters in

Down Below weren't as efficient as they were in other sections of the station. To some degree, that was understandable. The designers of Babylon 5 had never intended that anyone would actually live in the service corridors and excess storage area that constituted Down Below, and consequently they had not provided for the same amount of ventilation and the number of ducts there were throughout the rest of the place. Add to that the severe lack of proper sanitation facilities, and it combined to make Down Below someplace one avoided if one could at all help it.

At least no one was staring at Vir here. In that respect, as ironic as it sounded, it almost made Down Below preferable to up above. Every so often, someone would glance in Vir's direction, but only in terms of assessing whether or not he appeared to present some sort of danger. On those occasions, if Vir caught their glance, he would peer out from beneath his hood and flash a sickly little smile that practically cried out that he was no threat whatsoever. The mute questioner would then go on about whatever unseemly business he needed to attend to.

In his hand, Vir clutched the picture he had printed out. It was the last known image of Rem Lanas. Vir had stared at it for so long that he felt as if every curve of the man's face was permanently emblazoned in his mind.

He scanned the throng that was perpetually milling about, trying to spot some sign of his quarry. It didn't seem a particularly promising means of accomplishing what he needed to do, but he could see no other way. He tried not to draw any attention to himself, and that wasn't especially difficult. No one seemed to care about him . . . or, indeed, about anything.

He looked sadly at the assortment of makeshift tents and homes that had been erected hodgepodge throughout Down Below. He saw several people, a family by the look of it, grouped around an open flame and cooking something that seemed to have once been some sort of vermin. The very sight of it was enough to cause Vir's stomach to buck. In a way, it helped put his life in perspective for him. Here he had been so miserable over his personal situation, not liking the way that representatives from the Alliance had been looking at him. *Looking* at him. That should be his biggest problem. At least he had clothes, food, and shelter. At least he had all the amenities and wanted for nothing save companionship. But companionship was a very small thing compared to everything that these poor, needy people required.

He spent several hours wandering around, even becoming so bold as to start asking random people if they had seen Rem Lanas, holding up a picture to jog their memory. Most times he simply got blank stares. It might have been that they didn't know, although it was just as likely that they didn't care. First of all, Rem Lanas wasn't their problem. And second, this odd Centauri who was asking around was obviously an outsider, despite his ill-fitting clothes, possibly even operating undercover for some organization. Why should they cooperate with him? When had anyone cooperated with them, after all.

It was a rationale that Vir could easily understand, although he would probably have been even more forgiving if lives had not been potentially on the line.

Presuming, of course, that he was right, and hadn't simply conjured the entire thing out of some crack-brained misinterpretation of purposefully cryptic remarks made by Londo.

That was when he heard noises.

The sound came from a distance away. It was an assortment of voices, several of them trying to talk at once, but there was one louder than the others. Whereas the others were speaking with high emotion, the most commanding one came across as firm and reasonable. It was a voice that Vir knew almost as well as his own or Londo's. It was Sheridan's voice.

The tour was coming through. The "reclamation" project of which Sheridan had spoken.

Vir looked around, trying to see if there was any sign of Rem Lanas. There was nothing. Perhaps he had missed him, or perhaps Lanas had come in behind him, circled around somehow.

As he stood there, the residents of Down Below began to look around at one another in confusion, unable to figure out just what the commotion was all about. Clearly some of them thought they were being rousted, as had happened before during periodic security sweeps. However, there wasn't any sound of scuffling or of weapons being fired in warning. Everything certainly seemed peaceful enough.

There were side passages that extended off in a variety of directions. Maybe Lanas was lurking down one of those, Vir reasoned. It was still a long shot, though, and he was beginning to feel that he was handling this situation completely wrong. That, despite his assorted concerns, he should have gone to security. He should have trusted this business to anyone except himself.

He started to turn in one direction . . .

. . . and a flash of light caught his eye.

He was momentarily confused. He wasn't sure where it had come from or what had caused it. All he knew was that the flash drew his attention to another corridor—one he hadn't noticed before. Then he gasped in astonishment, unable to believe his luck.

It was Rem Lanas. He was around Vir's height, but thinner, with long arms and narrow shoulders. Vir was dumbfounded. Despite his memorization of Rem's features, he glanced at the printout nevertheless. Lanas looked a bit more dishevelled than he appeared in the picture, but it most definitely was him.

He was standing in a narrow alleyway, just around the corner from the main corridor, his hand resting against the corner of the wall. He was clearly listening for something. Listening, and glancing around the corner every so often, as if to try and determine just how quickly Sheridan and the others were approaching.

And now Vir could see Sheridan and the others, far down

the corridor. Lanas was positioned in such a way that he could walk only a few steps and easily intersect the group's path. Sheridan and the others were ringed by guards, with Zack at the forefront. Vir could see Zack scanning the crowd, scrutinizing anyone who came within range, glancing at their hands . . .

Their hands. Of course. To see if they were holding weapons.

Vir did likewise, staring at Lanas across the way. Lanas' hands were empty. He didn't seem to have a weapon on him. Nonetheless, there was something about him that practically screamed "threat." As quickly, as unobtrusively as he could, Vir began to move toward him. Drawing within range presented no immediate difficulty; Lanas was paying no attention to him whatsoever. His concerns seemed entirely focused elsewhere.

Let me get there, Vir was intoning to himself. *Let me get there.* The problem was, he had nothing concrete upon which to base his actions. But somehow he felt driven nonetheless, as if he were caught up in forces that were compelling him to behave in a certain manner. It wasn't the first time he had felt that way, certainly. But all the other times that feeling had come over him, it had always been Londo who had been piloting the ship, so to speak. This time it was up to Vir . . . presuming the "it" was what he thought it was. There was still always the possibility that he had totally misinterpreted everything, that this was all the result of his fevered imagination working overtime.

He drew closer, closer, and Rem still wasn't noticing him. Now Vir could clearly make out the look in Rem's eyes, and it was a look that he found frightening. It was as if Lanas wasn't even present in his own head. His eyes were wide but empty, as if his body were simply being worn like a cloak. His body was stock still, frozen, but poised, like a great animal preparing to pounce, or perhaps a trap waiting to spring shut. And his throat . . .

Vir's gaze was immediately drawn to Rem's throat, because—insanely—it seemed to be moving all on its own. It was pulsing gently, rhythmically. Vir had no idea what could possibly be causing such a thing.

Sheridan was still a distance away, getting closer with every passing moment . . . but then again, so was Vir as he drew nearer to Rem.

It was when Vir was only a few feet away that Rem Lanas noticed him.

Vir had no idea if he had made some movement, done something that might have drawn Lanas' attention to him. Maybe some sort of sixth sense that warned him of danger had come into play. Whatever it was, Lanas' head snapped around and his wide, eerily vacant eyes focused on Vir. His throat seemed to pulse more violently.

Vir froze in his tracks. He had no idea what to do. And then, his mind racing desperately for some sort of strategy, he did the only thing he could think of. He threw back his hood, a grin splitting his face, and he cried out joyously, "Rem! Rem Lanas! I *thought* that was you! It's me! Cotto! Vir Cotto! How are you!"

Lanas tilted his head slightly. He seemed to be having to make an effort to focus on Vir.

"Don't tell me you don't remember me!" Vir continued. "After all those crazy times we had together!" As he'd spoken, he'd drawn to within a couple of feet of Rem.

But Sheridan and the others were also drawing closer. Rem snapped his head back in the direction of Sheridan's path, started to move toward him. Vir stepped around to intercept, and Lanas really, truly focused on Vir for the first time. Something terrifying entered those eyes, something dark and fearsome, and Vir could almost hear voices screaming in his head.

And the throat was no longer pulsing. It was . . . undulating.

There was something in it. Something moved up the throat,

and Lanas began making a hacking, coughing noise in his
larynx, his lips trembling as if he were about to vomit.

Acting completely on instinct, Vir lunged. Rem took a step
back, tried to dodge around him, but his movements were
slow and awkward, and Vir collided with him. They went
down in a tumble of arms and legs, and Vir found himself positioned just behind Rem, Rem's head pinned against the
crook of his knee. Automatically, Vir reached around and
grabbed Rem's lower jaw, shoving it up while bracing Rem's
head against his own leg. Essentially, he had him in an utterly
awkward but nevertheless effective headlock.

Rem struggled violently, the gagging continuing. No words
were spoken, no one shouted for help. A group of people had
assembled at the far end of the alley, but their backs were to
Vir and Lanas. Instead they were watching Sheridan's approach. One or two glanced in the direction of the struggling
Centauri, but clearly decided it was some sort of personal
issue that did not merit their involvement.

"Stop it! Stop it!" hissed Vir. Vir wasn't one of the more
physically aggressive types around. He couldn't remember
the last time he'd been in a fight, and he had absolutely no
combat technique, no confidence in his ability to handle himself in a battle. But he was being prompted by pure despera-
tion, and from that was born the strength and determination
he needed.

Then he saw something starting to protrude from between
Rem's lips.

It was all Vir could do not to cry out in terror. The thing was
thin and black, like some sort of tentacle, and it was shoving
its way through Rem's mouth, trying to get free. The pul-
sating in Rem's throat had ceased. Clearly this was the thing
that was trying to get out of him. Vir was sweating profusely,
trying not to panic as another tentacle managed to slide
through, despite his best efforts. He yanked up as hard as he
could, and Rem's own teeth crunched through the tentacles,
severing them. They fell to the ground, writhing about on

their own for a moment before ceasing. But Rem's head began to shake furiously, the thing inside now either in agony or just wildly determined to get out. Vir redoubled his efforts, but his fingers, thick with perspiration, began to slip.

Then Vir realized that Sheridan was still talking, but his voice was moving beyond them. He had passed by, and the entourage was following him. That realization, that momentary victory, caused him to relax his guard for just a second.

It was enough. Lanas suddenly shoved backward, catching Vir on the side of the head. Vir fell back, his head ringing, and from his vantage point on the ground he saw Rem's mouth open wide. Some sort of creature leapt out of it.

It was small and black as its tentacles had been, covered with a thick layer of fur. It had four more functioning legs in addition to the two that had been truncated, and the force of its ejection from Rem's mouth caused it to smack against the far wall of the alley. It spun about a moment, orienting itself. It was no bigger than the palm of Vir's hand.

It screamed in fury, though the sound wasn't audible. Vir heard it in his head.

Vir, momentarily stunned by what he was seeing, lay helpless on the floor, and then he gasped as the thing scuttled at incredible speed across the way, straight toward his face. He had a brief glimpse of something sharp sticking out of the thing's back and he realized that it was some sort of stinger. There was no time for him to get out of the way, no time to do anything except let out a truncated cry of fear.

And then the black boot came down.

It smashed to the floor of the alley mere inches from Vir's face, crushing the creature under it effortlessly. Vir gasped in astonishment as the booted foot twisted back and forth in place for a moment, grinding the thing thoroughly into the ground. When it stepped back, there was nothing more than a black and red pulped mess.

—— chapter 11 ——

Vir looked up.

And he saw the individual that he had only thought he'd seen earlier. The man was dressed in grey robes, and although Vir couldn't see his hooded face completely, what he did see looked quite young. He couldn't have been more than thirty.

Rem lay on the ground, staring upward. The cloaked man stepped forward, crouched down over him and seemed to study him for a moment. Then he passed a hand over Rem's face, and Rem closed his eyes. His chest began to rise and fall in a natural sleeping rhythm.

"He'll be all right," said the cloaked man. When he spoke, it was in a very soft voice, so soft that Vir had to strain to listen. "He'll sleep it off for a time, and when he comes to, he'll have no idea why he's here. He'll be of no harm to anyone."

"What happened?" asked Vir, hauling himself to his feet. "Who are you?" Then he noticed the man was holding a staff. The ends of the staff appeared to be glowing softly. In barely contained astonishment, Vir said, "Are you a . . . a techno-mage?" The notion was both fascinating and frightening. Vir had had dealings with the science-based sorcerers nearly four years earlier, and he had found it one of the most daunting experiences of his life. When the techno-mages had finally left on their journey beyond the Rim, purportedly never to be seen again, Vir had breathed a sigh of relief. Yet now, apparently, he owed his life to one.

"Yes . . . but a cloistered one. My kind don't get out much. My name is Kane."

"It is? Really?"

"No. Not really," admitted the initiate. "It's a chosen name. I'm not about to tell you my real name, of course. Names have power, and I'm not going to give you power over me of any sort. Rather a foolish notion, really."

"That's a good philosophy," said Vir. "Thank you for squishing that . . . that . . ."

"Sleeper. Leftover biotech from the Shadows. Resided in your friend here," and he tapped Rem's body with the toe of his boot, "wiped his memory, and waited until it was ready to fulfill its mission."

"To assassinate Sheridan."

Kane nodded. "Yes. All Lanas had to do was get close enough, and the creature would have done the rest. It has quite a good jumping range. And once it landed on Sheridan, it would have stung him, and he would have been dead before they could get him to Medlab."

"Just like Kran."

"What?"

"Nothing. But why now? And why Lanas?"

"It wasn't just now. There were times before. There will probably be other times, although death may take different forms. As for why Lanas," and beneath his robes, Kane shrugged. "Luck of the draw. Purely random chance. They had to pick someone. They picked him."

"They who?"

"That," smiled Kane, "would be telling. You don't need to know . . . yet."

"But—"

"Tell me," Kane drew closer to him, studying him thoughtfully, "why you chose to handle this matter on your own, why you did not summon security."

"I . . . I didn't have enough to go on. Not for sure. I had guesses, hunches, that was all. Besides, the most upsetting thing was the thought of letting it get around that the Centauri were involved in an assassination attempt. Even if it turned out to be false, there would be inquiries, and interrogations, and word would leak to the other members of the Alliance. I didn't want that. Centauri doesn't need it. Things are bad enough as it is."

"So you risked your own life, limb, and neck in order to try and head it off and protect the Centauri reputation."

"I . . . guess so, yes," Vir agreed. Then, worried, he added, "You're not going to tell anyone, are you?"

"Why would I do that?"

"I . . . I don't know. I don't know a lot of things," Vir admitted. "Starting with—"

But Kane held up a hand to quiet him. "No. Do not start. Because if you do, there will be many answers that I cannot give you. Not yet. But I will tell you this much, Vir . . . your actions have been quite impressive. I was observing you to see what you would do, and you do not disappoint. It very much seems as if the darkness has not reached you."

"That's good to know, that—" Vir paused, and then said, "The, uh . . . the darkness?"

Kane took a step toward him, and there was hardness in his eyes. "It stretches its coils from Centauri Prime to here. It lurks hereabouts, but it thrives on your Homeworld. Knowledge is power, Vir. I seek knowledge on behalf of the techno-mages, and they in turn seek knowledge from your world, for it is there that the dark power will continue to grow. You will have to make some rather severe choices soon. Very, very soon."

"I . . . have no idea what you're talking about."

"Good," said Kane, apparently satisfied. "I was going for cryptic."

"You succeeded."

"That's a relief. I am somewhat new at this, after all. Now I have to work on mysterious. Ah . . . your associate is stirring sooner than expected."

Vir turned and glanced at Rem Lanas. Sure enough, he was sitting up, holding a hand against his head as if he had a seriously splitting headache. "What . . . happened?" he inquired.

"I'll tell you in a moment," Vir said, and looked back to Kane.

He was gone. There was no sign that he had ever been there, other than a crushed, red and pulped creature on the floor.

"He's got the mysterious part down pretty well, too," said Vir.

— *chapter 12* —

Londo had known it was a test. There was absolutely no doubt in his mind at all.

"Sheridan is to die, you know," the Drakh had said.

The comment had snapped Londo from his reverie. There, in his throne room—the place that was the symbol of his power and, for him, the further symbol of the sham that he was—he was startled as the now-familiar voice spoke from the shadows. What was truly chilling was that Londo had realized he was, in fact, *aware* that Shiv'kala was watching him. At least, he'd been aware on some sort of subconscious level. And it hadn't even disturbed him.

The notion that he could actually get used to this half life he was living—even take it for granted—terrified Londo more than anything that had come before.

It had taken a few moments for the comment to sink in. "What?" Londo had said.

The Drakh had laid it all out for him. Told him the plan, told him about Rem Lanas. Told him about the creature that lived within Lanas. He had been picked at random, taken off the streets. It was the randomness that they had felt would be the greatest strength. Someone with no established grudge toward Sheridan, no particular hostility toward the Interstellar Alliance. Lanas was just a nobody. A nobody who wasn't particularly strong willed, not particularly intelligent. All he was, in the final analysis, was useful.

When the Drakh had finally stopped speaking, Londo

squinted in the darkness at him. Shiv'kala just stood there, unmoving, unblinking, that same, frightening little smile in place. "And you have told me this . . . why?"

"He was your friend. I wished to let you know of his impending fate . . . so that if you desired to say your good-byes . . . you would have the opportunity."

A test. No . . . not just a test.

A trap.

Londo had known it, had been positive of it. The Drakh could just as easily have said, "Sheridan is to die soon. Drop him a nice note," and been done with it. No, he had told Londo everything there was to know because he wanted Londo to have that knowledge . . . in order to see what he would do with it.

Londo had not slept. For two days, he did not sleep. He had gone back and forth in his head, envisioning Sheridan as his great enemy, as the leader of an Alliance that had mercilessly assaulted his beloved Centauri Prime. Someone who had turned his back on them. And Delenn, his wife . . . she had a way of looking at Londo in the most insultingly pitying way.

But try as he might, he had not been able to erase from his memory all the times when Sheridan had been of service to him. Those years on Babylon 5 had been the best years of his life. He had not realized it at the time; it had merely seemed a period of slow, steady descent into darkness. But the fact was, Sheridan and Delenn had indeed been there for him on a number of occasions. Not only that, but he was positive that in their own way, they had been pulling for him, hoping that everything would turn out all right for him. The fact that everything had developed so abysmally—that he had become the single most powerful, and weakest, man in the Centauri Republic—was certainly not their doing, not at all. He had brought his fate solidly upon himself.

He had tried to sleep, but had managed only moments of rest, at most, before he would drift back to conscious-ness. During that time, he had felt the keeper shifting in mild confusion. Obviously the creature itself needed to rest as well, and had synchronized itself with Londo's own sleep period. So when Londo became mentally distressed, the keeper likewise experienced discomfort. The thought gave Londo some degree of satisfaction.

Finally he had not been able to take it anymore. But he had known that he would have to be crafty. He could not simply mount an obvious rescue mission, or inform Sheridan. Such an effort would probably be prevented by the keeper. In the event that the keeper could not stop him, certainly it would inform the Drakh, who might in turn change their plan . . . and let their displeasure with Londo be known in a most direct and unpleasant manner. Londo desired to save Sheridan, but not at the price of his own skin. Londo was not that generous.

So he had summoned Vir. The timing had been perfect, for the celebration in the palace had actually been Durla's idea. Durla had sponsored it, naturally, as a means of gathering all his allies and supporters and showing them his elevated position in the court. Since the idea had originated with Durla—Durla, the puppet of the Drakh who probably didn't even know who truly pulled the strings—the Drakh in turn would not question it or suspect some sort of duplicity on Londo's part. An invitation to Vir would be the most natural thing in the world.

So he had brought his old associate, his old friend—possibly his only friend in the galaxy, really—to visit. The invitation had attracted no attention whatsoever, as Londo had hoped.

Then had come the next step: Londo had started drinking almost as soon as the festivities had begun. The problem was, he had needed to walk a fine line. The challenge was to consume enough alcohol to render the keeper insensate, as he had found he was capable of doing. By accomplishing that, he would be able to speak to Vir more or less freely, without the keeper—and by extension, the Drakh—becoming aware of what he was doing. The problem was, if he imbibed too much, he would become so incoherently drunk that he wouldn't be of any use to Vir, to Sheridan, or even to himself.

So Vir had come, as invited, and Londo had taken him aside, fighting to remain on his feet while the liquor swirled around his brain, leaving a pleasant fog hanging over him. But Londo had proceeded with caution nevertheless, and it had been most fortunate that he had. For as he had begun to bring Vir current with the situation, as he had begun to unfold the plan in small bits . . . he had felt the keeper stirring to wakefulness. He had sent the creature into inebriated insensibility, but it had fought itself back to moderate sobriety with a speed that was both alarming and annoying. Apparently it was starting to build up some degree of tolerance to alcohol. Londo would have to reassess the amount of liquor it was going to require from now on to render the keeper unawares.

Londo dealt with the setback as best he could. He had tried to cue Vir to the danger presented to Sheridan by seeking historical precedent. Londo could sense that the keeper was suspicious of the conversation. It sensed that something was going on, but it wasn't entirely certain just what that might be. No pain was inflicted, no forcible commands were relayed into Londo's skull. But the creature had been most wary indeed, and so Londo had needed to be wary as well.

It had been tremendously frustrating for him. Part of him had simply wanted to drop the carefully chosen phrases, the historical allusions, and simply tell Vir what was going on. But he knew there would be immediate action of some sort taken by the keeper. Who knew the full powers of the monstrosity perched upon his shoulders? He knew it inflicted pain, and that it monitored his actions, but he had no reason to believe he had seen the outer limit of its capabilities. Perhaps it could blow out his brain stem with but the merest mental effort. Maybe it could send him into seizures, or stop his hearts, or . . . anything.

He wanted to do something to prevent Sheridan meeting a

gruesome death at the scaly hands of the Drakh, but the simple fact was that he wasn't especially inclined to sacrifice himself to that endeavor. He still valued his own skin above Sheridan's.

After Vir had left, Londo had monitored the news broadcasts carefully. The keeper had thought nothing of Londo's watching the news. He was, after all, the emperor. It was only appropriate that he should be keeping himself abreast of current events. And when the news had carried the item about Sheridan's leading a highly publicized tour of officials into Down Below at Babylon 5, Londo's spirit had soared. It had been everything he could do to prevent himself from shouting out with joy.

Then his enthusiasm had dissipated. He could almost feel a dark cloud radiating from the keeper, and it was at that moment—even as he saw news footage of the obviously unharmed Sheridan leading the tour—that he had it confirmed for him that, yes indeed, this had been a test. A test that he had failed, because he knew that they knew. He wasn't quite sure how he was aware of it. Maybe the telepathic bond was becoming two-way. But he did, in fact, know, and now all that remained was waiting for the retaliation to descend upon him.

"Was it worth it?"

Londo was sitting in the private library that had traditionally been the province of the emperor. The Centauri set great store by it. The emperor was considered to be something akin to a living repository of Centauri history, and it was intended that he carry within his head all the great deeds of his predecessors, and the many magnificent accomplishments of the Republic. Because that duty was so respected and sacred, the highest priority was given to providing the emperor with a secluded and well-guarded place where he could indulge his historical interests to his hearts' content. Indeed, there might not have been a more secure room in the entire palace. There were many books there, and many assorted relics from the illustrious past.

So it was that when Shiv'kala's voice emerged from the darkness and asked "Was it worth it?" Londo jumped, so violently startled that he nearly knocked over the reading table. He got to his feet, trying to maintain some degree of dignity in the face of such a clumsy response. The light was quite dim in the library; he couldn't see Shiv'kala at all. "Are you here?" he asked, wondering for a moment if perhaps Shiv'kala was only speaking in his mind but was, in fact, elsewhere entirely.

"Yes. I am here." Upon hearing the voice again, Londo could indeed tell that Shiv'kala was physically in the room. But his voice seemed to be floating from everywhere. "And you are here. How nice."

"Nice," Londo said tersely, "is not the word I would have used. What do you want?"

" 'Want' is not the word I would have used," countered Shiv'kala. "I do not 'want' to do what I must. What *we* must."

"I don't know what you're talking about."

"Do you not?"

Londo started to feel something, and braced himself. It was the beginning of . . . the pain. Except it was different somehow. They'd hit him with pain in the past, but he sensed that this was not going to be like the other times. Rather than hitting him suddenly and violently, this time around the pain was starting from a much lower baseline. It gave him cause to think that perhaps he was developing a tolerance for the psychic and physical torment they were inflicting upon him. For that matter . . . perhaps it was totally unrelated to the Drakh at all.

"Are you doing that?" demanded Londo, putting a hand to his temple.

"You have done it, Londo," replied Shiv'kala. There was that familiar resignation in his tone. "You . . . and you alone."

"I do not know—" The ache was increasing now, reaching

the previous levels and growing greater. Londo was finding it
hard to breathe, and it seemed as if his hearts were pumping
only with effort.

"Oh, you know," and any trace of sympathy or sadness was
suddenly gone from the Drakh's voice. There was only hardness, and cruelty. "You have made a fool of me, Londo."

"I? I . . ?" And suddenly Londo staggered. He tripped over
the chair in which he'd been sitting and crashed to the floor,
because he had been wrong. What he was feeling this time
was far worse than anything he had ever endured before at the
hands of the Drakh. Perhaps it was worse than anything he
had felt in his entire life. He realized belatedly that the agony
had started off slowly to put him off guard, to make him think
that perhaps it wouldn't be so bad. He had been wrong.

His body began to spasm as the pain rolled over him in
waves. He tried to distance himself mentally, tried to shut
down his mind, but there was no possibility because the pain
was everywhere, in every crevice and fold of his brain, in
every sensory neuron of his body. He opened his mouth to try
and scream, but he couldn't even do that because his throat
was paralyzed. All he was able to muster was inarticulate gur-
gling noises.

"I told the Drakh Entire," continued Shiv'kala, as if Londo
were not writhing like a skewered beast, "that you could be
trusted. That you knew your place. They requested a test. I
provided it. You failed it. That, Londo, is unacceptable."

Londo completely lost control. Every bit of waste fluid in
his body evacuated, something that hadn't happened since he
was two years of age. The sensation was humiliating, the
stench was repugnant, and then both of those spiraled away
as the agony continued to build. His soul, blackened and
battered as it already was, cried out for release. He remembered how he had wanted to die all those months ago, how he
had been ready to end it, but he realized that he had been a
fool, because he had never wanted to die the way that he did
now. At that moment, he would have given anything for the

release of death. He would kill his friends and loved ones, he would annihilate a hundred, a thousand innocent Centauri. He would do anything at all just for a cessation of the agony that was hammering through him.

And then it got worse.

He felt himself being torn apart, he felt every single organ in his body liquefying, and he knew, he just knew, that his brain was dissolving and flooding out his ears, he could practically feel it, and the pain was frying his eyes and his teeth were spiking through his gums, his tongue had swollen and was blocking his windpipe, there was burning in every joint that made the slightest movement pure agony, and so he tried to stay still, but the pain prodded him to move and then there was more anguish and it just kept building until it reached the point where he forgot what it was like not to hurt.

And then it stopped.

Just like that, all at once, and he couldn't move because he was lying there numb and foul-smelling, and he felt as if he would never be able to present himself with dignity ever again, he would never feel safe again, he never wanted another soul to look upon him because he was hideous and disgusting and had been reduced to a quivering, gibbering wreck of a man. The very thought was revolting to him, and yet he couldn't help it; he was so relieved that the pain had abated, for however short a time, that he cried copious tears, his body shuddering convulsively.

"Do you know how long you endured that?" Shiv'kala asked quietly. Londo tried to shake his head, but if he had been able to answer, he would have said it had been hours. Perhaps days. "Nine seconds," Shiv'kala continued, apparently knowing that Londo was not going to be in any sort of shape to reply. "You felt that way for precisely nine seconds. Would you like to endure that for twenty or thirty seconds? Or even better . . . twenty or thirty minutes? Or hours, or days?"

"No . . . no . . ." Londo's voice was barely recognizable as his own. It sounded more like the guttural grunt of a dying creature.

"I did not think so. I doubt that you would survive it. Even if you did, I likewise doubt you'd like what you became as a consequence."

Londo didn't reply. None seemed necessary, and he doubted he could have strung a coherent sentence together anyway.

Apparently not caring about Londo's newly discovered reticence, Shiv'kala said, "That was your punishment, Londo. Punishment, however, will not be enough. You must do penance. Do you understand? Do you hear what I am saying?"

He managed to nod.

"Good." Shiv'kala had moved from the shadows and was now standing directly in front of Londo. He tilted his head and regarded the emperor with curiosity. "Tell me, Londo . . . would you kill Sheridan yourself . . . if the alternative was more punishment?"

For all the world, Londo wanted to shake his head. He wanted to spit at the Drakh, he wanted to cry out defiance. He wanted to stumble to his feet and fasten his hands around the scaly throat of that grey-skinned monstrosity. At that point, he didn't care anymore if hidden bombs blew his people to bits. He didn't care if he died in attempting to strangle Shiv'kala. All he desired at that moment was the opportunity to try and, even more, the will.

Instead he simply nodded. For he knew it to be true; at that moment, he would do anything. Kill Sheridan, kill Delenn, kill Vir, kill Timov . . . anything, anyone, whatever it took, if it meant not getting another taste of that agonizing "punishment." Even though his body wasn't presently being subjected to pain, the memory was still fresh within him. He needed no reminder of what he had just been through; if nothing else, the stench floating from him made it very difficult to forget.

"Well . . . you do not have to kill Sheridan," Shiv'kala told him. "For the moment, we shall let him live. You see . . . there is a relatively recent development that has come to our attention. Sheridan is going to become a father, you see."

Londo was slowly managing to draw breath into his chest, steadying his racing hearts. So it took a few moments for Shiv'kala's comment to fully register on him. He was still lying on the floor, but he managed to raise his head ever so slightly. "Fa . . . father?" he asked.

"That is correct," said Shiv'kala. "Your penance, actually, will be quite simple."

Shiv'kala was moving then, and Londo could not take his gaze from him. He was heading toward the relics . . . toward a shelf with several urns of varying purposes. He studied them thoughtfully, and then reached up and took one from the shelf. It was silver, with a burnished gold inlay.

Londo knew the one he was taking. It had a very specific purpose in Centauri tradition, and he had no idea why Shiv'kala could possibly be interested in it.

And then a slow, horrible thought began to dawn on him. He brushed it aside just as quickly, though, convinced that he could not possibly be correct. It was unthinkable, beyond the pale, even for the Drakh. They could not, they would not . . . and certainly they could not think to make him a party to . . .

Then the Drakh opened the folds of his garment.

"No," whispered Londo. "No . . . please . . ." From the floor, he still could not move, but he began to beg, all thought of dignity long gone. "No . . ."

Shiv'kala did not even acknowledge that he had spoken. His chest was undulating in a most hideous fashion, as if it were alive with sentient cancer sores. He placed the vase on a nearby table and then unscrewed the base. He set it aside . . . and then put his hand to his chest.

"You wouldn't . . ." Londo pleaded. Even though he knew that it was hopeless, he continued to implore Shiv'kala to reconsider.

Once again, the Drakh made no response. Instead, ever so

delicately, he pulled a creature from within a fold in his body. The creature was similar to the keeper, but smaller. Its eye was closed. As alien a being as it was, Londo could nevertheless tell that it was sleeping, perhaps even hibernating.

Shiv'kala held the thing proudly in his palm for a moment. He ran a finger along the ridges of its body in a manner that appeared almost paternal. It was all Londo could do not to vomit. Then he placed the creature on the base and screwed it back onto the urn. Londo, at that point, couldn't even get a word out. He just shook his head helplessly.

"When Sheridan and Delenn go to Minbar . . . you will go there as well. You will deliver," and he touched the vase with a long finger, "this gift. You will order the bottom sealed to discourage inspection by Sheridan. The keeper within will be able to escape when the time is right."

"A . . . child?" Londo couldn't believe it. "A helpless child?"

"The son of Sheridan and Delenn . . . yes, it will be a son . . . but it will not always be a helpless child. When he is grown . . . he will be of use to us. The keeper will see to his destiny. And you . . . will see to the keeper."

"No." Londo, to his own astonishment, was managing to shake his head. "No . . . an innocent child . . ."

"If you shirk your penance, Londo," Shiv'kala said calmly, as if he had been expecting Londo to protest, "you should consider the consequences for all the innocent children on Centauri Prime. But before any of them . . . Senna will bear the brunt of our . . ." His lips twisted in that foul semblance of a smile. ". . . displeasure."

"Not . . . her . . ." Londo said.

"Emperor, you do not seem to realize how little say you have in the matter. Now . . . will you cooperate?"

Hating himself, hating life, hating a universe that would do this to him, Londo could only nod.

Then his vision began to lose focus as one more wave of pain washed over him. He shut his eyes tightly, letting it pass, shuddering at the sensation. When he opened his eyes again, Shiv'kala was gone. Gone, having left Londo alone with his humiliation and pain and weakness. Londo, who would forever know that not only did he have a breaking point, but it had been reachable through means that seemed almost effortless. It made him wonder just how much more the Drakh could do to him. As horrifying a notion as the thought suggested, was it possible that—until now—the Drakh had actually been going *easy* on him?

He wondered how much worse they could make it for him.

He wondered why threats to Senna struck so closely to him.

He wondered if he would ever know a time when he was actually, genuinely happy to be alive . . . even if the feeling lasted for only a few moments.

And then, as the brutalizing that his body had endured finally caught up with him, he wondered no more as he lapsed into merciful unconsciousness.

— chapter 13 —

The lady Mariel was busy writing a suicide note when the knock at the door interrupted her.

Her task was not one that she had undertaken lightly, or spontaneously. Indeed, she had been laboring over it for some time. She had worked over the word choice, selected one, and then discarded it, wanting everything to read properly. It hadn't been an easy business, this writing notion. She would choose a word, then pace the length of her villa—which was hideously small, a gift from her father when she reached her age of ascension and, at this point, the only piece of property remaining to her, sufficiently secluded off in the forest so that it had been spared the bombings of Centauri Prime—only to return to her work and cross out the word. "How do writers do it?" she asked at one point, although there was no one there to answer.

No one there.

Once upon a time, there had always been someone there. But not anymore. Thanks to Londo . . . they were gone. All the suitors. All gone. Fortunes, gone. Life, gone.

She wasn't entirely certain that she was actually going to go through with the suicide. Granted, she was depressed, but the more overwhelming concern for her was that she was bored. She lived this pointless existence, filling days, killing time, and accomplishing nothing. Society was closed to her, doors slammed shut . . . again, thanks to Londo Mollari.

When his holographic image had loomed over all of Centauri Prime, she had stood there at the window of her villa and screamed imprecations for the entire time that the figure had stood upon the horizon. Right after that, she had started the suicide note, deciding that a world where Londo Mollari was emperor was one in which she simply did not want to exist anymore.

But since the suicide note was going to be her last act of record, she wanted it to be just right. And since she was not a writer by nature or by craft, well . . . it was taking a while. Still, she was quite close to finishing a useable draft, and then—that would be that. The only thing remaining would be selecting the means, and she was sure that she would probably go with poison.

Certainly she knew enough about different types, and what would be both effective and painless. Her mother had taught her well in that regard, possessing rather extensive knowledge on that topic. Her father had also been well aware of her mother's erudition along those lines. It had served nicely to keep him in line, and he was quite candid in stating that his wife's mastery of terminal ingestion was the secret to the length and relative calm of their marriage.

When the knock came at the door, Mariel put down her work and called, "Yes?" while making no attempt to hide the irritation in her voice over being interrupted.

"A thousand pardons, milady," came the reply from the other side of the door. The speaker sounded rather youthful. "But your presence is requested at the Development office."

"The what?" Having been forcibly removed from the life of politics and the court, Mariel paid very little attention these days to the government or the way in which it was set up.

"The Office of Development, overseen by Chancellor Lione."

It wasn't a name that meant anything to Mariel. She began to wonder if this was some sort of elaborate prank. Or worse, a ploy to get her to open the door so that some sort of

assassination attempt might be carried out. After all, Londo
was emperor now. If he carried within him a need for revenge against her, certainly he would have the resources to
dispatch someone to attend to it.

Then again, she was preparing to kill herself anyway. If
someone was going to show up and do the job for her, certainly it wasn't that much different. Still, protocol had to be
observed.

"Just a moment," she said. She was wearing the sheerest of
nightgowns. She had little need to get dressed these days,
since she was on her own and no one came to visit her. Even
the fellow who delivered food to her once a week simply left
the supplies outside the door. Indeed, that had been one of the
considerations that had sent her thoughts toward suicide. It
wasn't just the humiliation and the ennui, it was also a matter
of practicality. Soon what meager savings she had would run
out. The delivery fellow had intimated that an "arrangement"
might be able to be worked out, and he had suggested it with
an unmistakeably lascivious grin. The thought of falling so
far that she was actually considering the "arrangement" had
been what had finally propelled Mariel's thoughts down the
road of embarking upon final festivities. It had also resulted
in the supplies being left outside the door.

For the sake of propriety, she tossed on a robe over her
gown—a sheer robe nonetheless—and answered the door.

There was a very serious-faced young man standing there.
She noted his discipline; his gaze did not so much as flicker
over the lines of her body. If her beauty had an effect on him,
he did not let it show. "Lady Mariel?" It was intended as
an interrogative, although there was very little question in
his tone.

"Yes."

"I am Throk of the Prime Candidates. Chancellor Castig
Lione wishes to see you."

"Does he now?" She arched one curved brow. "And he has
sent you to fetch me?"

"Yes, milady."

"And if I do not choose to go?" She said it with a slightly toying tone. She had not played with a young male in some time. Pleasantly, she found that it still amused her. "Will you take me by force? Will you sling me over your shoulder as I struggle and plead for mercy?"

"No, milady."

"Then what will you do?"

"I will wait until you choose to go."

"Then that is what you will have to do." With that, she closed the door.

It was getting late in the evening. She prepared herself a meager and carefully rationed dinner, ate it slowly and sparingly, worked on her suicide note, read a bit, then went to bed. When she awoke the following morning, she glanced out her front window and was dumbfounded to see Throk standing exactly where he had been the previous afternoon. As near as she could tell, he hadn't moved from the spot. He was covered with morning dew, and a passing bird had seen fit to relieve itself on his shoulder.

She opened the door and stared at him. "My, my. You're quite determined, aren't you."

"No, milady. I simply have my orders. Returning without you would not be following my orders. I was told to treat you with all courtesy. That, in fact, to treat you with discourtesy would result in my answering directly to Minister Durla."

"Who?"

"Minister Durla. The minister of internal security."

"Oh." She frowned. The name was vaguely familiar, but she couldn't place it. No matter. It probably was not important. "And so you have chosen to wait."

"One choice is no choice, milady."

"A good point. Come in."

"I will wait here, milady, if that is acceptable."

The edges of her mouth crinkled. "And if it is not acceptable?"

"I will still wait here. I was informed you could be quite seductive and was explicitly told not to enter your domicile for fear of being distracted from my mission."

"Ooo. 'Quite seductive.' I like the sound of that." She laughed lightly then. This was the most amusement she'd had in ages. "Very well, Throk. Remain there. I will attire myself in something more suitable and then go with you to speak with this chancellor of yours. Oh . . . and Throk . . ."

"Yes, milady."

"A pity you didn't come in. I was going to let you watch me change." She winked one eye lazily as she noted a telltale movement under Throk's shirt while the youth fought to keep an impassive face. She slid shut the door, then leaned against it and laughed some more, her shoulders trembling in silent mirth. She'd forgotten what it was like to entertain herself in that manner.

The day was getting off to quite a start.

The Office of Development was more than just an office. It was an entirely new building, tall and gleaming, part of the renovations that had been going on across Centauri Prime. Most impressive, she had to admit. Castig Lione's office was on the top floor, which, for some reason, didn't surprise Mariel in the slightest.

Lione rose from behind his desk as Throk ushered her in. "Milady Mariel," he said, the picture of graciousness. "Young Throk left to fetch you yesterday. We were beginning to lose hope."

"Your noble officer was delayed in rendering assistance to me. He is to be commended," Mariel said smoothly. Just to see Throk's expression, she cupped him under the chin and tickled him behind the ear. Nonetheless, he remained impressively impassive.

"Well done, Throk," Lione said. "You may leave us, now."

"Yes, sir," Throk said in a voice that sounded faintly strangled. He bowed quickly to Mariel and got out of there as quickly as he could.

"My congratulations, milady," said Lione, as he gestured for her to take a seat, which she promptly did. "You have managed the formidable feat of causing Throk to be disconcerted. I thought no one was capable of that."

"I am not no one," Mariel said.

"True. Quite true." He seemed to contemplate her for a moment, and suddenly said, "I have been remiss. Something to drink?"

"No, thank you."

He nodded, then pulled a bottle from his desk drawer, poured himself a glass, and downed it. "You are doubtlessly wondering why I desired to see you."

"No."

"You're not?"

She gave a small shrug of her shapely shoulders. "The world and the events that transpire within it are altogether too insane for my tastes. I prefer to simply allow them to unfold, rather than try to anticipate anything."

"Well said," he chuckled. "Best not to give things too much thought. That way lies madness."

"Speaking of madness, how is the emperor?"

The well-delivered jibe prompted an appreciative chuckle from Lione. "I, of course, would never dare to make such an obviously disrespectful comment," he said. "But I suppose that having been married to the emperor at one time accords certain . . . privileges. Are you sure you want nothing to drink?"

"Quite sure. What I would like," and she rearranged her skirts delicately around her shapely legs, "is to know why I have been summoned here. I do have a good many things to attend to . . ."

"Do you. Do you really." Something in his voice had changed ever so slightly. A slight coldness crept into it, perhaps even a hint of contempt. Lione glanced at his computer screen, apparently checking a file that was displayed upon it. "Once upon a time, milady, your activities were quite easily tracked. They consisted of a series of public appearances, parties, social engagements at high-profile establishments, and so on. However, I have no clue as to what you might be up to this fine afternoon. No sign of any activities at all. Or perhaps you're simply trying to keep a lower profile these days."

Her lips thinned as her smile dissipated, to be replaced by a hardened look of barely restrained impatience. "Are you endeavoring to make a point, Chancellor? If so, what are you trying to say?"

"I would assume, milady, that I am not saying anything you do not already know. As closely as we can determine, you have fallen on extremely hard times. You are nearly out of money." Apparently warming to his topic, he leaned forward, interlacing his fingers. "Furthermore, it was bad enough when you were simply divorced by Londo Mollari. But now your former mate has risen to the exalted rank of emperor. That makes you an imperial discard. The men who once flocked to you so eagerly now desire to keep their distance. They do not desire to tempt fate, in the event that the emperor might either form a new attachment to you, or else seek you out for some rather distressing punishment. Your beauty may well be without match, Milady Mariel . . . but there remain quite a few women out there to choose from, many of them well-connected. And few of them present anything resembling the potential difficulties that would face anyone seeking your . . . favors."

"Did you bring me here to insult me?" Mariel asked. She could feel her irritation mounting quite rapidly. She had not been certain why Lione had wanted to see her, but never would she have been able to guess that it was because he wanted to torment her.

"Not at all." He seemed stricken that she could think such a thing. "Milady, I have nothing but the utmost respect for you. I have brought you here at the suggestion and recommenda-

tion of Minister Durla, but also because I genuinely believe
that you will fit in nicely with our plans here at the Office of
Development. Although what we have in mind is, well . . ."
And he smiled. "Not precisely within the official purview of
this office, if you understand my drift."

"I would like to say that I do, but I would be lying."

He stood then. She remained where she was as he saun-
tered around the room. Since he had only half risen from his
chair earlier upon her arrival, she had not realized quite how
tall he was. "There is a great deal of resentment toward the
Interstellar Alliance, at present," he said.

"At present?" She chuckled lightly. "There has been for
some time, and that situation will continue, I'd wager."

"Yes, as would we. And since the IA promises to be something of a presence in the galaxy for some time to come, we
have a certain . . . obligation, shall we say . . . to protect Centauri interests in that regard."

"Protect them how? They have already dropped enough
bombs upon us to wipe out a less hardy race. It's a bit late for
protection now, is it not?"

He looked out his window, seemingly pleased with the
view. "It is never too late, milady. I am overseeing the creation of a . . . a department, if you will. A quiet section of the
government that is not of the government . . . if you see my
meaning."

"I am . . . beginning to," she said after a moment of consideration. "You're speaking of a bureau within the Centauri
government charged with spying upon the Alliance."

"Please, milady," protested Lione. " 'Spying' is such an
ugly word."

"Really. What word would you prefer?"

" 'Espionage.' Far more elegant, don't you think?"

"You speak of things that could potentially involve great
risk," said Mariel thoughtfully. "I do not embark on such un-
dertakings lightly. What would you have me do?"

"Only that which you are more than capable of accomplishing, milady," said Lione. He had been circling the room, but now he stopped next to her. In what might be seen as a somewhat bold move, he rested a hand on her shoulder. "Your beauty, if I may say so, is exceptional."

"You may say so," Mariel told him. "And you are implying that a beautiful woman may accomplish a great many things, particularly when it comes to eliciting information from easily manipulated men."

"Quite."

"But beauty, my dear chancellor, is very much in the eye of he who beholds it," she reminded him. "The most beautiful Centauri woman on the face of this planet may be considered quite hideous by a Drazi, for example."

"True enough," admitted Lione. "But you are overlooking two things. First, there are many cross-species standards for beauty that you already surpass. To Human eyes, you are exceptionally attractive. Also, your features would not be found displeasing by a Minbari. And my understanding is that the Narn . . . well, the Narn find pale skin rather exotic, so I'm told."

"You're told correctly," Mariel said, remembering the attentions paid her by G'Kar. Certainly part of their relationship had been spurred by the fact that G'Kar drew great pleasure from cuckolding his old opponent, Londo, but certainly the Narn was attracted to her as a female, as well. "And the second thing that I am overlooking?"

"Charisma, milady. You have a great deal of charisma, and I am certain that it would serve you in good stead, even with those races who would consider a Centauri female to be less than aesthetic."

"Why, Chancellor. You certainly know how to flatter a woman."

"But I do not do so idly, I assure you. I feel you could be a most valuable operative for us, Milady Mariel. And I speak not only in terms of espionage. There may be the occasional requirement for sabotage or . . ."

"Murder?" she finished the sentence. "Oh, but let me guess: 'murder' is a distasteful word as well."

"Since you bring it up . . . I personally have always preferred the term 'relocation.' "

"Relocation?"

"Yes. To the next life."

"Ah." She smiled. Clearly the chancellor was not without a sense of humor, however morbid it might be.

He came full circle around his desk and seated himself once more. "Doubtless you are wondering how this will benefit you directly."

"It did cross my mind. Unless you were intending that I should become involved out of the goodness of my hearts."

"I have no doubt that there is much in your hearts, milady, but how much could be honestly described as 'goodness,' I would not care to find out. In answer to your question: Titles and lands, I regret, presently would be out of my reach to provide you. This aspect of my office must maintain a low profile, and to elevate you in such a manner would be too conspicuous. It might draw questions.

"However, we can easily provide you with attractive remuneration, drawn from certain discretionary funds we have at our disposal. Furthermore, I believe you will find that certain doors to society will slowly begin creaking open for you once again. Your attracting some attention can only be beneficial to the cause. Just . . . not too much attention, if you——"

"Understand your meaning? Yes, Chancellor, it's quite clear."

"Your missions would come from this office, and you would answer directly to me."

"And if I were to find myself in any sort of difficulty derived from my espionage activities? If the truth behind one of my 'missions' were to come out, and I found myself facing charges of being a spy? What then?"

"Then," sighed Lione, "I am afraid that you would very likely find yourself in rather disastrous straits. Might I suggest that you not be found out?"

"So you are saying I would be considered . . . disposable." She smiled humorlessly. "It would not be the first time. Since Londo already disposed of Daggair and myself, I have some experience in being considered easily dispensed with."

"Do you think that the lady Daggair would be interested in becoming involved, as well? Or, for that matter, the lady Timov? Granted, she is still the emperor's wife, but our understanding is that there is no love lost between the two of them. She might be willing to accommodate us."

Mariel gave the question some serious consideration. Then, slowly she shook her head. "I would not, if I were you, Chancellor. Daggair very much enjoys playing at being the manipulator. Politics and gamesmanship are something of a hobby to her. But she remains a dabbler, nothing more, with overmuch confidence in her abilities. I doubt she truly would have the stomach for the stakes that you're describing.

"As for Timov . . . you underestimate her, I think. She is superb at developing rationalizations for disliking Londo, but in my opinion, rationalizations are all they are. She was quite young when she married Londo, and she was quite starry-eyed when she did so, although it was an arranged marriage. I believe that some of that stardust remains, although it is very much tucked away in the corners of her eyes where she thinks it will not be noticed. I would not count on her being willing to betray Londo. Furthermore she is far too outspoken, and certainly does not suffer fools gladly. There is no subtlety to her, which would make her a less-than-attractive candidate.

"There are, however, others," she added thoughtfully. "Other individuals who might very well be of the caliber that you are looking for. In my time, I have had the opportunity to make the acquaintance of many 'dubious' individuals. I can provide you with a list of names, if you are so inclined."

"You see? Your usefulness to us begins already." Then he

tilted his head slightly. "You seem thoughtful, milady. Is all well?"

"I am just . . . thinking about the other wives. Londo's, that is. Sometimes I look back on that part of my life as if it was someone else's entirely." She laughed softly. "Do you know what Londo used to refer to us as? 'Pestilence, famine, and death.' "

Lione shook his head politely. "I am afraid I do not understand the reference."

"Oh, it relates to Earth. Londo is quite the aficionado with Earth legend. One of their religions apparently states that, when their judgment day arrives, it will be heralded by four horsemen. And three of them would be pestilence, famine, and death."

"Earth customs seem to hold endless fascination, not only for Londo, but for his former protégé, Vir, as well." Clearly struck by a thought, he added, "Who would the fourth horseman in this mythical quartet be?"

She frowned, trying to recall, and then her face brightened. "Oh yes. War."

"War." Castig Lione chuckled. "Considering where Londo led us to, that is quite appropriate, don't you think?"

"I try not to think, Chancellor," Mariel said. "Oftentimes it gets in the way of living my life."

"So we have an understanding then, milady?"

"Yes. Yes, I believe we do." She extended a hand in a rather elegant fashion and Castig Lione took it suavely and kissed her knuckles. "I can trust to your gentlemanly nature, I assume, to make my 'remuneration' a fair one, so that we need not discuss such annoying matters as exact sums at this time?"

"I am quite certain, milady, that you will not be disappointed."

"And I thank you for thinking of me in this matter."

"Well, milady . . . as I mentioned earlier . . . to be honest, it was Durla who suggested your name to me in connection with our endeavors."

"Durla . . ." Her face blanked a moment, and then she recalled once more. "Oh, yes. That minister person. Do be so
kind as to pass my thanks along to him, then. And by all
means, Chancellor . . . do not feel circumscribed by the business nature of our relationship."

"Milady?"

Mariel, clearly not feeling any need to expound beyond
that, simply withdrew her hand from his, then walked out of
the room, stopping only to toss a small-but-knowing smile
over her shoulder.

It seemed to Castig Lione that Durla was taking extreme
pains to sound casual when he inquired, "Oh . . . and did you
have the opportunity to meet with the Lady Mariel?"

Durla had regular weekly meetings with Lione to discuss
an assortment of projects. Indeed, Durla had meetings with
all of the chancellors who answered to him. Lione was accustomed to them. In his case, he would sit there and speak at
length about plans of the Development Office, both short-
and long-term, and Durla would appear to be listening and
nodding, although whether he was truly attending to anything
that Lione was saying, Lione never really knew for sure.

This time, however, Durla seemed quite attentive. His
forced attempts to appear nonchalant came across as just
that: forced. Lione wasn't entirely certain why that would be,
although he did have his suspicions.

"Yes. Yes, I did."

"And how did it go?"

"It went quite well. She is an extraordinary individual, the
lady Mariel is. A great deal of charm and personal charisma.
Your assorted suggestions for our bureau of espionage have
been superb up until now, Minister, but the inclusion of
Mariel may well be one of your most perspicacious selections
yet."

"Good."

The minister said nothing for a time, and Lione couldn't

quite tell whether he was expecting Lione to continue speaking or whether Durla was simply lost in thought. To play it
safe, Lione said, "I have been giving some thought to naming
the division of the bureau, sir."

"Naming?" Durla momentarily seemed puzzled.

"Yes, Minister. Certainly we should have a means of referring to the division that is to oversee the gathering of information and other . . . activities . . . in regard to the Alliance.
However, calling it the Espionage Division would seem a bit
obvious."

"Yes. Yes, absolutely, I agree." Durla pursed his lips, considered it, and then said, "Designate it as the Division of
Public Works."

"Public works. Very well, Minister. May I ask how you—"

"Did she say anything about me?"

The question had come out all in a rush from Durla, and it
caught Lione momentarily off guard. "She, Minister? Do you
mean the lady Mariel?"

"Yes, yes. You did tell her that it was upon my recommendation that she was being brought into the Division of Public
Works."

"No, sir, because at the time, we were not calling it the—"

"Do not fence with me, Lione," said Durla, in a voice that
seemed to suggest Castig Lione was suddenly in danger.
By this point, Durla's attitude had more or less confirmed
Lione's evaluation of the situation, but Lione was not about to
say what was on his mind. He had a feeling that doing so
could prove to have rather nasty consequences. "Did you
mention me to her. I simply wish to know."

"Why do you wish to know, sir?" asked Lione.

"Because," Durla said steadily, "if I should happen to encounter her at a formal function, I wish to know if she knows
that I know of her involvement so that I do not say something
out of turn."

Lione slowly nodded, running Durla's last sentence through
his mind a couple of times to make certain that he had followed

it correctly. "I . . . understand, Minister. In point of fact, yes, I did mention your name to her. Twice, I believe, although I would not swear to it."

Durla suddenly seemed rather interested in tapping the surface of his desk with his finger. "Indeed. And . . . what did she say? In regard to me, I mean. She did indicate that she knew who I was."

It might have been Lione's imagination, but it seemed as if Durla was puffing out his chest slightly as he said that, as if completely absorbed in his self-image. "Yes, sir. In fact . . . now that I think of it . . . she did ask me to thank you for recommending her."

"She did!" Durla slapped his hand on the desk as if he'd suddenly had an off-the-cuff recollection of where he had left his wallet. "And why did you not say this earlier, Lione? If you are to be overseeing an intelligence-gathering division, it might behoove you to be more efficient in transmitting important information to me, without my having to drag it out of you. Do you not agree?"

"Wholeheartedly, Minister. I shall endeavor to do better in the future."

"Did she say anything else? You said she knew who I was. Of course she did," he answered his own question. "She must know. Everyone does."

"She definitely had an awareness, Minister. When I mentioned your name, she said . . . now what was it? Ah. She said, 'Oh, yes . . . that minister person.' "

The temperature in the room dropped substantially.

" 'That . . . minister person?' Are you quite certain that is what she said?"

"Word for word, sir."

Durla's face hardened, and it was at that moment that Lione knew precisely what to do. He leaned forward in his chair, his tall frame almost bending in half as he gestured in a conspiratorial way that Durla should lean forward. Clearly confused, Durla did so, and when Lione spoke, it was in the whispered tone of someone sharing a very great secret. "She is a very subtle individual, sir."

"Subtle."

"Sublimely so, yes. However, sir, she is still merely a woman . . . and I have always been a fairly astute judge of the breed, sir."

"I don't quite follow you, Chancellor."

"I believe, sir, that she may have more . . . consideration for you than she lets on. Oh, but . . . perhaps I'm speaking too boldly here—"

"No, no," Durla said quickly. "I need to know whatever might be on your mind, Chancellor. By all means, be bold."

"Well, Minister," the Chancellor said, warming to the topic, "although her words seemed dismissive, there was something about her tone of voice that indicated otherwise. Almost as if she was trying mightily to give the appearance of having only the slightest notion of who you were. But let us be realistic, Minister . . . who on Centauri Prime does *not* know Minister Durla of Internal Security? The idea that she would not be instantly familiar with your name is simply absurd. A far more reasonable supposition is that she was being—"

"Subtle?"

"Yes. Precisely. I could see it in her eyes, sir. It was quite evident . . . if one knows what to look for."

"Well . . . that is excellent. Most excellent," Durla said, looking remarkably cheered. Lione sat straight up again and Durla continued, "I have no doubt that she will be a valuable addition to the Division of Public Works. Good work, Lione. Good work all around."

They chatted for a few more minutes about assorted business matters: The current membership of the Prime Candidates, and how it could be increased. An archaeological project that Durla, for some reason, was in the process of commencing on some outlying world. But Lione wasn't listening. Instead his mind was racing in regard to the situation that had presented itself to him in such stark and clear relief. There was no doubt, as far as Lione was concerned. Clearly Durla was besotted with the woman. When it came to matters involving the lady Mariel, Durla obviously could not be counted on to think straight.

That was a useful piece of information to have. Lione had no idea quite yet how, or if, he would turn it to his advantage. But he had no doubt that, sooner or later, it would come into use. A useful little hole card . . . and one that would be his to play when it suited his needs.

part ii

2265-2267
Nighttime

— *chapter 14* —

Senna was becoming increasingly worried about the emperor.

Naturally she had something personal at stake. In her nearly two years at the palace, she had become rather used to the comforts. Her continued residence there was contingent upon not only Londo's good graces, but his continued health.

But it was more than just that. She had a feeling about him, a sense that in some way, he was truly aspiring to greatness. He wanted so much for his people. He loved Centauri Prime with a passion that she felt was unmatched by anyone else in the palace.

That, of course, was no great measure, because Senna did not particularly like anyone else in the palace. Durla seemed to be omnipresent, watching her with those cold and deadly eyes, like a great animal waiting to spring upon unwary prey. Durla's preferred right-hand man, Castig Lione, was not much better. Then there was Kuto, Durla's newly chosen Minister of Information, although as near as Senna could tell, Kuto's major activities involved the suppression of genuine information . . . or, at least, the free flow of ideas. From her vantage point in the social strata, Senna could watch clearly the slow disappearance of any persons who expressed opinions contrary to the directives the government foisted upon the people.

The people. Great Maker help the people.

A number of times during the many months she had

resided in the palace, Senna had made forays into the city. She had made certain to leave behind her richly stitched and elaborate dresses, and instead had favored simple, relatively unattractive garments. She had moved among places that Londo would most likely—and most unhappily—have disapproved of. And the things she heard were most disturbing to her.

There was constant talk of anger toward the Alliance, indicating emotional wounds that had never been healed. She remembered the child who was hobbling about with one leg gone at the knee, his lower leg having been crushed by falling debris and amputated; his parents hadn't had the money to pay for prosthetics to replace it. She recalled the woman who said she never slept anymore, that every small sound during the night awakened her as she believed that more bombs were about to be dropped upon her. From the woman's haunted visage, Senna could tell that the woman wasn't exaggerating her plight. Senna's hearts went out to her, and she wished once more that there was something she could do.

Although their stories of horror and mental anguish were all different, their current sentiments seemed to be consistent. The resentment toward the Alliance still burned hotly, and even as Centauri Prime was being rebuilt, it appeared to Senna that it was being rebuilt for a reason. And that reason was the launching of some sort of attack against the Alliance. The specifics of it didn't seem clear to anyone. It was more a free-floating sense of anger, which permeated the social structure of Centauri Prime, from the top through to the very bottom.

The truth was that Senna had no more love for the Alliance than anyone else. But some aspects of her education, including her all-too-short time with Telis Elaris—whom she continued to think of at least once a day, and always with a sense of grief and loss—had led her to conclude that the path upon which the Centauri Republic seemed determined to tread could not be the correct one. Indeed, it could very well lead to an even greater disaster. Centauri Prime had been pounded into the ground but, ultimately, most of the Republic's citizens were at least still alive. They were being permitted to rebuild, and even the economy was showing signs—slow signs, but signs nonetheless—of beginning to recover.

If the Republic, once it was rebuilt, resumed its old ways and came into conflict once more with the Interstellar Alliance, things might go far worse for them the next time. How apt, how poetically just would it be, if the illegal mass drivers—the ultimate in ground punishment, gathering in space debris and raining it down in concentrated form—were used against Centauri Prime, just as the Centauri had wrongfully used them against the Narn? By the time the Alliance got through with them, there might not be a single Centauri left alive. Rather than recapture the glory of republics past, the Centauri might find themselves extinct. Within a generation everything that the Centauri Republic had ever accomplished, for good or ill, would be dust and forgotten.

Senna did not want to let that happen, but she didn't have the faintest idea how to go about preventing it. One female could not possibly prevent the Centauri Republic from committing mass suicide, which seemed the likeliest outcome if Centauri Prime continued on its present course.

The only hope she could possibly discern lay with the emperor. He, however, seemed to be slipping farther and farther away with each passing day.

Oh, there were the occasional good days. On those occasions, Londo would laugh or joke with her, tweak her cheek in an affectionate manner that could not possibly be considered anything other than paternal. Sometimes he would regale her with tales of the Republic in the past, or share with her some examples of his impressively extensive collection of slightly ribald jokes. In short, there was any number of times when the emperor was someone she genuinely wanted to be with.

The rest of the time, however . . . well, when he would look at her, it was as if he was staring at her from the bottom of a very deep pit. His were the eyes of a man who somehow, in some manner that she could not begin to comprehend, had seen his own future. And it was apparently not something that was going to be pretty or desirable.

Now, as she approached the emperor's study, Senna hoped that perhaps she would encounter Londo during one of his more convivial moods. Because if he were in that sort of state, then she might actually be able to share with him her concerns over the future of the Republic. Certainly there was no one else in the palace with whom she could speak on any sort of open basis. Everyone else had the misfortune of being male, or the sort of political in-fighter who wouldn't hesitate to use anything that Senna said against her. She had no desire to provide any potential enemy with that sort of ammunition. But the emperor . . .

The emperor, for some reason, she was not afraid of. If anything, she was afraid *for* him.

She peered in through the study, and saw him slumped at his desk. For the briefest of moments, she thought he was dead. That was until she heard the snoring, however; at which point she knew that Londo was still among the living . . . although barely so, it seemed.

And then she thought morbidly, *A shame he's not dead. He'd stay well preserved for some time if he were.* As soon as the notion went through her head, she chided herself for it. What a horrible thing to think, particularly when it was obvious that the emperor was hurting emotionally.

She studied him thoughtfully and wished that there was some way that she could reach directly into his mind. Sense his thoughts, ease the pain. Do something, *anything* possible to help this basically good man, or at the very least have some idea of what it was that was eating away at him.

Then she noticed that he had been working on something. His hand was resting on it. She dared not touch him in order to move his hand and see better, but then—as if he were unconsciously urging her to look—he moved his arm. In his slumber, it slid off the desk and hung limply at his side.

She looked more closely and saw that it was a book. A book that he was apparently writing by hand. How very, very quaint. Most people, it seemed to her, preferred data crystals and such. She could only guess why he might want to work in what some would consider an archaic fashion. Perhaps he felt it added a sort of personal touch. Or maybe he was inspired by the numerous books of history, many of them handwritten by past emperors, which were said to line the walls of the private library. By continuing in that tradition, he was making himself a sort of living link to the past.

From a purely pragmatic point of view, by confining his writings to one book that he carried with him, it also meant that his thoughts and musings would be kept in his possession at all times. The moment anything was put onto a computer, even as a private file, there was always the danger that someone, somewhere would be able to carve their way into the system and access it.

She toyed with the notion of picking up the book, examining it. Certainly there was nothing to stop her from doing so, with the sole exception of her conscience. Obviously this was a work in progress, and it was unlikely that Londo would want anyone perusing it before he felt it was ready.

Even so . . .

Well . . . if she didn't actually turn the pages, that wouldn't be so invasive, would it? After all, she was simply looking down at the open ones. Why . . . who could fault her for that? It wasn't as if she had been seeking it out. Besides, certainly Londo meant for it to be read sooner or later. What point was there in writing a history if no one was going to see it. And it was a history, she was quite sure of that. Because she had just kind of, sort of, well . . . just happened to lift the title page ever so slightly and spotted the word, carefully delineated in Londo's own script. Then, ever so delicately, she laid the book flat again so that she could see just what Londo was writing about at that particular moment. The book appeared already to be half full. Apparently Londo had been quite busy.

She started to read, although she wasn't touching the book at that point. But when she saw just what it was that she was reading, her eyes went wide with surprise.

Minbar! The emperor had been on Minbar! She remembered when he had disappeared from Centauri Prime, some five months before. His departure had been unannounced and rather unexpected. Durla had tried to act as if he had been expecting it, but even he had seemed a bit caught off guard.

Londo had been gone for three weeks, and there had been a bit of confusion and nervousness bandied about, although Durla had done an excellent job of staying atop all the problems that had cropped up. And then, after a time, the emperor had returned. Senna realized that it was from that point on that she had really noticed the change in him. He seemed . . . smaller than he had before. Diminished somehow. It was nothing she could truly put her finger on, but she was certain that she wasn't imagining it. Something very bad had happened, and she now knew that whatever it was that had happened to so dispirit the emperor, it must have occurred on Minbar.

Despite her better judgment, Senna set aside all pretense to the contrary and started reading what Londo had written. She still didn't pick up the book, as if not touching it would somehow negate any invasion of privacy or breaking of trust. Instead she leaned with her knuckles on the table and read in earnest.

Apparently Londo had gone to Minbar to meet with Delenn and Sheridan. Delenn was with child, and at the point in the narrative where the page began, Londo was recording an encounter with the president of the Interstellar Alliance and his "lovely wife," as Londo put it.

Senna continued to read:

It was clear to me that they were to be somewhat guarded in my presence. I could see it in Sheridan's eyes, feel it even when he wasn't looking at me. He was suspicious and unsure. I suppose I could not blame them, truly. They were not expecting me simply to show up on Minbar. Now that I was here, they had no clue as to what to anticipate. It had to be especially perplexing for Sheridan, since he believed himself a superb strategist, and my appearance on Minbar did not fit any proscribed pattern he could anticipate.

As for me . . . I had my own difficulties to deal with, my own "secrets" to attend to. So not only was I a bit more boisterous than I normally would have been, left to my own devices, but certainly more effervescent than the moment called for. No doubt that increased the level of their suspicions.

We were seated in the dining room which, I must admit, was not particularly lavish. These days it seems to me that the palace on Centauri Prime is more of a prison than a home. Nonetheless, at least it is a decorative prison. The food, as far as I was concerned, was mostly inedible; even the most elaborate Minbari delicacies are, at best, bland. But I smiled through it as we chatted—once more—about how surprised Sheridan and Delenn were to see me. Surprised . . . and even a bit disconcerted. When I commented on it, they promptly denied it, of course. They wished to be polite. Considering the purpose of my being there, it seemed almost quaint that such was their concern.

Our conversation broadened to surprising people in general. "Another of the benefits of being emperor . . ." and then I added, almost as an afterthought, "or president in your case . . . is not so much the people who are pleased to see you in office. It's the people who are furious that you're even alive, let alone holding a position of power. Knowing that every day you succeed, they die a little inside . . . makes the endeavor eminently satisfying."

Sheridan cast an uncomfortable glance at Delenn and

then forced a polite smile. "I hadn't really thought of it in those terms," he said.

I thought of the looks I get from my ministers, and the scheming eyes that watch my back as I pass, thinking of how delightful my spine would look with a dagger protruding from it. "Oh, you will. You will," I assured him.

There was an uncomfortable silence—one of many in the evening—and then Delenn said, "If you don't mind my saying so, Emperor Mollari—"

I waved a scolding finger. "Londo, please."

"You told *me* to call you Emperor Mollari," said Sheridan.

Indicating Delenn's ensemble, I replied, "You don't look as good in that outfit as she does." This actually prompted the first genuine smile of the evening. "Go on, Delenn."

"I was just going to say that your attitude toward us is . . ." She paused, searching for the right words. ". . . quite improved over the last time. When we were all on Centauri Prime, you said some . . . unkind things."

I waved dismissively. "Playing to the audience, Delenn, nothing more. I need to get my people fired up in order to begin the long and difficult process of rebuilding. There's politics," and then I looked significantly at them, "and there's friendship. And when I learned that you were with child, and that you were finally coming here to stay . . . how could I not come and convey my personal best wishes."

When she read that, Senna's hearts leapt. So grim Londo had been as of late, so sullen. Was it possible that he indeed presented one face to his people and advisors, and another to those he truly considered his friends? For some reason, it made Senna want to know the real Londo even more. The one who genuinely cared about reconciliation. Already she could see that it made sense, although she wasn't entirely sure that she agreed with the tactic. She understood it, though. Saying whatever was necessary to get the people stirred up. Yes. Yes, it did make sense. After the battering, the bombings . . . their spirit was at a low ebb. First and foremost, he had to get them to *care* about something, to manufacture some sort of passion and energy. And if it was directed at first in a negative manner, well . . . at least it was there. Once it was present, he could then steer it whichever way he wanted it to go.

She looked back at the book and continued to read . . .

Delenn and Sheridan looked at each other, and I could tell what was going through their minds. They were hoping that what I said was the truth . . . but they were not certain.

I suppose I could not blame them. I have been living so many lies for so long, even I am not certain what the truth is anymore.

Senna's face fell when she read that. It certainly wasn't the sentiment she was hoping he'd express. "Living so many lies?" What did that mean?

As Sheridan and Delenn tried to make up their minds, my own thoughts began to race as to possibilities under which we might . . . chat in an open manner. I had, after all, certain considerations that needed to be attended to. "I would raise a toast to you, but there doesn't seem to be anything at hand. Do you have a little Brivari, Mr. President? Some of that excellent Earth whiskey tucked away in a box somewhere?"

"No," said Sheridan. "Since alcohol is dangerous for Minbari, I decided to leave all that stuff at Babylon 5."

Immediately I remembered, and could have kicked myself for the oversight. Lennier had told me that alcohol engendered murderous rages in Minbari. Foolishness. Foolishness of me to forget that. For now there was no way I would be able to . . . relax sufficiently, to be able to truly open up. With flickering hope, I asked, "Surely there must be a little . . ."

"Not a drop," Sheridan said firmly. "I'm surprised that you didn't bring your own supplies."

I glanced at my shoulder and felt a slight twinge of warning. "My associates do not allow me such pleasures anymore. I suppose they feel I am dangerous enough sober. No reason to make things worse."

We continued to eat in silence once more, and then I felt a slight qualm in my mind, through that damnable connection. But this time it was not a warning that came from within, but from without. I glanced up and immediately saw the problem. Delenn was looking at me, her eyes narrowed, as if she was perceiving that which she could not . . . indeed, must not . . . be allowed to see. And yet I was

Senna stopped reading, thoroughly confused. What could Londo possibly be talking about? What was Delenn "perceiving" that she should not? The only thing Senna could guess was that Delenn was intuiting something about Londo's state of mind. He wanted to retain his privacy, keep his purposes and thoughts obscure. After all, he had spoken of "living lies," a comment that bothered Senna greatly. Obviously, Londo was worried about letting anyone get too close to him emotionally.

Although the comment about "that damnable connection" still mystified her.

And yet I was almost tempted to do nothing. Perhaps . . . perhaps if she perceived, if she knew and understood . . . then they would be able to take the proper action, know the precautions that they should employ.

That was when a little voice in my head urged me to stop stalling. It wasn't words that I heard so much, but a sense that I should get on with it . . . lest there be dire consequences for all concerned. And I knew that I had no choice. No choice at all.

His conscience. He was wrestling with his conscience over some sort of decision, probably having to do with whether he could trust Sheridan and Delenn. Senna felt herself utterly caught up in the drama of the moment.

"So, Delenn," I said quickly. That startled her from her concentration and she muttered an apology. "You haven't asked me about my gift."

"What gift?" Delenn responded. She still seemed a bit befuddled by her long gaze into the dark places of my life, and she turned to Sheridan.

Sheridan, ever the diplomat—and, of course, eager to distance himself from the great Centauri Republic and its even greater emperor—said, "We really can't . . ."

"Oh, it's not for you," I quickly assured them. Then I clapped my hands, and one of my retainers entered with the urn. It was draped with a white cloth, so naturally it drew some degree of curiosity, particularly from Delenn. At least there are some aspects of females that cross all races, and inquisitiveness appears to be a universal womanly trait. Sheridan just looked suspicious. Of course, he had long practice at it.

The retainer set the vase down and left, and I removed the cloth with just a bit of a flourish. I have to admit, it was a rather impressive looking bit of pottery . . . at least, from the outside.

Sheridan picked it up, and it was everything I could do to repress a shudder. Instead, sounding remarkably sanguine about it, if I do say so myself, I said, "It is a Centauri tradition to give this to the heir to the throne when he or she comes of age. It is very old."

"It's beautiful," Delenn said. "But we cannot possibly accept."

Naturally, I would have been more than happy to oblige them. Instead I had to say, "I insist."

"Won't they miss it back home?" asked Sheridan.

They were asking so many questions, so many damned questions. It was an annoying trait. They never accepted anything at face value, never took the word of others. They had to keep asking and probing until they themselves were satisfied.

"The tradition is not well known outside the palace," I said. "Besides, I have no heirs and, when I am gone, I suspect the Centaurum will do all it can to eliminate the position of emperor. If I am going to be obsolete, and that is going to be obsolete, then I may as well make sure it goes someplace where it will be appreciated."

Lies intermingled with truth. I was becoming quite facile with it. Truthfully, I did not think there was any chance whatsoever that the position of emperor would be eliminated. There are far too many people who crave the ultimate power of that office. The very people who would be in a position to do away with the office of emperor would be the very same people most eager to don the white themselves. Little good may it do them.

And besides . . . I knew of the prophecy. I knew I was ordained to be followed by an emperor . . . by at least one . . .

This revelation stunned Senna for a moment. A prophecy? She had read assorted books of Centauri prophecy. Certainly there were women who were quite legitimate seers, and their forecasts were well known. But she didn't recall any published prophecy that specifically mentioned Londo. Or that cited when or if the position of emperor would be done away with. Was it some sort of private reading that had been done just for him?

She hoped that his next words would spell out what the prophecy was, or where he had divined it from. Instead, as she read on in eager anticipation, she felt a flicker of disappointment . . .

At that moment, a Minbari entered and whispered something into Delenn's ear. I suspect that he was of the same "caste" as Lennier, for he had that same, quiet manner as the star-crossed Ranger. Delenn nodded and rose. "Something has just come up," she said. "If you will excuse me."

For a moment I thought that perhaps somehow, through some miracle, she had figured it out. That she actually knew. But then she walked out of the room without so much as a backward glance, and that was how I knew she remained blissfully oblivious.

Sheridan then faced me, and I hoped that he was going to continue to try and dissuade me from presenting him with the gift. Instead he picked that horrendous moment to allow me to be magnanimous. "Well, if I can't talk you out of this," he said, ". . . well, thank you. When should I . . . ?"

The words I was about to speak felt as if I was allowing poison to drip from my mouth. "When your child, male or female, turns sixteen years, then you hand it over."

"I notice the bottom part is sealed."

Great Maker, nothing slipped past the man. I kept my expression bland, though, as I fabricated on the spot, "Yes. I'm told that it contains water taken from the river that flowed past the first palace, two thousand years ago."

He actually looked intrigued as he gently set the vase down.

We chatted for a bit more, but with every passing moment I became less and less enthused, more and more anxious to simply get out of there. I felt as if the walls were closing in. My breath was heavy in my chest. I tried to tell myself that it was simply the different atmosphere on Minbar, but I could not ignore the fact that I was likely suffering from some sort of attack of anxiety. Suddenly I knew that if I did not get out of the dining room, if I did not get away from the urn, I would go mad right there, right on that very spot. They would mark the floor as a historical site, the place where the great Emperor Londo Mollari lost his mind and collapsed from the strain of a tormented conscience.

I began to make my excuses to Sheridan, talking about how I was needed back on Centauri Prime. How they could not function without me. I tried to make it sound like a great trial and task. I laughed about it, shared with him how daunting such awesome responsibility could be. And all during that time, I wanted to do nothing more than flee the room. But I tend to think that, had I done so, such an action might well have piqued his curiosity and sent him off in directions that it would be best not to go.

Mercifully, Delenn returned before too long. She seemed distracted, saddened. Her smile was a forced thing, her luminous spirit momentarily diminished, but she did her best to try and bring herself back up to her normal levels of cheerful and thoughtful social interaction. Then I was in the midst of saying my good-byes as we walked down the corridor toward the exit.

"Are you sure you can't stay a little longer?" asked Sheridan.

I was not entirely certain how serious he was. I think, in a perversely ironic way, he actually meant it because he was moved by my magnanimous "gift."

"No, the affairs of state weigh on me just as they do on you," I said. "Besides, I'm sure you would like to settle in and get down to creating the greatest empire in history, yes?"

It was a good exit line. Nice, noncommittal, even a tacit acknowledgement of the inevitable greatness of the Interstellar Alliance. I could depart their lives with a smile and the knowledge that, at the last, I was the same charming and amusing Londo as in the earliest days of Babylon 5, rather than this dark and forbidding presence that I have become.

I wanted to turn away, to say nothing more . . . but I

could not help myself. There was so much more that
needed to be said, that should have been said and never
would be. I felt a gentle stirring, a mild warning, a rebuke
in advance that seemed to say, *Keep your distance. You
have done your duty, your penance, now leave. Simply . . .
leave.*

That, more than anything, spurred my next words as I
said to them with terrible earnestness, "One thing I want
you to know, to understand and to hold in your thoughts in
the years to come . . . I want you to know that you are my
friends, and you will always be my friends, no matter what
may happen. And I want you to know that this day . . . this
day in your company means more to me than you will ever
know."

Then I sensed their presence. Durla's guards, two of his
closer and more dedicated followers, hovering there. Obviously Durla had a sense of how long I should be spending
with Sheridan and Delenn, a mental approximation that I
can only assume was provided for him by means he does
not truly understand himself. He had imparted those time
limits to the guards, and they were coming in search of me,
their presence a gentle but firm reminder of just who was
watching whom.

The word *Go* filtered through my brain, and I did not
even have to bother to look in the direction of my watchers
to know that they were there. "It appears I must go now."

"I know," said Sheridan. Of course, the fact was that
he did *not* know. He thought he did, thought he compre-
hended, but he understood nothing. Not really. The odds
are that he never would.

And his lack of comprehension was underscored by the
last words he would ever speak to me on the surface of
Minbar. Because if we were to face each other again, I
knew it was likely to be across the interstellar plain
of battle, perhaps snarling at one another via view screens.
Or else we might, just might, meet as keeper and prisoner,

should Sheridan's fates turn against him and he wind up a prisoner on Centauri Prime. Of course, in my own situation, the concepts of prisoner and keeper are extremely fluid, and I constantly find myself occupying both positions at the same time. I am he who holds the fate of millions, and I am he whose fate is held by other keepers.

And I know that the situation will never be reversed. I will never face Sheridan with myself as a prisoner, for were it to come to that, I will be dead before such an encounter took place. They will certainly attend to that.

So Sheridan spoke his last, unknowingly sardonic words to me then as we stood for the last time as peaceful equals: "You're always welcome to come back, Londo."

"More than welcome," echoed Delenn.

They were good people, I knew that. They deserved better than what was coming to them, better than what I had done to them. Then again . . . so did I. Except my living hell was of my own making, whereas their future living hell . . . was also of my making. Is there any more blackened and stained soul in existence than mine?

I could hardly get out any words. I managed to say, "Thank you . . . good-bye . . ." And then I was gone, my guards walking on either side of me, escorting me back to my ship. I thought I overheard Sheridan and Delenn discussing Lennier just before I was out of earshot, and I wished I could have heard more. He was a good lad, Lennier. I spent some time with him. In retrospect, he may be the only individual who ever spent extended time in my presence without becoming tainted in some manner. A good and pure soul is his. I envy him that.

Through the glass of my cruiser, I watched Minbar receding, and then, naturally, I heard an all-too-expected voice. The voice that said *You*

"You! You! What are you doing?"
Senna jumped back, completely startled, her hand jumping

and knocking the book off the table. Londo had awoken, and he was looking up at her with pain-filled and bloodshot eyes that were seething with anger.

"What are you doing! How much did you read? *What did you read!?*"

Senna's mouth opened, but no words emerged. Londo was on his feet, and he had risen with such fury that he knocked aside the writing table, sending it crashing to the floor. He sounded more than just angry.

He sounded terrified.

"I . . . I . . ." Senna finally managed to get out.

Londo grabbed up the book, slammed it shut. "This was private! You had no right . . . *no right!*"

"I . . . I thought—"

"You didn't think! Not for a minute! What did you read here! Tell me! I will know if you are lying, tell me!"

She remembered how just a short time before, she had been thinking how she had never been afraid of Londo. That sentiment was gone. She had never been more terrified, not just of Londo, but of anyone, as she was at that moment. "About . . . you and Sheridan and Delenn. You gave them the urn."

"And then?" He grabbed her by either shoulder, shook her, and there was such tumult in his eyes . . . she remembered being a very small child, looking to the skies as her father, Refa, held her tightly, and there were storm fronts rolling in. And those darksome clouds had been the single most frightening thing she had ever seen . . . until this moment, when she looked into the eyes of Londo Mollari.

"And then?!"

*"And then you left, never to come back, and I'm leaving too, all right, **all right?!**"* Senna cried. And she tore away from him, sobbing and choking so hard that she couldn't even catch her breath. She thought she was going to be ill. She ran then, ran as fast and as hard as she could, ran from the room and almost crashed into Durla. His eyes widened as he took

in Senna's agitated state, and the condition of both the furniture and the emperor.

"It's your fault, it's *all your fault*!" she howled in his face.

"Young lady . . ." Durla began, but he got no further as her hand flew, almost on its own accord, to smack against his face and leave a huge flaming red area the size of her palm on his cheek. Durla staggered from the pain of the impact, but Senna didn't stay around to see the results of her action. Instead she ran down the hallway, her arms pumping, her breasts heaving.

In her room, she tore away the fine dress she was wearing. The cloth, the beautiful, gilt-edged, shimmering cloth made a most satisfying ripping sound as she shredded it. Naked, she yanked together some assorted articles of clothing, tossed them on in a hodge-podge manner, and threw a cloak around her shoulders.

She heard a crack of thunder from outside. The skies were opening up and rain was starting to hammer down. She didn't care. She couldn't stay in the palace a second longer, not when she knew what she knew. And as she ran out into the rain, she realized that the most frustrating thing was that she knew what she knew . . . was nothing. And it was the nothing that she feared more than anything.

— chapter 15 —

When Senna had not returned after a week, Londo summoned Lione. To Londo's utter lack of surprise, Durla showed up with him. "I had some matters to discuss with you, Majesty," Durla said, "and since Chancellor Lione stated that you desired to—"

Londo was gazing out the window at the city. Without even bothering to turn around, he said to Lione, "I have a little task for your Prime Candidates, Chancellor."

"They, and I, are at your service, Majesty," Lione said, bowing slightly.

"Senna is out there somewhere. I want her found, and I want you to alert me as to where she is. I will handle matters from there."

Lione and Durla exchanged glances, and then Durla cleared his throat and took a step forward. "Majesty," he said politely, "are you sure that would be for the best?"

"She is one young woman, Durla. If I cannot save one young woman," and he gestured out at the city, "how can I save all of them?"

"That's not quite what is at issue, Majesty. I was simply thinking that perhaps this is a matter that should not be pursued."

"Indeed." Londo's voice was carefully neutral, his back still to them.

"Obviously, Majesty, the young woman is . . . how shall I put this? . . . an ingrate, Majesty. After all you have done for her, after all the time she has resided here . . . and this is how she treats your hospitality?"

Londo was silent for a time.

"Majesty?" Durla said carefully.

At that point, Londo turned to face them. His eyebrows were knitted in apparent surprise. "Chancellor . . . you are still here?"

"You have not dismissed me, Majesty," Lione said in confusion.

"I did not think it necessary. I have given you your orders . . . or," and his voice took on a cutting edge, "were you operating under the assumption that I was coming to you as supplicant, putting in a request that you could attend to or disregard, at your discretion?"

"No, Majesty, it's just that . . ."

"I have told you what to do. Your only response should be to bow, say, 'Immediately, Majesty,' turn and leave. Apparently you did not comprehend that. So . . . we shall try it again. I will give the order. You will respond as expected. And if you do not do so . . . I will have you executed within the hour." He smiled and spread his hands as if greeting an old friend. "That sounds fair, yes?"

Lione paled, and he visibly gulped. Durla looked in confusion from Londo back to Lione.

"I have a little task for your Prime Candidates, Chancellor," said Londo, without waiting for Lione to reply. "Senna is out there somewhere. I want her found, and I want you to alert me as to where she is. I will handle matters from there."

"Y-yes, Majesty."

Londo fixed him with a deathly glare. "You were supposed to say, 'Immediately, Majesty.'" Lione's back stiffened so abruptly that there was an audible crack. Then Londo smiled wanly and said, "Close enough. Go to, eh?"

Chancellor Lione almost sprinted from the room, and Londo turned his gaze upon Durla. Londo's eyes seemed almost hooded, as if a veil had been drawn over them. "Now . . . what business have you, Durla?"

"Majesty, perhaps the Senna matter should be examined in more de—"

"What. Business. Have. You."

It was quite evident to Londo that Durla was wrestling with the notion of continuing the discussion . . . but then he very wisely reconsidered. Instead, he said, "You have inquired about the archaeological dig on K0643."

"Yes. I have."

Londo felt a slight stirring on his shoulder. And he knew why.

Several months previously, he had been examining various budget items, and he had come across Durla's fringe world project. The reasons behind it completely eluded him. At that point, he had dictated a computer memo to himself to speak with Durla about it. Before he could follow through, however, the shadows had moved ever so slightly and Shiv'kala had emerged from them. Londo had not known he was there, and by that point had given up trying to figure out whether the Drakh was simply omnipresent, or whether the keeper summoned him and somehow he managed to materialize on an as-needed basis.

"That is a worthy project," Shiv'kala had told him. "I do not suggest you challenge it."

"May I ask why?"

"Yes."

There was a pause, and then Londo had said, "Very well: why?"

And Shiv'kala, naturally, had made no response, unless one counted melting back into the shadows as a response. Londo, feeling haggard and weary by that point, had simply signed off on the item, reasoning that any project that got the people of Centauri Prime interested and involved was worthwhile.

But now . . . now things felt different. It wasn't that they necessarily *were* different. However, they *felt* that way. For ever since he had left that urn with Sheridan and Delenn, forever damning not only their unborn child, but himself, it was as if he had hit rock bottom.

After the explosive conflict with Senna, though, something within him had simply . . . snapped. It was like a mental bone had broken, and now it was beginning to reform, tougher and harder than ever. It was most unexpected to Londo, who had been so accustomed to despair that he had almost forgotten what a glimmer of hope could look like.

He still knew better than to go head-to-head with Shiv'kala, for that was certainly a lost cause. But he was beginning to reacquire a bit of his fighting spirit. Major acts of defiance, particularly face-to-face, might well be beyond his capabilities. But smaller such actions or inconveniences . . . what was the phrase? Nibbling to death by cats? Yes . . . that was it. What a marvelous turn of phrase those Humans had.

"Majesty," Durla was saying, "what do you wish to know about the project?"

"I do not understand the reason for it," Londo said. He felt the tingle of alertness on the part of the keeper, but he ignored it. "I wish you to explain it to me."

"It is all in the original proposal, Majesty, which you appro—"

"The report is not here, Durla. You are here. I am here. We can speak to one another, yes?"

"Well . . . yes, of course, Majesty, but I . . ."

"So? Explain."

Ohhhh, the keeper was not happy with the direction of the conversation. In a way, the keeper's reaction was of morbid fascination to Londo, for Londo was curious as to whether or not Durla knew of the Drakh's existence. His actions, his attitudes, had led Londo to wonder about it, but he could not be sure. So by pushing Durla, gently but firmly, Londo was taking a stab at answering the question for himself. If Shiv'kala or one of his associates made themselves known right then and there, that would certainly settle the question, wouldn't it.

"Well . . . unemployment is obviously a serious problem

for us, Majesty. A number of key businesses were destroyed during the bombing." Durla shifted uncomfortably from one foot to the other. "So my office felt that reclamation and exploratory projects might be of benefit in terms of building a sense of accomplishment and pride. The salaries paid to the excavators in the case of K0643 are minimal, but they have room and board, in addition to—"

"This world," Londo said, tapping some research he had done, "is reputed to be haunted, yes?"

Durla laughed scornfully at that. "Haunted, Majesty?"

"A place of lost souls. A world of darkness, tainted by evil. Have you heard these things?"

"Yes, Majesty," Durla said, his lips thinned nearly to a sneer. "I have also heard tales of Rokbala, the evil soul-stealing monster who hides under beds and swipes the souls of naughty children. My older brother told me of him when I was three. It kept me awake at night at the time. Now, however, I sleep quite soundly."

Londo nodded slightly in acknowledgement of the apparent childishness of the concern, but then continued. "Nevertheless . . . we certainly have projects that could employ willing members of our race in a fulfilling manner right here on Centauri Prime. K0643 is on the Rim, of all places."

"Majesty," said Durla slowly, "we must look for that which no one else knows about. There are other worlds, worlds that the Alliance is not interested in. Remote worlds such as this one. We must mount archaeological investigations. We must dig. We must locate. While we do this, the Interstellar Alliance will laugh at us. They will sneer and say, 'Look at the once-great Centauri Republic, rooting around on barren worlds and scraping about in the dirt like the basest of creatures.'" Durla's voice hardened. "Let them say these things. Let them lull themselves into a false sense of security. It will not last, and they will see the error of their ways . . . but by then, it will be too late. We must look outside Centauri Prime, Majesty. There, and only there, will we find our true greatness."

Slowly, Londo nodded. "That is a very impassioned speech, Minister."

"Thank you, Majesty. I believe passionately in the things that I do."

"Oh, I'm sure you do," Londo told him. "But I would be most curious to know . . . from where you got the idea."

"From where? Majesty . . ." And he shrugged. "It just came to me."

"Just . . . came to you."

"Yes, Majesty."

He felt an even more pronounced stirring on his shoulder that told him all he desired to know. "Very well, Durla. Since you have such passion for your work . . . who am I to gainsay you, eh?"

"Thank you, Majesty. And now, if you wouldn't mind, there are some other—"

But Londo put a hand to his temple and sighed heavily. "In point of fact . . . I am a bit fatigued. Let us discuss other matters later, if that is acceptable to you, Durla."

"I am but here to serve your wishes and the best interests of Centauri Prime," he said graciously, and walked out rather quickly. Londo had the sneaking suspicion that he had been quite anxious to get out of the room.

He sat back and waited.

It didn't take much time at all. He sensed Shiv'kala's presence, and he turned to face the Drakh. Shiv'kala stared at him for a long moment, and then said quite softly, "What are you playing at, Centauri?"

Londo smiled, and said two words:

"Quack. Quack."

Shiv'kala tilted his head slightly, looking at Londo—for once—with utter lack of comprehension. Then, to Londo's delight, he simply glided back and away into the shadows without another word.

"Quack quack," Londo said once more, this time with relish.

— *chapter 16* —

It had not been one of Senna's better weeks.

Although sections of the capital city had been rebuilt, there were entire areas that still were in desperate need of renovation and recovery. But the money had been slow in coming, for there were only so many directions that the government could go. By startling coincidence—or perhaps not so startling, in truth—it was the areas of the city inhabited by the poorer inhabitants of Centauri Prime that were getting the least attention.

And there were fewer sections, it seemed, that were getting less attention than the area known as Ghehana.

Ghehana had a reputation that long preceded it, as a place where one could live if one was in extreme financial difficulty. And if one was willing to do whatever it took in order to survive, then one could easily find a home there.

Even during the time that she was on her own, Senna had heard horror stories about Ghehana. It was where no decent person truly wished to go, and yet it was where an amazing number of people seemed to wind up. Senna had never thought that she herself would ever seek refuge there.

But it had been to Ghehana that she had fled. She had tried to remain in the central parts of the city, but those were for the well-to-do or, at the very least, for those who had money to spend and places to live. She had not wanted to be reduced to begging in the streets, but as it turned out, she hadn't had the opportunity. Soldiers attached to the Office of Development had been instructed to make sure that no one was loitering around, because it was felt that seeing homeless or out-of-work people would only reduce the morale of those who really counted on Centauri Prime.

This was a city, a world, a race that was on the upswing. Prospects were bright. Employment was up. Destiny was manifest. Everyone knew that—sooner or later—there would be a reckoning between the great Centauri Republic and the supremely arrogant races who comprised the Alliance. Piddling, backward, nowhere species who once wouldn't have been worth the Republic's time to conquer. Oh, yes . . . the score would be evened, there was no doubt of that. To that end, however, work, dedication, progress, and a patriotic heart were the orders of the day.

Homeless beggars, on the other hand, were just too depressing for words. And so, every effort was made to shunt them elsewhere. Where they went did not matter, so long as they went there.

On one or two occasions, as soldiers sent Senna scuttling out of a doorway in which she had taken refuge, or away from a street corner that she was standing on for too long, a soldier would look at her with curiosity, as if he vaguely remembered her from somewhere. But Senna would quickly hustle along, and withdraw from their sight as quickly as possible.

So it was that she found herself in Ghehana.

The area frightened her. Even after two years, there were still piles of rubble in places where buildings had been. Worse, there were people actually living within the piles, having carved out spaces for themselves. The streets, rarely cleaned, were thick with dirt and grime. Isolated fires flickered in areas where people gathered to warm themselves.

Senna had managed to get a small amount of money to tide herself over by selling a few of the fineries that had belonged to her at the palace, objects that she had grabbed up at the last moment. She had used the money sparingly, managed to buy food with it, but she was running extremely low on funds, and the growling of her stomach made her realize that she was once again going to have to spend some of them.

She was also tired of sleeping outside, hunkering down in doorways, lying in alleys. Her clothes were filthy, she desperately needed a bath, and she had so much dirt under her fingernails that she was convinced they would never come clean, even if she had the opportunity to cleanse them.

She leaned against the corner of a building, trying to decide just what in the world she was going to do, and then she heard someone clear their throat quite loudly. She turned and saw a Centauri male, slender, about medium height, short cut hair, with a generally disreputable look about him. He was grinning widely at her and she could see the glimmer of a gold tooth on the right side of his mouth.

"How much?" he asked.

She stared at him. "What?"

"How much for your time?" He coughed once. There was an ugly rattling sound in his chest.

She still didn't comprehend . . . but then she got it. "Oh. No. No, I'm not . . . I don't do that."

"Oh, I think you do. Or would." He seemed to be looking right through her, dissecting her with his eyes. His gaze made her feel filthy down to her soul. She drew her tattered cloak around her, but then he stepped closer and roughly drew it aside. "If you were cleaned up a bit, you'd actually be quite pretty," he allowed. "You're young. How experienced are you? How many have you done at one time? Three? Four?"

"Get away from me!" she said hotly, pushing him. He staggered slightly, and then suddenly took a step forward and pushed her back. The movement caught Senna off balance and she fell, hitting the ground hard. Passersby, on their hurried way to this or that activity, most likely illegal, didn't so much as slow down.

"Don't stand around out here, my dear, unless you intend to do something with what you've got," the man said to her.

And then someone was standing behind him, and the

someone said in a calm, measured and controlled voice, "I believe the young lady said she wished you to get away from her. You had best do as she says and move along."

Senna gaped in astonishment as she saw who the newcomer was. Her assailant, however, did not bother to turn around. "Oh really. And who died and left you in charge?"

"Cartagia. And, after him, the regent."

Something about the voice prompted the man to turn slowly and see just who it was that was addressing him. He looked into a very familiar face, and his spine stiffened and his legs began to tremble slightly.

Londo Mollari, dressed in rather ordinary garb that was attracting no attention from anyone, continued, "And if you wish to be the next to die, I can certainly oblige you." He snapped his fingers and there were two men on either side of him. Although they were likewise clad in unmemorable clothing, from their look and bearing it was clear that they were guards. In synch, they opened their coats slightly to reveal gun butts tucked just inside. Furthermore, each of them had fairly vicious blades dangling from their belts.

The man who had been harassing Senna immediately backed up, and now his legs were shaking so violently that he could hardly stand. "Muh . . . muh . . . muh . . ."

" 'Majesty,' I believe, is the word you are seeking," Londo said drily. "I believe it would be best for you if you went on about your business now, yes?"

"Yes. Yes . . . absolutely," said the man, and he bolted from there so quickly that he practically left a vapor trail behind him.

Londo watched him go with a vague look of satisfaction on his face, and then he turned to Senna.

Senna, for her part, couldn't quite believe it. Londo extended a hand to her and it was only then that she remembered she was still on the ground. "Well," he asked. "Are you going to let me help you up? Or are you, perhaps, going to bounce a rock off my head?"

She took the hand and stood, dusting herself off. "How . . . how did you know where I was?"

He shrugged as if it were a trivial matter. "An emperor has ways, my dear. Come," and he gestured in front of her. "Let us walk for a bit."

"Majesty," one of the guards said in a low voice, looking around with clear suspicion. "Perhaps it would be wise not to remain. From a security point of view . . ."

"Is the most powerful individual on this planet to be the most helpless, as well?" Londo asked. "Any other Centauri, from greatest to least, can move about with confidence. Is that to exclude me? These are my people. I will deal with them as such. Come, Senna." And he began to walk.

She hesitated, and Londo turned to her, indicating once more that she should follow. This time she did as he specified, falling into step beside him. As they walked, various passersby recognized him and reacted with assorted degrees of amazement. Some bowed. Others looked confused. One or two exhibited airs of scorn. Londo serenely ignored them all, acting as one of them but apart from them.

"I . . . did not expect to see you again, Majesty," Senna told him. "After the . . . after . . ."

"After you invaded my privacy?"

"I . . . did not mean to—"

He wagged a finger at her. "Do not say that. Do not think you can fool me. I've had experience with enough wives to know how the female mind works. You did precisely what you set out to do."

"But I thought you were writing a history book. One that would be publicly available anyway. It didn't occur to me that you were writing so private, so personal . . ."

"It is a history nonetheless. However, it is one that I assume will be published posthumously. Once I am gone," and he shrugged, "what do I care of what people know of my innermost feelings and concerns."

"If people knew those, though, Majesty, they . . ." Her voice trailed off.

He looked at her with interest. "They what?"

"They would feel better about the future of Centauri Prime," she said. "Perhaps even about themselves. I . . . Majesty, lately I don't feel as if I even know you. And I have been living in the palace for some time, so if I don't know you . . . who does?"

"Timov," Londo said ruefully. "If anyone knows me, it is she. She is my first wife. My shortest wife. My loudest wife. Not my most dangerous . . . that would be Mariel. But Timov, she was . . ."

"Is she dead?"

"No. She has sworn to outlast me. She would not give me the satisfaction of having her precede me to the presence of the Great Maker." He waved it off. "It is pointless to speak of her. Why did you run off?"

"Because you frightened me, Majesty."

He took her by the elbow and turned her to face him. "I was angry with you. I shouted at you. That was the extent of what you faced . . . and that frightened you? My child, if you accomplish only one thing in the time that you spend with me, it has to be to raise your tolerance level in terms of what does and does not frighten you. There are terrifying things in this galaxy, Senna. Things so monstrous, so evil, so dark, that it takes tremendous courage simply to look them in the eye . . . eyes," he quickly amended, although she wasn't sure why. "If you are to make your way in life, you must not be so easily daunted by something as relatively trivial as an old man shouting at you."

"You are not old, Majesty."

"Aging, then, if that preserves your delicate concerns. An aging man shouting at you." He paused and then said, looking as if a great deal hinged on her answer, "How far . . . did you get in the narrative? Where did you start, for that matter?"

"At the beginning and end of your dinner and time with President Sheridan and Delenn."

"And no farther?"

She shook her head, looking so earnest that no reasonable person could possibly doubt her. "No, Majesty. No farther. Why? Is there something there I should not read?"

"You should not read any of it," he told her flatly, but it seemed to her as if his body was sagging in visible relief. "It is . . . first draft, if nothing else. It is not ready to be read by someone else. What I write in those pages are my initial thoughts, but as I prepare the history for publication, I will craft it into something that is more . . . appropriate to an emperor, and less politically charged, if you understand my meaning."

"I . . . I think so, Majesty. It's just that . . ."

"What?"

"Nothing."

"No," he said firmly. "You are not to do that with me, Senna. Not ever. You do not start a thought out loud, and then seek to pluck it back as if it was never released. Finish the thought."

"I . . . just did not want to hurt your feelings, Emperor."

Londo made a dismissive noise. "My feelings, Senna, are beyond your ability to hurt, I assure you. So . . ." And he waited for her to continue.

"Well, it is just that . . . when you grabbed the book from me, you not only seemed angry . . . but you were also . . . well . . . afraid. At least, that was how it looked to me. Afraid that I had read something that I should not have read."

"It was simply the timing," he said easily. "I had been having—shall we say 'unpleasant'—dreams, and then I awoke, confused and disoriented, and found you there. Was there fear in my eyes? Perhaps. All manner of notions were tumbling around in my head. But you should not read too much into what you saw at that moment."

The way he said it and explained it, it almost all sounded

reasonable. She wanted to believe it. She wanted to be able to return to the palace because, truth to tell, she had become comfortable there. She had come to think of it as her home. Yes, there were people there she found distasteful, even somewhat frightful. But that would certainly be the case wherever she resided, wouldn't it? And she also felt that Londo . . . needed her somehow. Not on any sort of romantic level, no. She didn't think for a moment that that was entering into the picture, and she was quite certain that he would never even try to take advantage of her in that way, because of her youth and out of respect to her late father. She was certain Londo would think such a thing utterly inappropriate.

"Was there anything else in there," Londo said slowly, "that caused you any confusion or concern? Now is the time to speak of these things, Senna."

"Well," she admitted, "the things that you wrote in that book . . . they made it sound as if you have some great secret that you keep hidden within you. There was such curious phrasing, and it seemed as if you felt you were being watched all the time."

He nodded. "A fair comment. And understandable, since you did not read earlier parts of the narrative. The secrets are—"

He was cut off as a man bumped into them at that moment. He wore grey, enveloping robes with a hood drawn up, and he seemed quite intent on hurrying on his way. His hurried movement actually brought him into contact with Londo for a moment. The guards immediately stepped forward, alert, and Senna didn't blame them, since such an incident could easily cover a knife thrust. But the hooded man moved right on past, and Londo seemed barely to have noticed him. For one moment, though, the man glanced in Senna's direction and smiled. She couldn't help but notice that he was quite handsome, and then he vanished into the crowd . . . a crowd that was slowly becoming more dense as word of the emperor's presence began to spread throughout Ghehana. The guards relaxed their defensive posture only slightly, and still kept a wary eye on the crowd.

"The secrets," continued Londo, "involve that which you must already know. Sooner or later, it is the destiny of the Centauri Republic to try and reclaim its place in the power structure of the galaxy. When, and if, I encounter Sheridan again, we will be enemies. There was a time . . . I have not felt like that since . . ."

His voice had trailed off. "Since when, Majesty?"

"I had coordinated a military assault against the Narn," Londo told her. "The details are not important; suffice to say that it was the first strike by the Centauri Republic in our endeavor to obliterate the Narn. When the assault was already in progress, before word of it had become public . . . the Narn ambassador to Babylon 5, a fellow known as G'Kar, bought me a drink, shook my hand in friendship, and spoke of a bright future. He did not know—though I did—what was about to happen. It was not a pleasant feeling for me. It still is not. Sometimes, Senna, you look upon an enemy and wonder what it would have been like in another life, if you and he were friends.

"Well, I genuinely was friends with them. I look back upon those days as if I am watching someone else's life, rather than my own. I did not realize . . . how very fortunate I was at the time. All I felt was the discontent. Discontent that rose within me until it pushed out every other attribute I had. In those days, when I spoke in anger of what Centauri Prime had once been, I breathed fire. Here is the interesting thing, Senna: when you breathe fire, you are usually left with ashes in your mouth."

"But then . . . then why go down that same path again? If it brought you nothing but unhappiness . . ."

"Because the people need it, Senna. The people need something to believe in. That might not have been the case even as recently as a generation ago, when the memories of what it was like to be feared throughout the galaxy had grown faded and dim. But the current generation of Centauri know what it was like to be world beaters. They have tasted blood, Senna. They have tasted meat. They cannot be expected to go back to grazing on plants. Besides . . . this time it will be different."

"How? How will it be different?"

"Because," he said with conviction, "those who were running Centauri Prime were power mad or insane or both. They lost sight of what was truly the important thing: the people. The people must always come first, Senna. Always, without exception, yes?"

"Yes, absolutely."

"I will not ever forget that. My goal is simply to obtain for the Centauri people the respect that they so richly deserve. But we will not mindlessly destroy, we will not endeavor to lay waste to all that we encounter. Before, we overreached ourselves, became greedy and overconfident, and we paid a price for that . . . a terrible price," he said, glancing at a fallen building. "But having paid that price, having learned from our mistakes, we will proceed down a path that will bring glory to the Centauri Republic without taking us to ruination."

"That . . . does not sound all that unreasonable," Senna said slowly. "You . . . might have put it that way to President Sheridan . . ."

"No," was the firm reply. "He cannot be trusted, Senna. For the time being, we cannot afford to trust any except each other. We must proceed with caution. Who knows, after all, how Sheridan might misinterpret or inaccurately repeat anything that I say to him. So I speak of friendship and stick with generalities. That is the way such encounters must be handled, at least for now. Do you understand?"

"I . . . think I do, yes. I just wish that you didn't have to be, well . . . so lonely."

"Lonely?" A smile played on his lips. "Is that how I come across to you?"

"Yes. In the journal, and even in person sometimes, yes. Very lonely."

"Believe me, Senna . . . there are many times I feel as if I am never alone."

"I know exactly what you're talking about."

"You do?" He raised an inquisitive eyebrow. " 'Exactly' how?"

"The guards all the time, and Durla, and Lione, and Kuto, and all the others . . . they hover around you . . ."

"You are a very perceptive girl," he said, letting out what seemed to Senna to be another sigh of relief.

"But that's not the same as having companionship. It's just not the same at all."

"I suppose you are right."

"I am . . . at least I could be . . . company for you, Majesty. As . . . you see fit, that is."

"Senna . . . what you can do for me is return to the palace and live safely and happily there. To be honest, that is all that I require of you. Will you do this for me?"

"If . . . it will make you happy, Majesty. Sometimes I think few enough things do. So if my presence would help in that regard . . ."

"It would," Londo said confidently.

"Very well. Although I just want you to know . . . I could have survived out here, on my own, if it was necessary. I just want us both to know that."

"I understand fully," Londo said. "I appreciate you clarifying that for me."

One of the guards stepped in close and said with some urgency, "Majesty, I *really* think it is time for us to go."

Senna looked around and saw that it was becoming more and more crowded with each passing moment. People seemed to be assembling from everywhere. Within a short time it would become impossible to move.

Londo surveyed the situation a moment, and then said softly to the guard, "Step back, please." The guard did so, a

puzzled and concerned look on his face, and then Londo
turned to face the crowd. He said nothing, absolutely nothing.
Instead he stretched his arms out in front of himself, held
them level for a moment . . . and then spread them wide,
making his desires known simply by a gesture.

To Senna's utter astonishment, the crowd parted for him,
creating a clear avenue down which he could proceed.

That was precisely what he then did, walking down the
avenue, nodding to people, and as he did he worked the lines
that were on either side of him. He would nod to this person,
touch another's hand, speak a few words of encouragement to
yet another. It was one of the most amazing things Senna had
ever seen. Just like that, with no apparent effort, Londo had
created an impromptu parade, with himself, Senna, and the
guards as the entirety of the procession.

And as they moved through Ghehana, someone called out
Londo's name. "Mollari." And then someone else followed
suit, and another and still another, until they were chanting it
over and over.

"Mollari. Mollari. Mollari . . ."

Londo basked in their adulation, smiling and nodding, and
Senna realized that there had been a great deal of truth to
what Londo had said. The people needed something to believe in, something to elevate them above themselves. And
for the time being, that "something" was going to be Londo
Mollari himself. Londo the Emperor, Londo the Rebuilder,
Londo the Lover of the People, who was going to bring prosperity to Centauri Prime and rebuild the Republic into something that every Centauri could be proud of.

But he still seemed lonely.

And that was something that Senna decided she was going
to do something about.

The Centauri worker wished that he were anywhere else but here.

He had wandered off from the main dig site, feeling tired and thirsty and fairly fed up with the company of his fellows. All of them seemed hideously happy to have some kind of employment, however marginal, and they were laboring under some sort of bizarre delusion that somehow the needs and interests of the great Centauri Republic were going to be served by working at a useless archaeological dig on some damned backwater planet, using antiquated tools and having no clear idea of what it was that they were actually looking for.

"Idiots," he said, not for the first time. It was at that point that he decided he had had it. He took his dirt cruncher, aimed it just below his feet, and fired it straight down. By all rights, by all instructions, there shouldn't be anything there in particular. He was determined to take out his ire by burning the cruncher out completely, operating it at high speed for longer than it was meant to operate.

The cruncher pounded about ten feet straight down, and then something came back up.

The worker never really had the opportunity to figure out what it might be. All he knew was that one moment he was happily pushing his cruncher to the maximum, and the next some sort of black energy was enveloping him and he heard a scream, which he thought was his own except he realized it was inside his head, and not quite like anything he had ever heard before.

Then he heard nothing else, ever again, as his body was blasted apart in a shower of gelatinous body parts that spattered over a radius of about fifty feet. Since he was spread so wide and far, no one who subsequently stumbled upon any part of his remains truly understood what it was they were looking at.

When he didn't show up for sign-out that evening, he was marked down as absent without leave, and his pay was docked accordingly. Meantime, eighty feet below, something went back to standby mode, and waited for a less abusive summons.

— *chapter 17* —

Vir tossed about in his bed as the giant sucker-woman approached him.

There was a look of pure evil in her eyes, and her arms were outstretched, and she was waggling her fingers, and at the ends of those fingers—Great Maker protect him—there were the suckers. Each one smacking its "lips" together, hungering for him, ready to attach themselves to him and try to suck the life clean out of him. Somewhere from all around him, he heard Londo's voice shouting, "Run, Vir! Run! Don't let her get to you!" Vir, however, was rooted to the spot, his legs refusing to obey his commands. He wanted to run away, but he simply couldn't.

She drew closer, closer still. Her bald pate gleamed with a pulsing black light, and she laughed with a sound that had once filtered from the forest as primitive beings had squatted around their fires and glimpsed fearfully into the darkness. When her lips drew back in a hideous simulated rictus of a smile, he could see her fangs dripping with blood, and the suckers were nearer, still nearer, and there was no escape . . .

That was when Vir finally managed to get a scream out, and the scream was so powerful that it roused him from his dream, forcing him to sit up, gasping, looking around, trying to figure out what in the world had just happened.

As he did so, he realized that there was the insistent buzzing of the door chime. His bleary eyes focused on a clock near his bed. It was the middle of the night. Who in the world was showing up at this insane time.

"Go away!" moaned Vir, flopping back onto his bed.

There was no reply from outside other than the renewed pushing of the door chime.

A warning trilled in the back of Vir's brain. What if it were an assassin, hoping to catch him confused, disoriented, and particularly vulnerable. At that point, however, Vir simply didn't care. The notion of someone blowing his head off, at that moment in time, seemed preferable to trying to go back to sleep, where sucker-fingered women might be lurking about in the recesses of his consciousness, waiting to prey upon him as soon as he relaxed his guard.

"Lights dim," he snapped irritably, and the lights in his quarters obediently came to half. Even that modest lighting was enough to make him feel as if his eyes were being seared from their sockets. He rose from his bed, snagged his robe, put his right arm in the left sleeve, twirled in place as he sought in futility to catch up with the trailing sleeve, snagged it, realized his error and then yanked the robe off and put it on correctly. The buzzing continued throughout all of it, to the point where Vir didn't even bother to find his slippers, but instead padded barefoot across the room as he shouted, "I'm coming, I'm coming! Hold on already!"

He got to the door, disengaged the locking mechanism, wondered if he was going to be staring down the muzzle of a vicious weapon when it slid open and decided that he definitely didn't care at this point.

The door opened wide, and he let out a short, high-pitched shriek.

"Is this a bad time?" asked Mariel.

Vir couldn't quite believe it. *What is she doing here?*

She was waiting for his response, and he sought to find his voice. "Uh . . . no. No is . . . fine. I wasn't doing anything. Well . . . I was sleeping . . . but, you know, that really doesn't require too much effort. In fact, it's a bit of a waste of time.

There's so many other better things I could be doing. You know, I think I'm just going to give up sleep altogether. There's far more efficient ways to go about living your life, you know, than wasting time sleeping. I mean, I've been getting nine, ten, twelve hours sleep, but I think I could do with a lot less. Like . . . one. One would be good. Or . . . three, which is what I had tonight," he said, double-checking the clock to make sure he had that right. "Yes, three is good. Three is plenty. I can't believe how well I'm functioning on just—"

"Ambassador . . . may I come in?"

Again, as was often the case, Vir had to fight the impulse to glance behind himself. "Yes. Yes, by all means. Come in. Come in."

She did so, glancing around the suite as she did. "My, my. I like what you've done with the place, Vir. Back in Londo's day, it tended to look a bit like a museum. A Londo Mollari museum, considering he had portraits of himself all over. How long has it been, Vir?"

Not long enough. "Quite . . . some time, Lady Mariel," Vir told her. "Four, five, six years. Time flies when you're having fun. Or when you're having . . . well . . . whatever it is that I have."

"I remember quite clearly the last time I was in this room."

"Really? When was that?" Vir was hoping that his sense of feeling flustered would depart soon.

"When Londo had a small orgy with myself and Daggair. Both of us, at the same time. Would have been three had Timov been willing . . ."

That was definitely more than Vir wanted to know. He stepped quickly away, wishing that he could cover his hands with his ears, but that would hardly seem professional. He also dismissed the notion of shouting "la la" at the top of his lungs. "I was . . . not expecting to see you here, Milady . . ."

"Mariel, please. We have no need for formalities," she said softly. "You are, after all, an ambassador. I am simply the former wife of a sitting emperor. I see no differences between us."

Eyeing her uncomfortably, Vir said, "I . . . see a couple." He cleared his throat loudly. "Can I get you something? Something to drink or . . . something?"

"That would be quite nice. Are you sure this is not a bad time?"

"Oh, don't be silly!" he said as he poured her wine from his private stock; the stuff that he only consumed when he was extremely nervous. He tended to go through a bottle a day. "You just caught me a bit off guard, that's all. I wasn't expecting you."

"I wasn't expecting to be here myself," Mariel said as she picked up the wine and sipped it daintily. "I was to connect on a shuttle through here, but the connecting flight met with a bit of an accident."

"No one hurt, I hope," he said.

"Not hurt. Just dead. I'm told the fireball was quite spectacular, although naturally it didn't last all that long, since it was in space at the time."

Vir felt his tongue drying up. He tossed back an entire glass of the wine in one shot and started pouring himself another.

"Anyway . . . since I am here on Babylon 5 until a new ship is dispatched, I thought I might touch base with you. See how you are getting along. I have such fond memories of you, Vir."

"You . . . you do?"

"Yes, indeed." She stared into the contents of her glass and smiled, apparently from a pleasant recollection. "Do you know what I liked about you then, Vir? Shall I tell you?"

"You don't have to."

"You made me laugh. It's not always easy for a man to get a woman to laugh, but you managed it so easily. You had a charming facade you created back then, although I could see through it rather easily, of course."

"What . . . facade would that be?"

"An air of barely controlled panic."

"Ah. Well," and he laughed uncomfortably, "you saw right through that, I guess. Clever you."

"Yes, indeed, clever me. So . . . fill me in, Vir. I have been away for quite some time." She interlaced her fingers and leaned forward. "Tell me what's been going on, on Babylon 5."

"Oh, *uhm* . . . well . . . all right." And he proceeded to rattle off as many major events as he could recall that had occurred in the past five to six years, including the Shadow War, the in-auguration, and the telepath wars. Mariel took it all in, every so often interrupting with a question, but most of the time simply nodding and listening. When he was done some time later, Mariel looked almost breathless. "My," she said. "It's been rather busy. And how exciting this must have all been for you."

"I don't know if 'exciting' is the word I'd use," Vir admitted. "That almost makes it sound as if I was enjoying it. It's been more like, that my life has been moving at high speed, and I've been doing everything I can, not to be thrown off."

She laughed. She had a beautiful laugh. Vir wondered why he had never noticed that earlier.

"And you," he then said. "You must have been very busy, too, I'm sure."

She said nothing.

He stared at her as he waited for her to pick up her half of the conversation. But nothing was forthcoming. "Mariel?" he prompted.

"I'm sorry," she said coolly. "I just assumed you were having a little joke at my expense."

"What? No! No, I'd never—! What joke? What do you mean?"

"Londo tossed me away, Vir," she said. "I mean nothing to him, and he let the entire world know it." She had been standing until that time, but now she sat on the edge of one of

the chairs. And Vir began to see that she was actually not remotely as cheery as she had originally appeared. Indeed, it
now looked as if she was doing everything she could to hold
back tears. "You have no idea what it is like, Vir, to be so
completely diminished in society. To be tossed aside. To have
people looking at you and laughing behind your back, because you're considered a joke."

It took no more introspection from Vir than to consider his
own life up until that point. To consider the fact that he had
once been the family joke, tossed away to Babylon 5 and
made attaché to the ludicrous Londo Mollari, so that he
would be out of the way and not embarrass anyone.

"I think I do," said Vir. "But . . . but look at you!" he added,
waving his glass of wine around so vehemently that he came
close to spilling it. "How could anyone treat you as a joke!
You're so . . . so . . ."

"Beautiful," she said hollowly. "Yes, Vir, I know. And as
such, men would seek me out as a symbol of their own status.
But another symbol hangs over me in addition to my beauty. It
is that of castoff. Cast off from Londo Mollari. It stays with
me, haunts me. No man wants to be seen with me because . . ."
Her voice sounded as if it were going to break, and Vir felt his
hearts going with it. Then, with visible effort, she composed
herself. "I . . . am sorry, Vir," she said softly. "I . . . miss my
old life. I miss the parties, the social whirl. I miss the company
of men who wanted to be seen with me . . ."

"There's a party tomorrow! Right here, on B5," Vir said
quickly. "A diplomatic gathering being hosted by Captain
Lochley. It's not a big deal, she has them every other month or
so. Feels it's good for morale, that kind of thing. I haven't
been going lately, figuring that—well, never mind. In any
event, I could go tomorrow, with you. That is to say, we could
go. You and I."

She looked up at him. Her eyes were glistening. "That's
very kind of you, Vir. But I don't really think you'd want to be
seen with me . . ."

"Don't be ridiculous! Truthfully, I'm not sure why you'd want to be seen with me."

"Are you serious?" she asked. "To be seen with the ambassador of the Centauri Republic to Babylon 5? Any woman would be honored. But you may be harming your own status by squiring me . . ."

"Are you kidding? Practically everyone here hates Londo," he laughed. Then he stopped laughing. "I . . . guess that wasn't so funny, actually. Besides . . . who's to know?" he added quickly, as he hunkered down next to her. "Listen . . . when you look at a Drazi . . . can you tell one from the other?"

"Not . . . really," she admitted.

"Well, neither can I. And I'll bet you that Centauri probably look as much alike to Drazi as Drazi do to us. Drazi and all the others. The point is, they're not even going to know who you are, most likely. Not unless you wear a sign that says 'Londo Mollari's ex-wife.' "

"I had one, but I think I left it back home."

He laughed at that, and so did she, and when he laughed he patted her on the hand and she put her hand atop his, and he felt something akin to electricity upon her touch. He almost jumped from the contact.

"Are you sure about this, Vir?" she asked.

"Absolutely sure. Look, you'll go—"

"We'll go," she corrected him.

"We'll go, and it'll feel just like the old days for you. You'll have a great time."

"We'll have a great time."

"Right. We. I'm sorry, it's just that . . . well . . ." and he sighed, "I'm not all that accustomed to thinking of myself as part of a 'we.' Not for a very long time."

And then, to his shock, she tilted his chin back and kissed his uplifted lips gently. Very, very gently, no heavier than a butterfly's flutter. It was still enough to send a wave of static running along his hair.

She asked what time the party was. He told her. She told him where she was staying in Babylon 5, and where he should come to pick her up. He nodded. Then she kissed him again, not quite as lightly this time, and Vir suddenly felt as if there was too much blood in his body.

When their lips parted, with a faint smacking sound, Mariel said to him, "You are such a sweet man. I had forgotten what it was like to be with a sweet man. I'll let you get back to sleep." And with that she excused herself and left. It wasn't until Vir's aching knees informed him, some minutes later, that he was still crouching, that he thought to stand up. Then he eased himself onto the chair and sat there, stunned.

When Mariel had first shown up at his door, he had been seized by waves of panic. He remembered the horror stories Londo had told of her, remembered the chaos that had seemed to be left in the woman's wake. He remembered that Londo had almost died thanks to a present that she had given him, although she had claimed that she'd had no idea that it was remotely dangerous when she'd given it to him. He remembered the aura of darkness that had seemed to cling to her, that had made her almost frightening to look at.

All that had been washed away by the utter vulnerability she had projected upon arriving in his quarters. He had felt all his hesitations, all his concerns melting away, one by one, until he had been left with only one raw, stunned thought:

*She's one of the ones Londo got **rid** of? He must have been out of his **mind**!*

The ambassadorial reception turned out to be one of the turning points of Vir's entire career . . . if not his life.

It was almost as if he were attending it while having an out-of-body experience. Normally, if Vir attended such functions—as he had once or twice in his career—he remained firmly planted, back against a wall, nodding to some people, making small chitchat with others, and frequently holding Londo's drinks when Londo ran out of hands to hold them with—which was often. In short, when Vir had been there, his entire contribution to the evening was that he had . . . been there.

Lately it had been something of a horror show for him. He had spent many years making what he felt were friends among the population of Babylon 5. But he had spent the past year and a half watching them disappear, one by one. Londo, Lennier, Delenn, Ivanova, Sheridan, Garibaldi, even G'Kar— he who had made Vir more uncomfortable on one occasion, dripping blood from his hand in an elevator, than Vir had ever been in his life before or since. All of them were gone.

Oh, Captain Lochley was there, and she was polite enough, but she tended to keep him at an emotional distance, as she apparently did with everyone. And Zack was there, but Vir always felt as if Zack was regarding him with suspicion, waiting for Vir to pull a weapon or something. That might have been Vir's imagination, but nevertheless, that was how he felt.

As for the rest of the members of the Alliance, well . . . they had very little patience for him indeed. It wasn't personal; they hated and feared all Centauri. Somehow, that didn't make it any better. It was little wonder that Vir had stopped attending the gatherings altogether.

This night, though . . . this night was very, very different.

This night, Mariel was there in full force.

When Vir went to pick her up, he was stunned to see how small her room was. It was barely large enough for someone to turn around in, and it certainly wasn't located in one of the more upscale sections of the station. Nevertheless, Mariel managed to look radiant. She was attired in a remarkably simple, unadorned dress, but its lack of decoration was part of its strength, for there was nothing to distract from her pure beauty.

And beauty she possessed in abundance, for all that she seemed to devalue it. When the door to her room opened, she was simply standing there, in the middle of the room as if she were on display, her hands folded daintily in front of her.

Vir busily tried to remind his body that breathing was an autonomic reflex, and his lungs really shouldn't be forgetting how to expand and contract. His lungs didn't seem to be listening, and breath remained in short supply for some moments.

When he finally did start breathing regularly again, Mariel asked, in a voice barely above a whisper, "Do I . . . please you, Vir? You would not be ashamed to be seen with me?"

Vir literally couldn't find words to reply. When he did speak, the result was an almost incoherent string of syllables, rather than useful phrases. Fortunately enough, the utterances managed to convey the fact that he was not the least bit ashamed.

She took a step closer to him and said softly, "I think . . . when you first met me . . . I was very likely a bit arrogant."

"No! No, not at all."

"If I was, you would certainly be too polite to say so. So in the event that I was . . . I apologize to you now. I hope you will forgive me." She kissed him once more, and this time Vir's head fell off.

At least, that was what it felt like. He stood there stupidly for a moment, then felt around for his head, reattached it to his shoulders, and somewhere during that activity, Mariel said, "Shall we go?"

They went.

Vir couldn't believe the evening. It was like a dream . . . except, of course, for the absence of women with suckers on their long fingers.

For the entirety of the dream, Mariel was a delight. If the ambassadorial gathering was a vast ice field, as far as relations with the Centauri went, Mariel was a spring thaw, she was the warming sun, she was . . .

"All that *and* a bag of chips," Zack Allan commented, and he nudged Vir in some sort of comradely fashion that caught Vir flatfooted.

"Excuse me?" Vir said.

"Your date," Zack said, pointing toward Mariel who was, at

that moment, gaily capturing the interest of half a dozen ambassadors at once. There was a roar of laughter at some comment she made, and most of the ambassadors were smiling widely, except for one who was frowning furiously. But that wasn't of major concern, since that was how his race showed that they were happy. Fortunately the Divloda ambassador, who tended to display extreme pleasure by urinating uncontrollably, had not been able to make the gathering, to the dismay of no one at all. "She's all that and a bag of chips."

"Is that good?" asked Vir.

"What do *you* think?"

They watched Mariel working the room. The female ambassadors, Vir noted, regarded her with cool disdain bordering on outright distrust. But the male ambassadors from any race came flocking to her. Mariel was lucky that she didn't slip on the drool that was rapidly collecting on the floor.

And Vir laughed. He had forgotten what the sound of his laughter was like. "I think that's very good."

Zack chucked him on the shoulder. "You lucky dog. Where did you find her, anyway?"

"She's Londo's . . ." Vir caught himself. ". . . old . . . friend."

"And now she's your new friend. Well, don't you let her get away, Vir."

"I'll certainly try not to."

Zack Allan wasn't alone in his comments. Other ambassadors, one by one and even in pairs came over to Vir during the evening, and asked him about Mariel. The problem was, Vir wasn't the world's greatest liar. He had little talent for it. As long as he had been working with Londo, that hadn't been a problem, for Londo had been more than capable of attending to that function. Now that he was on his own, however, Vir had no fallback.

So this time, rather than rattling off a long, implausible story, he operated on the notion that less was more, and proceeded to be extremely vague. He met all inquiries with raised eyebrows, smiles, and occasional winks.

"Tell us truly, Vir," one ambassador said, "is she of the nobility?" Vir shrugged, looked mysterious, and rolled his eyes as if to indicate that a higher guess should be forthcoming. "A duchess? A . . . a princess?" Vir then gave a slow, lazy wink, and the ambassadors nudged one another and smiled knowingly, as if they had managed to wrangle some dark secret from Vir.

Every so often, Mariel would return to Vir as if he were home base, taking him by the arm, drawing the conversations back over to him. It all began to make sense to Vir. People tended to judge one by the company one keeps. All these years, Vir had kept company with Londo Mollari, and that had worked against him terribly, in the long run. Londo was a man who held much darkness within him, and he cast a long shadow. Vir had been swallowed up in that shadow. The murkiness had clung to him long after Londo's departure. But that was now in the process of changing, as the light of Mariel broke up those shadows and left Vir standing in the light.

By the wee hours, Vir felt as if he was flying. It was at that point that Mariel came up to him once more, as she had several times before, and entwined her arm through his. "Now is the time to leave," she said softly.

Vir had a drink in his hand, and several more working their way through his system. "But the party's still going on!" he protested.

"Yes. And it is never good to be among the last to leave. By departing earlier, you see, it gives them time to speak of you with one another in glowing terms after you have gone."

"Ooooohhh," Vir said, not really understanding.

"Not only that, but it makes it seem as if you have things of greater importance to do. That also makes you desirable."

"Oh. That's clever. I like that. That's very clever. I only wish it were true."

And Mariel took his face in her hands and looked him

squarely in the eyes, and there was great significance in her voice. "It *is* true. You do have more important things to do."

Then Vir understood. He very quickly said his good-byes, and to his amazement, not only did the ambassadors seem regretful that they were leaving, but several of them made noises about wanting to see Vir again. They must get together, have lunch, have dinner, their aides would be in touch, have a good evening, have a wonderful evening, we must do this again soon. All the niceties, the traditional little pleasantries that were the standard coin of the realm of social interaction, but coin that had long been missing from Vir's personal treasury.

When they left and stepped into the transport tube, Vir—still just the least bit uncertain—said softly to Mariel, "Should I . . . escort you back to your room?"

She smiled at him with a smile that could melt steel. "I'd rather you escorted me to yours."

Feeling more bold than he ever had in his entire life, Vir took her by the shoulders and kissed her. It was rather clumsy and he succeeded mainly in clonking his upper teeth against hers. "Oh! I'm sorry! I'm . . . I'm . . . suh . . . sorry!" he stammered.

"It's all right," she assured him, and she returned the kiss with such expertise that Vir felt as if his entire body was aflame.

When their lips parted, Vir whispered to her, "You are all that . . . and a . . . a . . . a box of popcorn."

She frowned. "Is that good?"

"I think that's very good," he said.

And later that night, as their bodies intertwined, Vir whispered to her, "Don't leave . . ."

"If you want me to stay, I will," she told him.

"Yes . . . yes, please stay."

And she did.

— *chapter 18* —

The months passed quickly.

Vir could not remember being happier. It wasn't as if Mariel was with him all the time; far from it. She came and went, heading off visiting friends or associates. But Babylon 5 apparently had become her home base, and every so often Vir would be delighted to learn that she was returning. During their time together, he was deliriously happy. And when they weren't together, Vir nevertheless still felt like a new man. He walked with more spring in his step, new confidence in his attitude.

Not only that, but when others on Babylon 5 looked his way, he would greet them boldly or snap off a salute. He would walk right up to people, address them by name, ask them how they were doing. In short, he started behaving as if he had every right to be there. And others began responding to him differently, as well, treating him with the respect he should be due. When Mariel wasn't with him, they invariably asked how she was. When she was with him, they would look at Vir with open envy.

He loved every moment of it. He finally felt as if he, Vir Cotto, was coming into his own—when his world came crashing down on him.

Mariel had just departed Babylon 5 again when Vir strode into his quarters—using that same snappy stride despite the fact that it was quite late. As he had in the past, he stood for a moment in the center of his quarters, already regretting her absence. She had a certain scent to her, a perfume that clung to her. He'd never asked her the name of the scent. It hadn't mattered. It was a beautiful scent. Everything about her was beautiful, wonderful . . .

He picked up a picture of her that now permanently adorned his shelf, and smiled at it.

The picture began to speak.

"Greetings, Chancellor. It continues to go well."

Vir let out a yelp and dropped the picture. It crashed to the floor, and he stared down at it in utter confusion.

The photograph began moving, the equivalent of a video screen image. And with Mariel's voice it was saying, "Tomorrow, as per your instruction, I'll be departing for the Nimue Homeworld. The undersecretary of Defense has offered me a standing invitation—he extended it last month during an early morning brunch, and I'm taking him up on it. I believe he will share with me some interesting insights into the Nimue Department of War." Then she paused, smiled, and nodded, as if listening to a conversation that Vir couldn't hear. "No, Chancellor, I doubt that he knows he's going to share them with me. But I can be . . . persuasive . . . as you well know."

Vir remembered the brunch. He had been there. And now that he thought about it, the Nimue undersecretary had been lavishing a great deal of attention upon Mariel. But he had thought nothing of that; so many people clearly found themselves drawn to her, yet at the end of the day, he was the one she went home with . . .

But . . . what was of far greater consequence was that the picture was inexplicably still talking. How could that possibly be? It had to be some sort of trick. For Mariel hadn't gone to Nimue . . . she had returned to Centauri Prime, to visit relatives. That's what she'd told him, that's what—

"No, Chancellor, I doubt Vir suspects. He remains a fool.

A useful fool. He has, however, been an aid to the cause, albeit an unwitting one."

"Stop it!" Vir shouted at the picture, which gave no indication at all that it heard him. "Stop doing this! *Stop it!*"

And suddenly, the picture did stop talking. The image of Mariel was restored to normal. Vir stared down at it, his chest heaving, and he didn't even realize at first how hard he was breathing.

"The truth hurts," a voice said.

Vir whirled. Then he stared in amazement, before that amazement turned to anger. "Of course. Kane. I should have known."

The techno-mage initiate bowed slightly, as if he were on a stage. He kept his staff clenched tightly in his hand. He was standing just inside the door, which was closed behind him. "The very same," Kane acknowledged.

Vir hadn't seen him since the incident with Rem Lanas. In looking back upon it, Vir had almost felt as if the entire thing had been some sort of strange dream. Kane had appeared at a crucial moment in his life, only to slip away again, as if he had never been there. Though Vir had been certain that he would hear from the initiate soon thereafter, when he hadn't, he'd begun to wonder if he hadn't been suffering from some sort of delusion.

The delusion was back now. This time, however, Vir didn't feel the slightest bit of intimidation. He pointed a trembling finger angrily at the fallen photo. "That . . . was a cruel joke to play. Why . . ."

"It was no joke, Vir," Kane replied. "It was an actual recording. We've been observing her ever since she set foot on the station. Once it was clear that she was going to remain here . . ."

"We?" demanded Vir. "There are more of you?"

"No," Kane said quickly, although he looked subtly chagrined. "I meant to say 'I.' "

"I don't care what you meant to say!" Vir told him,

abandoning any attempt to hide his anger. "Making up that thing about Mariel, changing her image to—"

"Vir, *listen* to me. I didn't make up anything. That really happened. Even an initiate has ways."

"Then have a way out!"

He stepped toward Kane as if to grab him, but Kane extended his staff and shoved one end under Vir's chin. "I wouldn't," Kane said dangerously, "if I were you."

It brought Vir to a halt, and enabled his senses to come swimming back to him. "I just want you out," Vir said stubbornly. "And I want you to stop making things up about Mariel. That trick you just did . . . it's a trick. That's all."

"You do not understand," Kane told him, slowly lowering his staff. "The way of the techno-mage is the way of truth. All of our 'magic' is based in, and adheres purely to, reality. We don't deviate from that path . . . ever. For any of us to use our powers to misinform, that would be a violation of our most sacred beliefs."

"And to buy into the words you're putting into Mariel's mouth would be a violation of *my* most sacred beliefs," Vir countered sharply.

"You should not blame yourself, Vir Cotto. Mariel is far more than she seems. Even she is unaware of her full capabilities . . . and you can feel some relief that that is the case. For if she did . . ." He actually shuddered slightly.

Vir once again indicated the door. "There's nothing you can say to convince me that Mariel is anything but—"

"Perhaps her own words could have a bit more impact," Kane said.

Before Vir could protest, the image of Mariel started speaking to the unknown "chancellor" once again.

"Poor Vir . . . I almost feel sorry for him, in a way," Mariel purred. "The other ambassadors have no love of the Centauri, certainly . . . and as a result, they draw particular entertainment from a Centauri female who speaks in rather withering tones of her 'paramour.' Of course, the amusement I share with the ambassadors makes them that much more pliant when they are speaking with me, so who is the greatest fool in the end, yes?"

"This is evil," said Vir. "I have witnessed evil, I've seen it in action, and this is one of the most evil things I've ever seen anyone do, Kane." His voice rose along with his fury. "You are to shut that down, right now, or I'll—"

"He only goes as high as three, did you know that? And usually not even that," continued Mariel.

Vir, who had been looking at Kane, whipped his head back to the picture frame. Every drop of blood drained from his face.

"What does she mean by that?" Kane inquired, seeming genuinely interested. "I confess, I don't quite understand the reference. It—"

"Shut up," Vir demanded hollowly.

Mariel laughed in the picture. "I know, Chancellor, I know. It is all I can do to feign interest. Perhaps I should start bringing something to read while Vir entertains himse—"

"*Shut up!*" Vir bellowed, but this time it wasn't at Kane. Instead he grabbed up the picture and threw it with all his strength at the wall. The frame shattered, and Vir stood there leaning against a table, trying to keep himself upright even as he felt the strength draining out of his legs. Kane started to speak, but Vir raised a finger and said, "Be quiet. I need to check something."

Moments later he had Zack Allan on the Babcom screen. The security chief didn't appear the least bit tired, but because of the lateness of the hour, Vir felt obliged to say, "I hope I didn't wake you."

"Me? Nah. I only sleep on duty," Zack said with his customary deadpan expression. He tilted his head slightly and asked, "Vir, are you okay? You look . . ."

"I need you to check something for me. Mariel . . . when she departed the station several hours ago, do you have a record of where she was bound?"

"I couldn't say for absolute sure, because she could easily make connections. But we'd have checked her outbound ticket. That's SOP."

"Where was it for? Hers, I mean?"

"Is there a problem?"

"I'm not sure. Can you just check please."

"Because if there is, I—"

"Would you just check please?"

Clearly taken aback by the fervency in Vir's voice, Zack nodded and said, "Hold on." The words "Please Stand By" appeared on the screen and then, an eternity later, Zack reappeared. "Nimue. She was heading for Nimue. Does that tell you what you need to know?"

"Yes. Yes, it does. Thank . . . you."

"Is Mariel all right?" asked Zack. "I hope there's nothing wrong, and if there is, then let me know how I can help. Because she's . . ."

"Yes, I know. She's all that and a box of cookies. Thank you, Mr. Allan," and Vir shut down the connection before Zack could say anything else well-meaning—something that would cut like a knife to Vir's soul.

There was an uncomfortable silence for a time, except that to Vir, it didn't seem uncomfortable at all. He sat and stewed in it, thinking about the world in which he lived. Thinking about the fantasy life he substituted for real life. Thinking that, until Mariel had come along, the last time he had really felt good about anything had been when he was looking at Morden's severed head atop a pike.

He had known. Deep down, he had really known that Mariel had been up to something. That she was using him, that she was up to no good. But he hadn't wanted to believe it, displaying what appeared to be an infinite capacity for self-delusion. The proof was that he hadn't spoken to Londo of it. Not a word had he breathed to his former mentor, about his association with Mariel, because he had known without question what the response was going to be. He would have told

Vir that he was completely out of his mind. That he had no business associating with someone like Mariel, that she would be using him, and so on and so forth. That knowledge should have been Vir's barometer, indicating what he was truly involved with. But once again, he had ignored all the warning signs with single-minded determination.

"For what it is worth," Kane said softly, looking genuinely contrite, "I am sorry."

"It isn't worth a damned thing," Vir said.

"Then perhaps this will be worth something: Mariel is not the problem. She's merely the pawn of others. Even those who appear to guide Mariel are themselves guided. There is a great darkness residing on Centauri Prime."

"A great darkness." Vir echoed the words without putting much inflection to them. "Is that a fact?"

"Yes. It is."

"And is that supposed to make me feel better, somehow? Less used? Less foolish?"

"No." Kane approached him and came uncomfortably close. Vir's instinct was to take a step back, but filled with a newfound stubbornness, he held his ground. Kane didn't appear to notice. "What it is supposed to do is fill you with a deep burning rage. It's supposed to make you realize that there is more at stake than your ego, or your hurt feelings. It's supposed to make you realize that you, Vir Cotto, have a destiny. And you must—you *must*—rise to the level of the man that you can be, in order to fulfill it."

"I see. And is it your job to help bring me to that destiny? To help me rise up and become all that I am capable of becoming?" asked Vir sarcastically.

"Well . . . no," admitted Kane. "In point of fact, I should be keeping out of it entirely. My job is simply to relay information to others, but otherwise stay completely out of the line of fire. Unfortunately, I find that I can't. I can't simply stand by and allow the Drakh to—"

"The who?"

"The Drakh," Kane said with an air of portentousness. "Servants of the Shadows."

"The Shadows are gone."

"But the servants remain," insisted Kane. "And their darksome influence is all throughout Centauri Prime. Ultimately, it is their hand behind Mariel's involvement. They also control Londo Mollari."

"And you know this for a certainty."

"For a time, I only suspected. So I took steps to make sure. It took some time, I admit. I stayed outside the palace and waited for Londo to emerge, since I didn't want to chance setting foot into the palace itself."

"Afraid?" Vir said challengingly.

Kane did not hesitate. "Absolutely," he said.

That, more than anything, Vir found absolutely chilling. If an initiate of the techno-mages was afraid, then Vir should by rights be bordering on total panic. He gulped and tried to appear undaunted.

"My patience was eventually rewarded as Londo finally emerged, dressed in fairly informal garb, and headed into a section of Centauri Prime which I believe is called Ghehana."

"Ghehana? Why would he go there?"

"He was seeking a young woman who had been residing at the palace, apparently. While Londo was there, I came into close enough contact with him that I was able to place a recording device upon him. As I feared, the Drakh detected it before long. It may have put them even more on their guard, but at least I was able to confirm for myself their presence."

Before Vir could say anything further, Kane stretched out his hand and a holographic image appeared on it. "It recorded everything within the room," Kane said, "for a few moments, until it was discovered. I thought you might want to see."

There appeared a small image of Londo, flickering ever so gently in Kane's hand. And he was talking to . . .

Vir gasped. Not since the last time he had seen Morden had he felt that he was looking upon the face of pure evil. The creature he saw Londo speaking to . . . even without all the warnings that Kane had voiced, Vir would nonetheless have trembled just to see it.

The Drakh was speaking to Londo about something . . . Vir caught the word "dig" and a designation . . . K0643, although he had no idea what that referred to . . . and then the Drakh appeared to react to something. He stretched out a hand and the picture fritzed out of existence.

"He was a bit more perceptive than I anticipated," Kane admitted with a touch of regret. "After going to all that effort, all I managed to get was that small bit. Still . . . at least it should be enough to convince you."

"To convince me of what?"

"That," Kane said cryptically, "you shall have to determine for yourself."

"No, no, *no*," Vir snapped, biting off each word. "Don't start going enigmatic on me. I'm having a rough enough night as it is. What are you expecting me to do with this . . . this information you've tossed in my lap? For that matter, how do I know that this, above all else, isn't some sort of trick?"

"If your interest has been piqued, then I suggest you get together with Londo, and get him quite intoxicated, if that is possible. Once he is sufficiently inebriated, say to him the word, 'Shiv'kala.' Watch him carefully to see his reaction. But only say it to him when he is truly drunk, because I suspect that if you speak the word while he is sober, then you will surely die before much time has passed.

"As for what I'm expecting you to do, Vir, I'm only asking whatever it is that you are personally capable of. No more, and no less, than that."

He bowed slightly and headed for the door.

"Wait a minute!" Vir called, but the door slid shut behind the initiate. He headed after him—the door opened mere seconds after Kane had passed through it . . . and Vir wasn't, for some reason, even remotely surprised to find that Kane was gone.

At that moment, Vir wasn't sure who it was he hated more: Kane, Mariel, the Drakh, or himself.

He turned back into his quarters and sat down on the bed. Thought of the press of her warm flesh against his. Had there been any of it that she had truly enjoyed? Had it all been a sham? Did she ever feel the slightest twinge of regret over the true motives behind what she was doing? What would he say to her when she returned? She'd show up, expecting that things were going to be exactly as she had left them, unaware that anything had changed. If he said anything to her, she'd likely deny it. Perhaps she would deny it because none of it was true. Perhaps . . .

No. No, it was true. Because as far as Vir was concerned, it all made so much more sense than the notion that a woman like that could become besotted with a man like him.

Vir had absolutely no idea what to do. He desperately felt as if he needed someone to talk to about the matter, but he couldn't think of anyone. Everyone he might vaguely have trusted was gone.

He didn't fall asleep that night, which wasn't surprising. He dressed the next morning as if in a fog. Stepping out into the corridor, he encountered two ambassadors who solicitously asked after Mariel and looked at him in a way that he would have once seen as genuine smiles, but now saw only as smirks. He turned right around and headed back to his quarters.

He sat on the couch, trembling with fury and indignation, and then he began to cry. It was unmanly, it was undignified, but he was alone and he didn't care. He grabbed a pillow and sobbed into it, felt as if his soul was emptying out into that pillow. He would expend all his strength into expelling all his misery and loneliness—and just when he thought he had no more strength to continue, a new fit of weeping would seize him and he would collapse all over again. When he had finally gotten all of the misery and self-pity out of his system, he found that most of the day was already gone.

What was left within him was a cold, burning desire for revenge. Revenge against the shadowy forces that had twisted and turned his life back on itself for years and years now. He had stood helpless before the advent of the Shadow ships that swarmed across the skies of Centauri Prime. He had watched Londo's slow descent into a darkness from which he could never return, and he had been unable to prevent it. He had experienced his own personal hell as he had found the blood of an emperor on his hands.

Once more he thought of Mariel, and the merest passing thought of her was enough to enrage him. Ordinarily, he would have been quick to let such feelings go. Life, he had always felt, was too short to let it be caught up in fantasies of vengeance. Not this time, though. This time the hurt had been too personal, the cut too deep. This time someone, or something, was going to suffer consequences for what they had done to him.

Perhaps what drove Vir the most was that, for the first time in his life, he didn't care about himself. At least that much of the self-pity remained with him, but it had been forged into something else. It wasn't as if he was despondent. Instead, he was taking that lack of concern for his own well-being, and crafting it into an attitude that he sensed would serve him in the months—perhaps years—ahead. He was not particularly anxious to die, but the notion of life wasn't holding any exceptional allure for him either. Vengeance was beginning to ascend over concerns for his personal safety.

He picked himself up and turned his attention to the computer terminal, checked the schedules and saw that there was a transport bound for Centauri Prime the very next morning. He told himself that the serendipity of the timing provided yet another sign that he was embarking upon the right course.

He lay upon his bed that evening, quite convinced that he

would never be able to so much as close his eyes. To his sub-sequent surprise, he fell immediately asleep.

The next morning he headed straight over to the departures area, walking as if he had blinders on, looking neither right nor left, barely acknowledging anyone he passed, even if they greeted him. He purchased a one-way ticket to Centauri Prime, wondered whether he would ever again set foot on Babylon 5, and came to the realization that he didn't care.

As Vir departed B5, he didn't notice Kane watching him go, nor did he see two other similarly robed figures who were standing beside Kane, one male, one female.

"You play a dangerous game," said the female, "as does Vir. He has no true idea of what he faces."

"Neither do we," replied Kane.

"But we, at least, have an inkling. He has nothing except what small pieces of information you have been dropping upon him."

"That will have to do."

"I mislike it," the woman said firmly.

The man standing next to her chuckled. "You mislike everything, Gwynn. At least Kane is stirring things up."

"Perhaps. Let us simply hope," said the woman known as Gwynn, "that we do not get caught up cooking in the stew being stirred."

Usually for Vir, the time spent in space travel seemed posi-tively endless. He didn't particularly like such journeys, and usually spent them on the edge of his seat, waiting for some-thing to go wrong, waiting for the bulkhead to buckle or the oxygen to leak or the engines to go dead or some other catas-trophe to hit. For Vir was always all-too-aware of the fact that a very unforgiving vacuum surrounded them, and only the relatively thin ship's hull stood between him and a violent death. On this voyage, however, he gave it no thought at all.

His thoughts were focused entirely upon Centauri Prime and what he would do once he arrived there.

Unfortunately, he didn't really know. He wasn't sure how he would approach Londo, or what he would do about the Drakh, or what he *could* do. These and any number of other considerations tumbled about in his mind.

No one was there to meet him when he arrived at the Centauri Prime spaceport, which was fine. He hadn't told anyone he was coming. He wanted his arrival at the palace to come as a total surprise. Somehow he sensed that the only thing he really had going for him was surprise. He wanted to make his movements and actions as unpredictable as possible.

The bottom line was, the only person he trusted anymore was himself. As much as he wanted to trust Londo, he had seen far too much for him to be able to place any real confidence in the emperor.

Nor did he trust the techno-mage initiate. His first encounter with techno-mages, on Babylon 5, during their great migration, had led him to think of them as tricksters. The terrifying illusion they had cast, of a monstrous creature threatening to rend Vir limb from limb, still occasionally haunted his dreams.

Techno-mages, as a group, had their own motivations, their own agendas. There was still the very distinct possibility that Kane had fabricated this entire thing. That there was no such thing as a "Drakh." What he had shown Vir had been so short, so conveniently minimal, that it was impossible for Vir to know for certain just how forthcoming Kane was being. He might have fabricated the entire thing from whole cloth, as a means of undercutting Vir's support for Centauri Prime—and that for reasons Vir could only guess. Which might have meant that the business with Mariel was also fabrication . . .

But no. No, Vir was positive that wasn't the case. The farther he was away from Babylon 5, the longer he was away

from that arena that they had shared, the more clear it became
to him.

Vir arrived at the palace and was greeted with polite surprise by Londo's personal guard. He was escorted to a
waiting room, there to wait until there was a hole in the emperor's schedule that would allow him to meet with Vir. "Had
we only been expecting you, we would have accommodated
you with far greater efficiency," Vir was told. He shrugged. It
made little difference to him.

And as he sat in the waiting room, he couldn't wipe the vision of Mariel from his mind. But he was determined that that
was exactly what he had to do. He pictured her face, lathered
with contempt, and mentally he started to disassemble it, feature by feature. Plucked out the eyes, removed the nose, the
teeth, the tongue, all of it, until there was only a blank space
where a woman had occupied so much of his attention.

And when she was gone—or at least, when he believed her
to be gone—he knew one thing for certain. He knew that if he
never, ever, saw a wife of Londo Mollari again, it would be
too soon.

The door to the waiting room slid open and Vir automatically started to stand. He rose halfway and froze in position.

It wasn't Londo standing there in the doorway. Instead it
was a diminutive Centauri woman, her face round, her eyes
cool and scornful, her lips frozen in a perpetual pucker of disapproval, her demeanor glacial.

"You've lost weight, Vir. You look emaciated. You should
eat something," said Timov, daughter of Algul, wife of Londo
Mollari.

At that moment, Vir seriously considered gnawing his leg
off at the knee just so he could escape.

Rumors had begun to filter through the dig.

There had been the reputation, of course. Everyone knew the stories. But no one had taken it seriously, not really seriously. There had been discussions of it in the evening hours, but in the early days of the dig, the chats had been like the laughter of children camping out.

But months had passed, and there was a sense that they were getting close to something. Nobody knew what that something was, but there was a general and unmistakeable air of foreboding, even among people who were of such a sober-minded nature that they would never have bought into a concept as quaint as a place being "haunted."

Then, there was the question of the disappearing diggers.

When one had vanished, no one had thought anything of it. But over the long months, several more had disappeared. At first this had been chalked off to simple desertion, but several of the men who had disappeared had been workers who had absolutely no reason to depart. In fact one of them, a fellow named Nol, just before he had gone missing, was talking about how the dig was the best thing that had ever happened to him. It had gotten him away from a wife he could not stand, children whom he didn't comprehend, and a life that had done nothing but go sour for him. So when Nol had disappeared, that really got eyebrows lifted and tongues wagging.

In short, no one knew what was going on. There was some brief discussion of a mass desertion, but representatives of the Ministry of Internal Security had caught wind of it and come in short order to calm the agitation of the workers. Still, to play it safe, workers had started traveling in groups of three or more at all times, never wandering off on their own, never searching around in areas that were considered off limits.

They also started spending more time in town. Ironically, there had been no town there before. But, in a case of form following function, a small trading community had arisen primarily to accommodate the workers. The odd traveler passed through from time to time, but for the most part it was a tight-knit, normal community. Or at least, as normal as could be expected with the aforementioned air of foreboding hanging over it.

Meantime, the digging drew closer and closer to that which had been hidden and forgotten for millennia . . .

— *chapter 19* —

Two years before Vir Cotto found himself in Timov's presence, Londo Mollari had looked at the expression on the face of his aide, Dunseny, who had just bustled into the throne room, and had known instantly.

"She's here, isn't she," was all Londo had said.

Dunseny managed to nod, but that was about all. This was an individual who had served Londo's assorted needs for years, and he had never seemed daunted by anything that Londo had thrown at him, or any duty that had been required of him. But now he wore a look of total befuddlement, bordering on intimidation, and *that* signaled to Londo the arrival of the diminutive terror known as Timov.

Londo sighed heavily. He'd had a feeling that the time would come. He just hadn't known when.

It was somewhat like death in that regard. Although maybe not; he actually had a fairly clear idea of what that felt like, and of when his own mortality would finally catch up with him. This led him to realize that Timov was even more fearsome and unpredictable than death. *She probably would be rather taken with that notion,* he mused.

"Send her in," was all Londo said. The aide nodded gratefully. Londo could easily understand why. Obviously the last thing the poor bastard wanted to do was go back and tell Timov that the emperor had no time for her.

Moments later, Timov bustled in, looking around the throne

room with a vague air of disdain, as if she were trying to determine the best way to redecorate.

Then she looked straight at Londo. "The curtains in here are ghastly. You need more light."

"No surprises," Londo murmured.

"What?"

" 'What' indeed—that is the question before us, Timov. As in, 'What are you doing here?' "

"Is that all I get from you, Londo? A coarse interrogation? Waves of hostility? I am your wife, after all."

"Yes. You are my wife. But I," and Londo rose from his throne, "am your emperor. And you will show proper respect to me, as befits a woman in the presence of the supreme ruler of the Centauri Republic."

"Oh, please," Timov responded disdainfully.

But then Londo stepped down from the throne and slowly advanced on her. "Down to one knee, woman. If you had taken this long to respond to a direct command from Emperor Cartagia, he would have had your head on a plate in an instant. You will genuflect in my presence, speak only when I permit you to speak, and obey my orders, or by the Great Maker . . . I will have you taken out and executed immediately, and your head placed on a pike as a warning to other disobedient wives everywhere! *Do you understand me?*"

Timov didn't budge. His face was only a few inches away from hers. And then she took out a handkerchief from her sleeve and dabbed at the right corner of his mouth.

"What are you doing?" asked Londo.

"You have a bit of spittle right there. Hold still."

Londo couldn't quite believe it. He felt as if he were trapped in some bizarre dream. "Have you lost your mind? Didn't you hear one word I said?"

"Yes. And if you're about to order soldiers to come in here and take me away so that my head can adorn your exterior fixtures, then you needn't look like a crazed animal while you're doing it. As wife of the emperor, *I* at least am aware that I have an image to protect. You should start considering yours. There." She tucked the handkerchief away, then serenely folded her hands in front of her. "All right. I'm ready," she said, her chin pointed upward. "Summon the soldiers. Take me away because I'm not subservient enough. I know it's what you've always wanted."

He stared at her for a time, gaping in open incredulity. And then, slowly shaking his head, he walked back to his throne.

"I am curious, though," Timov continued, as if the conversation was meant to continue. "Will the means of execution be the actual beheading? Or will I be killed in some other fashion, my decapitation to occur subsequently. It will make a difference in terms of the last outfit I wear. For example, there's liable to be much more blood in a beheading, so I'll probably want to wear something arterial red to get a better blend. But if something more bloodless is chosen, such as the administering of poison, then I'll probably want to wear one of my blue dresses—probably the one with a bit more scoop at the neck. I know, it's somewhat more daring than my usual ensemble, but since it will be my last public appearance, why shouldn't I leave tongues wagging? Of course, the one with the gold brocade could—"

"Oh, shut up." Londo sighed.

She was actually quiet for a moment, and then, sounding rather solicitous, she said, "You seem fatigued, Londo. Shall I get the guards for you?"

"Great Maker . . . I do not believe it. It cannot be possible." She folded her arms. "What cannot be possible?"

"That I've actually missed you," he said with slow disbelief. "Yes. I know you have."

"I never would have thought it could come to this."

"Would you like to know why you miss me?" she asked.

"Could I stop you from telling me?"

As if he hadn't spoken, Timov slowly circled the perimeter of the throne room as she said coolly, "Because you are surrounded by people who treat you as emperor. But you have not been an emperor for most of your life. You are much more accustomed to being treated as simple Londo Mollari. That is your natural state of being, and I believe you long, to some degree, for a return to those days. That is why you are so lonely . . ."

He looked at her askance. "Who said I was lonely?"

"No one," she said with a small shrug. "I simply surmised that—"

"Noooo." He waggled a finger at her. "It is all coming clear now. You've been speaking to Senna, yes?"

"Senna." Timov made a great production of frowning. "I don't seem to recall anyone by that name . . ."

"Don't try lying to me, Timov. I have far too much experience with it, so I can spot it when even the most expert of liars is engaging in the practice. And you are not at all expert, because you are much too accustomed to saying exactly what is on your mind, always, without exception. I think that if you tried to lie, your jaw would snap off."

"I will take that as a compliment." She sighed. "Yes. Senna contacted me."

"Eh. I knew it."

"She is worried about you, Londo. Heaven knows too few people around here are. They care about you only in regard to how they can use your power to further their ends, or how you can best serve their needs."

"And you know this how?"

"Because I know the mentality, Londo. I know the situations that draw certain types of players to certain sorts of games."

"And what is your game, Timov?" he asked, waving a finger at her. "Am I supposed to believe that you are here motivated purely out of concern for me? I will accept that about as readily as the claim that you never heard of Senna."

"I make no bones about it, Londo. I'm tired of having you hold me at arm's length. There is status, power, money that are owed me as the wife of an emperor. You've made no effort to contact me and bring me here, no effort to make me a part of your court, as is my due."

"You have wanted for nothing."

"That is true. The titles and lands of House Mollari are quite nice, and my lot in life is certainly of a higher caliber than poor Daggair or Mariel . . ."

" 'Poor' Daggair or Mariel?" He snorted. "Are you going to tell me that you actually have some degree of pity for them?"

"No, I wouldn't insult your intelligence by claiming that. But their situation was somewhat dire, last I heard."

"And have you done anything to improve that situation for them, using the resources you have at your disposal?"

"Of course not," sniffed Timov. "I do for them exactly what they would have done for me."

"As always, Timov, you can be counted on."

"You meant that sarcastically, I know, but the truth is that you know you always can count on me. I'll wager that even as we speak you're surrounded by backstabbers, yes-men . . . all manner of bottom feeders. You need someone who will be honest with you, tell you precisely what she thinks—"

"What 'she' thinks," Londo echoed mirthlessly.

"—and will never betray you. You said it yourself, Londo. With me, you always know where you stand."

"Except my situation is quite different now, Timov. I am emperor now. The stakes have been raised."

"Not for me. For the Durlas, the Liones, the others of this court, there is a certain advantage to trying to get you out of the way, for they can then attempt to seize power themselves. Whatever power I have, on the other hand, derives solely from you. If you are gone, so am I. So I would have far more at stake."

"So you are not simply in this for the money. That is not all you care about?"

Slowly Timov walked to the window and looked out across Centauri Prime. Londo couldn't help but notice that she ran her white-gloved hand across the windowsill and looked at the fingers. Obviously she didn't like what she saw, because she shook her head in mild reproof. Londo made a mental note to speak to the cleaning staff.

"If all I cared about was money, Londo," she said after due consideration, "I would not have provided the blood donation that saved your life when you were comatose on Babylon 5, some years ago. All I had to do was allow you to die, and I would have inherited—along with the other two wives—the entirety of your estate."

"I thought you were never going to tell me about that."

"I wasn't. But I felt that—" She stopped suddenly, turned and looked at him. "Wait. How did . . . you knew? You *knew*?"

"Of course I knew. Do you think I am stupid?"

"But . . . but how?"

"One of Franklin's medtechs let slip that I had undergone a transfusion. I know I have a rare blood type, and I know that you have the same, from back when we had our premarital medical exams. So I asked the medtech if you were the donor. He admitted that you were, but begged me to keep the information to myself."

"So that was the reason that you chose me as the wife to keep." There was a small settee with a thin cushion along the window, and she sat in that now, shaking her head in amazement.

"He begged me to keep the knowledge to myself, because he didn't want Franklin knowing that he had—what is the Earth saying?—spilled the peas. So why are you telling me now, after all this time?"

"Because," she said, looking slightly put out that her dramatic revelation had been preempted, "I want you to know you can trust me."

"If you mean that I can trust you not to betray me . . . no, of course I do not believe that. Then again," he added as he saw that she looked slightly crestfallen, "I cannot afford to trust *anyone* that far. That is a simple and sad fact of my life."

"I will stay here for a time, Londo," Timov declared. "I can certainly keep myself occupied during the days and nights here. If nothing else, Senna could use a positive female role model in this place."

"And you think you can locate one for her?" Londo queried.

Timov's lips thinned in her best "we-are-not-amused" expression, which was the one she most often wore and had thoroughly perfected. "If you are truly lonely, as Senna suspects . . . then you will have me to turn to. As for me, I will be able to avail myself of the rights to which I am entitled as your wife."

"Unless, of course, I divorce you as well," Londo said quietly.

She studied him carefully. "Is that what you intend to do?"

"I do not know. I will be considering all options."

"Fine. You do that," she said primly. "In the meantime, kindly assign someone to aid me in transporting my things to my room. I assume that somewhere in this decorated mausoleum you can manage to locate some sort of accommodations. I know better than to assume that I will be sleeping with you." She shuddered. "I still remember that ghastly display you put on with Daggair and Mariel. Shameless."

"Ah, yes," he said nostalgically. "What did you call it? Oh yes. My 'sexual olympics.' "

She made a loud *tsk tsk* noise.

"This is an absurd situation, Timov, you know that. To have you here, floating about the palace, expressing your disapproval of me? Undercutting me in front of—"

"I did not say that, Londo. Kindly do not put words in my mouth, or attribute to me actions that I do not intend to engage in. While in the presence of others, your courtiers and other rabble, I would never think of saying anything the least bit demeaning or, in any way, challenging your authority."

He stared at her, feeling as if he'd just been hit in the head with a brick. "Are you serious?"

"Of course I'm serious. Respect for the man is one thing; respect for the office is something else again. Private is private, Londo, and public is public. It would be nothing less than hypocritical of me to embrace the privileges of being the wife of the emperor while tearing down that same emperor in the eyes of his subordinates. I am here to help you rule, Londo. To rule wisely and well. But you cannot rule without the respect of others, and a woman who diminishes her ruler husband while others are within earshot, by extension, diminishes all of Centauri Prime. Because while you are emperor, you *are* Centauri Prime, heaven help us."

"I see."

For a long moment he said nothing, and then he reached over and tapped a small button on a stand nearby his throne. It sounded a chime that immediately brought Dunseny running. The aide glanced with clear apprehension at Timov.

"Kindly bring my wife, and her belongings, to the Empress Suite at once."

"Yes, Majesty," said the aide, his head bobbing obediently. Then he paused and inquired, "Where ... would that be, Majesty?"

"Wherever my wife says it is," Londo replied.

"Thank you, Londo," Timov said. "I will withdraw now, to bathe and wash off the dust of travel." And then, to Londo's complete astonishment, Timov bowed in a perfect curtsy, bobbing her head, bending her knee in such elegant fashion that it seemed as if she'd been doing it all her life. As she did so, she extended one hand and let it hang there for a moment.

Londo, surprising himself to a degree, stepped down from the throne, took her hand and gently kissed her knuckles. Timov looked up at him, then, and there was actually a sparkle of merriment in her eyes. "If we do this right, Londo," she said in a low voice, "we might actually have some fun."

With that, she rose, turned her back, and strode from the throne room.

He sat there for a moment in silence, and then, very softly, he began to count out loud. "Three . . . two . . . one . . ."

"Why are you counting?" came the voice of Shiv'kala.

"A private joke," Londo said to him, not even bothering to turn in his direction. "You will allow me my occasional indulgences in such things, I hope. I have so few these days."

"The woman."

"What of her?" asked Londo.

"She is . . . unexpected."

"Women often are."

"Her presence could be . . . troublesome. Have her leave."

"For no reason at all?" Londo demanded.

"You are emperor. You do not need a reason."

At this, Londo stood, stepped down from the throne and walked straight toward the shadowy edges of the room from which Shiv'kala always seemed to materialize—it was as if he stepped sideways out of space. "Even an emperor does not like to do things for no reason," Londo told him. "Emperors who do so tend to lose things, such as their popularity. That is often followed by the loss of life, or at very least certain bodily appendages to which I have become quite accustomed, thank you very much. I can handle Timov."

"We are not convinced." Shiv'kala paused a moment, then stepped ever so slightly into the light. His customary expression of amusement, mixed with disdain, was firmly in place. "You like the woman, don't you. Through your bluster . . . and her abrasiveness . . . you still like her."

"It is not about 'like.' "

"What then?"

"You," Londo said, stabbing a finger at the Drakh, "have no idea how it felt. That woman, and her fellow wives, pushed at me and yammered at me to advance through the ranks of society. They wanted me to obtain power so that they, in turn, would know comfort and privilege. It never stopped. And Timov was the loudest in proclaiming that I would never amount to anything. When the post to Babylon 5 came available, I knew it was considered a joke. I seized it anyway, because it meant that I would be as far away from them as possible. Now I have reached the pinnacle of Centauri status. I admit it: it will amuse me to have her nearby, so that she can see firsthand just what I—the *nothing*—have amounted to. That I am the pride and puissance of the Centauri Republic. That I am the living history of the imperial line of Centauri Prime. That I am—"

"Our servant."

The words, harsh but true, hung there. Londo had nothing to say in response.

"Let her remain, if it pleases you," Shiv'kala said quietly. "But do not let her get too close to you."

"That will not happen," Londo said confidently. "She has no desire to get close to me. She wants to enjoy the power and prestige, but I know her. She will become bored with it soon. And she will tire of watching people treat me with respect. She will find that she cannot hold her tongue; it will be too galling for her. She will leave of her own accord, and in that way I will be spared a needless conflict."

"Very well. But know this, Londo . . . if it does not develop as you say . . . the consequences will be on your head." And with that, Shiv'kala had faded back into the shadows.

"The consequences will be on my head." Londo had replied, making an amused noise deep in his throat. "Aren't they all?"

"You've lost weight, Vir. You look emaciated. You should eat something," said Timov, daughter of Algul, wife of Londo Mollari.

Vir was immediately on his feet, putting his hand on his stomach. "I've . . . gotten many compliments, actually."

"Well, let's have a look at you," Timov said. She walked up

to him, gripped him by the shoulders, and turned him this way and that as if inspecting a side of beef. He started to say something, but she shushed him as she continued her examination. Finally she turned him around to face her and said brusquely, "I suppose it's healthier for you . . . still . . . you're not quite as huggable as you once were."

"I'm not as . . . what?"

And Vir was dumbfounded as Timov threw her arms around him and squeezed him tightly. "It's good to see you, Vir," she said. She stepped back and looked up at him with an amused sparkle in her eye. "You poor, horribly abused, put-upon fellow. I never thought you'd last out the year when I first saw you. And yet here you are, the ambassador to Babylon 5." She looked closely at his face. "You do look a good deal more wan, though. Far more worry lines. And your eyes . . ." She held his chin, staring into them, not unkindly. "They've seen terrible things these past years, haven't they. Things you'd much rather have closed them to."

"Well . . . yes . . . but if I had, I would have kept bumping into furniture."

She laughed at that, and then gestured that he should sit. He did, and she did likewise.

"Not to sound presumptuous, Lady Tim . . . Empress Timov—"

"Timov, please. We're old friends."

"Are we? I mean . . . yes, of course." Vir felt as if his entire world was spinning off its axis. He needed time to cope with the shifting ground beneath him. "Timov . . . what are you doing here? How long have you been here?"

"The better part of two years, actually," Timov told him. "I very much doubt that Londo thought I would be here this long. Truthfully, I wasn't expecting it either. Things have just . . . worked out."

"Worked out . . . how? Are you and he . . ?" Vir wasn't quite sure how to proceed with the sentence.

"The secret of our marriage's success has always been our

lack of communication," said Timov. "I wouldn't say that we communicate all that much more now. But when we do, there is a . . . relaxed manner about it. We have been through much in the past years, Vir . . . particularly him. It has changed him. Made him more than he was . . . and less. I think he is trying to strike a balance now."

"And you're providing that?"

"After a fashion, in a small way," she allowed. "There is still much that needs to be done, much that needs attending to—"

At that moment, the door opened. Durla stepped in quickly . . . and came to a dead halt when he saw Timov and Vir. He forced a smile, and it was rather obvious that it was an effort to push it onto his face. "Ambassador Vir," he said with so much cheerfulness that he sounded as if he were medicated. "I heard that you had arrived. Shame on you for not advising us ahead of time. Highness," and he bowed to Timov, "I can attend to the ambassador's needs from this point. I'm certain you have other matters of far greater importance that need attending to . . ."

"Greater importance than chatting with an old friend?" she said, scoffing. "Not at the moment, no. Of course, to some degree I owe that to you, Minister. The Minister here," she said, turning to Vir, "has gone to great effort to try and minimize my calendar of activities. Is that not so, Minister?"

"With all respect, Highness, I have no idea to what you could possibly be referring."

"I'm sure you don't," Timov said flatly, in that particular tone that still caused Vir's bladder to feel slightly weakened. "Now if you don't mind, Minister, Vir and I were in the midst of a conversation. I'm certain you wouldn't want to disturb us, would you?"

"Certainly not," said Durla, as he bowed deeply and exited backing up.

All business, Timov turned back to Vir and said, "That man has got to go. He oozes bile. I have no idea why Londo keeps

him around, but he is a frightening little person. He has ar-
rayed an entire support group of key appointees, all of whom
are loyal to him rather than Londo. I will do whatever it takes
to find a way to rid the palace of him and his ilk. That, at the
moment, is my major concern. Well, that and Londo . . ."

"He's my concern as well."

"Is there some specific thing that has prompted you to
come here?" she asked.

Something in Vir's head prevented him from being utterly
forthcoming. He wasn't sure precisely what it was, but he
knew he just wasn't comfortable with telling Timov about
Kane. Perhaps she might think he was being used, or that he
was foolish for becoming involved with techno-mages, even
initiate techno-mages.

"I've . . . been hearing things," he said carefully.

"What sort of things?" She leaned forward intently, and
it was quite clear that she wasn't going to settle for vague
generalities.

But thanks to his lack of talent for dissembling, he knew
that if he tried to make something up, he would fail miserably
in the endeavor. So he cast his mind back to his conversations
with Kane, and something came to him. "K0643," he said.

She looked at him oddly. "What would that be?"

"It . . . has to do with digging," he told her.

"Digging?" Timov looked rather confused.

Small wonder. Vir was somewhat befuddled about the
matter himself. "Yes. I've just been hearing . . . well . . . odd
things in connection with it. I was hoping to see what Londo
knew about it . . ."

"Let us see what I can find out first," Timov said thoughtfully. "I will make certain that Londo knows you're here.
He'll probably want to see you this evening. In the meantime,
I'll make a few inquiries into this . . . K0643, you said?" He
nodded. She rose and said, "Come. I'll show you to your
guest quarters."

"Thank you. And . . . if I may say so, Timov . . . I'm really pleased over the way this has been working out. After my recent experiences . . ."

"Experiences?" She looked at him curiously. "What sort of experiences?"

"Oh, well . . . it's nothing you really need to worry about. It was my problem . . . well . . . not anymore . . ."

"Vir," she said with an air of impatience, "just tell me what you mean."

"Well . . . it's just that, when I saw you, I was . . . I'm a little ashamed to say it . . ."

"You needn't concern yourself, Vir. Just speak your mind."

"Well . . . I took one look at you and thought, 'Oh, Great Maker, not another of Londo's wives. Not after my involvement with Mariel.' But I realize now that I was completely—"

She took him by the arm and sat him down so forcefully the bench shuddered under him. She sat opposite him and said, very slowly, "What . . . 'involvement' . . . with Mariel?"

He told her everything, and as he did, Timov grew paler and paler. The only thing he left out was the exact details of what Mariel had been saying to the unseen "chancellor." But he gave enough generalities to put across his sense of personal violation. When he was finished, she whispered, "You . . . incredibly lucky man . . ."

"*Lucky?*" He couldn't quite believe what he'd just heard. "Timov, with all respect, how could anything about that experience possibly be considered lucky?"

"Because," she replied, "you're still alive."

That which had been hidden for millennia was only days away from discovery.

The casualties were rising.

And in the darkness, the Drakh stood ready. They spoke among themselves, communed. How many casualties would there be? How many workers would be sacrificed to the defenses that belonged to something that had been hidden for so long that it had been forgotten by all save the most loyal.

The answer came back: fifty percent. Perhaps sixty percent of the workers would be lost in that first burst of energy. The Shadows, of course, could have started the homing device with no casualties at all. For the Drakh, however, it was trial and error. And the Drakh had no desire to sacrifice any of their own. So naturally it made sense to use their pawns. They were a trivial concern.

All that mattered was the Hidden Base. The base that could only be reached through K0643. The Hidden Base, known to the Drakh as Xha'dam. Xha'dam, the place that would enable them to bring the power of the Shadows to the galaxy once more. And if they did their job properly, why . . . perhaps the Shadows would see the greatness of their work and would return. Return to praise the Drakh, and raise them up above all that lived, or at least, all that remained living.

The Drakh Entire was becoming impatient. To be so

close . . . so close . . . and yet have to proceed with caution. It was maddening.

But they maintained their patience, for time was on their side. It was not, however, on the side of the rest of the galaxy . . .

— *chapter 20* —

Kuto swayed into Durla's office with his customary wide gait. Durla stared at Kuto and wondered if it was possible for the man to get any fatter. As it was, Kuto's girth was so impressive that it was difficult for him to ease himself into a chair and, once he was there, disengaging himself from it became equally problematic.

For all that, Kuto had a rather avuncular manner that made him quite pleasant to spend time with, and a boisterously loud attitude that was well suited to someone who was designated the minister of Information.

"A moment of your time, Minister," he boomed to Durla, sliding into a seat before Durla could possibly have the opportunity to tell him to come back later. The chair creaked protestingly under his bulk, but Durla was used to that. "I assure you, it won't take long."

"What is it, Kuto?" asked Durla, putting aside his work.

"Well . . . there has been a good deal of interest being expressed lately in relation to K0643. Since I oversee information, people tend to come to me about such matters, and I address their queries, particularly when public statements might become necessary. Plus, when the inquiries come from high places . . ."

Durla put up his hands in the hope of getting Kuto to focus. The minister of Information had a habit of going off on annoying tangents. "Could you be just a bit more linear, Kuto. What inquiries? What high places? And why should a public statement be necessary? K0643 is simply one of the assorted job works being overseen by this ministry. I don't see how the public need concern itself overmuch."

"Well, I would have thought that to be so, Minister," said Kuto, scratching his copious chins. "The interest has been happening by degrees, however. First . . . we've been getting quite a few inquiries from families of workers who went to the site . . . those who disappeared and haven't been heard from again."

"If workers get tired or bored or simply depart their posts, we can hardly be held responsible," Durla said impatiently. "A certain degree of attrition was anticipated."

"Attrition is one thing, Minister. But outright disappearances?"

"If some are viewing this as an opportunity to begin a new life elsewhere, we cannot be held accountable for that, either. Is there anything else?"

"I'm afraid so. You see, the emperor's wife has also been making inquiries . . ."

"Timov?" Durla let out a long, frustrated sigh. "Why?"

"I couldn't say. But she's been checking about, and has garnered some information—"

"Why was anything told to her at all!" Durla demanded.

"Because what she sought was not classified information," Kuto said reasonably. "Should anything have been kept from her?"

"No. No, I suppose not." Durla leaned back in his chair, rubbing the bridge of his nose, feeling suddenly very, very tired.

Thinking of the project made him think of Mariel. After all, it had been she who had come to him in the dream and urged him on. There had to be an answer to it all, of that he was quite certain.

He had deliberately distanced himself, however, from Mariel's activities, and particularly those activities that were coordinated through the office of Chancellor Lione. He suspected that Lione was beginning to intuit something about Durla's feelings for her, and those feelings might be misinterpreted. If there was one thing that Durla did not want to allow, it was anything that might be seen as weakness.

Still . . .

"Kuto," Durla said, leaning forward in a manner meant to suggest that great secrets were about to be imparted. Kuto tried to respond, but leaning forward wasn't his forte. So he stayed where he was. "I am a bit . . . concerned about several individuals. Several people have attained important positions in a variety of . . . projects. Since I have you here, I thought perhaps I might entrust you with their names, and that you might check into their current whereabouts for me. However . . . it might be best if you did this without letting anyone know that the request came from me. And I would also prefer if you did not speak to Chancellor Lione about the matter."

"Chancellor Lione?" Kuto raised an eyebrow. "Is there a reason to doubt—"

"No. Not at all. But . . . this is my preference. I can trust you to honor it?"

"Of course."

Durla rattled off a half dozen names, the vast majority of whom he was picking at random off the top of his head. One of the names mentioned, however, was that of Mariel. Kuto didn't appear to react to her name any more than he did the others whom Durla mentioned. "And once I've found out what you wish to know?"

"Then relay the results to me."

Kuto nodded. "And what about Timov?"

"She is becoming rather tiresome, that one," Durla admitted. "Still, as long as the emperor expresses no wish for her to leave, we must honor his desires in the matter. Mustn't we?"

"And if his desires change?"

"Why then," Durla said quietly, "so does her . . . location."

* * *

Kuto nodded, smiled, left Durla's office . . . and went straight to Castig Lione to inform the chancellor that, yes indeed, his hunch had been right, and Durla had inquired about Lady Mariel.

Wheels within wheels. And moving like a wraith, through the minds of each and every player, flowed Shiv'kala, smiling from the darkness of their innermost ambitions, and secure in the knowledge that the Drakh would ultimately benefit from all . . .

chapter 21

When Vir came to, he felt a throbbing at the base of his skull, and when he tried to rub it he discovered that his hands were chained to the wall of the cell that he was occupying.

He pulled at the manacles and had absolutely no success in budging them. As the reality of his situation started to dawn on him, he pulled with greater and greater aggressiveness, but his only response was the loud rattling of the chains. By rapid degrees, his panic level began to elevate, and he pulled with even more ferocity, still to no avail.

Then he shouted, but that was an even bigger mistake, because he only succeeded in making his head hurt mightily. It was at that point that he managed to come to the realization that he was experiencing a thumping great hangover.

That, in turn, led him to remember the previous night, which had been one of great festivity and merriment. He was utterly perplexed as to how something that seemed to be going so right could possibly have ended up so wrong . . .

Some fourteen hours earlier Vir had puttered around in his quarters and wondered when, or even if, Londo was going to take the time to see him. Indeed, he was wondering a great many things, up to and including whether or not his presence on Centauri Prime was one great big mistake.

Then he reviewed, once again, the reasons he had come. The claims of a great darkness that had fallen upon Centauri Prime, that some sort of strange race had gained a hold over

Londo. And above all of that, he recalled the sense of personal humiliation over the entire business with Mariel. All of that served to steel his resolve, and made him more determined than ever to see through what he had committed to do.

The door to his quarters chimed, and he went to open it. Timov was standing there, and there was an unmistakeable look of concern on her face. "I have some information for you regarding K0643," she said without preamble. "It's a planet."

In quick, broad strokes she laid out what she had learned of the world. Of how it was a pet archaeological dig that had been initiated by Minister Durla. Of how some spoke of it as being haunted, as unlikely and improbable as such a thing might be. Of how people were vanishing from the site. "I'm wondering if there isn't some sort of cover-up attached to it," Timov said suspiciously.

"But what would they be covering up? Is there any concrete example of wrongdoing?"

"No, but I—"

"Well!" boomed a familiarly loud voice. "Well, well, *well*! And what is this, eh? Is my former aide-de-camp dallying with the wife of the emperor, eh?"

Vir was astounded at the change that had come over Londo. What he was seeing here was the Londo of old. A man in good spirits, in good cheer, a man who appreciated the presence and even the companionship of others. He didn't simply walk into the room, he practically exploded into it, with huge strides that ate the distance between himself and Vir in no time. He embraced him as he would an old friend, and Timov as well, which astounded Vir all the more.

It was at that point that Vir became convinced Kane was completely wrong. This wasn't a man who was being controlled by fearsome beings, whose life was beholden to creatures lurking in darkness. No, it was simply impossible. Londo was no good at concealing things from Vir; Vir knew far too much.

But . . .

Londo *had* known about that attempt on Sheridan's life. He had found that information somewhere, and from his attitude and actions the last time they'd been together, it had very much seemed as if Londo was acting like a man who knew he was under constant observation. Could that have been the case, at the time, but he was no longer under such scrutiny? Or was it that he had simply become so accustomed to it that he acted as if it meant nothing anymore?

Vir decided he didn't dare relax his guard. He did, however, return the embrace.

"You must come to my private dining room this evening . . . this very hour!" Londo declared. "We shall discuss old times . . . we will laugh as of old . . . we will make sport and make merry, eh? We shall celebrate your return home, Vir, for whatever the reason is that you have chosen to bless us with your presence. What is the reason, eh?"

"Just lonely, Londo," Vir said quickly. "Just anxious to feel the ground of Centauri Prime under my feet again. And I wanted to breathe the fine air of our Homeworld instead of the recycled atmosphere of Babylon 5. You must know the feeling."

"Ohhh, I know it very well. Very well, indeed. And Timov, you are looking fit this evening." He kissed her suavely on the knuckles. "You will bring the illustrious Vir to the private dining room, and join us, eh? We will make an evening of it. It will be like the old times for the three of us."

"The three of us didn't have any old times together," Vir said reasonably, "unless you count your coming into your quarters while I was trying to stop Daggair and Timov from killing each other."

"Ah, well Daggair will not be with us this evening, so you can rest assured that this night will go quite smoothly, Vir. Timov, I can trust you to make sure that Vir does not get himself lost in this vast abyss that is our home."

"You may count on me, Londo."

"You know, Timov . . . these days, I believe I am finding

that to be the case more and more. Well!" And he clapped his hands and rubbed them together briskly. "I have a few more stops to make during my early evening circle of good cheer. I will see you in . . . shall we say . . . an hour?"

"Sounds great!" Vir said cheerfully. It was the first time in ages that he was actually looking forward to spending time with Londo.

"Excellent! Excellent!" Londo then draped his hands behind his back and walked out of the room.

"My! He certainly is . . . boisterous," Vir observed.

"That was how he used to be all the time, when we were first married," Timov said. "And you know, the thing that I consider most upsetting, is that in those days, his outspokenness and boisterousness were remarkably annoying to me. More . . . they were an embarrassment. But now I look upon it, and it's taken me this long to realize . . . that he can be a rather charming individual."

"I've always thought so," Vir said diplomatically. Indeed, the apparent change in Londo's attitude was enough to lend a certain amount of hope to Vir's expectations for his stay on Centauri Prime. Nevertheless, the words of Kane stayed with him, and he had brought along several rather potent bottles of wine just for the occasion.

When he joined Londo that evening, Timov was already there, and after a brief pause, while his thoughts appeared to be elsewhere, Londo seemed delighted when Vir produced his alcoholic donation. Before long he was completely involved with the evening's private festivities.

What impressed Vir the most was the easy camaraderie that had grown between Londo and Timov. He couldn't get over it. When he had seen the two of them together on B5, there had been nothing but hostility between them. It was as if they were born unable to stand the sight of one another. But here there was laughter, merriment, an open appreciation of each other's presence.

And as Londo had become more and more inebriated, his

attitude seemed to go beyond that of a man who was becoming drunk. He seemed liberated, deliriously so. His laughter rang out so loudly that occasionally guards stuck their heads in to make certain that nothing was amiss.

"Vir, where have you been all this time!" Londo cried out, clapping Vir on the back and then sliding off a chair. "I had forgotten what it was like to have you as a drinking companion!"

"That's probably because I don't really drink very much," Vir replied.

This just caused an even bigger reaction of hilarity from Londo, who poured himself another drink, decided that the glass was too time-consuming, and took a swig directly from the bottle. Timov hadn't had nearly as much to drink as Londo, but she was quite nicely toasted herself. Vir was amazed to see that, in that condition, the woman was positively giggly, more like a teenage girl than the stern and severe woman she normally tended to be.

"To Centauri Prime!" Londo called out, raising the glass, which was still full. He took another swig from the bottle, then threw the glass. It shattered against the wall, spreading thick purple liquid across it. Londo stared, bleary-eyed and said, "I suppose that should have been empty, yes?"

"It should have been empty, yes!" Timov said, laughing. She hauled herself to her feet. "Londo . . . I'm going to call it a night."

Londo looked out at the dark sky. "That certainly would have been my guess," he agreed.

"Good night, my dear," she said, and then she kissed him. It was quite an overt gesture for Timov, and Londo was clearly surprised by it. Their lips parted, and then she touched Londo's cheek and said softly, "Perhaps I will see you later." With that, she walked out.

"What do you think she meant by that, eh?" asked Londo, taking another swig of liquor.

"I . . . think maybe she meant that she would see you later."

"You know, I think she did." Londo looked wistfully in the direction that she had departed.

It was at that point that Vir took a deep breath, and then he said, "So . . . tell me about Shiv'kala."

At first, Londo said nothing at all. It was as if his alcohol-saturated brain needed extra time to process the comment. Then, slowly, he turned his gaze on Vir. His eyes were so hazed over that it was impossible for Vir to get a feeling for what was going on behind them. "What . . . did you say?" he asked.

"I said . . . tell me about Shiv'kala."

Londo waggled a finger and Vir drew closer. With a sodden grin on his face, Londo said, "I would not . . . say that name again . . . if I were you . . ."

"But . . . is there a reason you can't tell me about Shiv'kala?"

That was all Vir remembered.

In his cell, Vir realized that that was the point when Londo had whipped the bottle of wine around and knocked Vir cold. That was where the dull ache at the base of his skull had come from. Knowing it, however, didn't make the knowledge any better, nor did it improve on his situation.

"Help!" he called experimentally, but no one responded. He shouted once more for aid, but it was no more forth-coming the second time than it had been the first.

The evening had gone terribly, terribly wrong . . . to put it mildly.

Londo had never in his life sobered up so quickly, so completely. The moment that name had escaped Vir's lips, every bit of inebriation had dissolved.

Part of it was that the keeper, which was enjoying the same blissful alcoholic haze as its charge, had been snapped to full attentiveness when the Drakh's name was mentioned. Part of it was Londo's immediate realization that something had to be done, and done instantly. Unfortunately, he had no idea what that something might be, and so he had reverted to the simplest and most straightforward means of handling a problem, especially when it involved hearing something that one did not want to hear. He silenced the source.

In this instance, silencing the source entailed nothing more involved than knocking him cold. That he had managed with no effort.

He stood over Vir's prostrate form, and naturally, as he had already suspected would occur, Shiv'kala emerged from his state of perpetual hiding. Never had the Drakh seemed more grave than he was at that moment. "This one must die," Shiv'kala said.

"No," Londo said.

"Pleading will not help."

"That was not a plea. That was a statement."

Shiv'kala looked at him with pure danger in his face. "Do not defy me."

Without a word, Londo crossed the room to a sword hanging on the wall—ornamental but nonetheless lethal. He pulled it from its sheath and turned to face the Drakh. He held the sword firmly in his right hand. His intent for its use was clear.

"I defy you," said Londo. "I will kill you if I have to."

"You are insane," the Drakh told him. "You know what I can do to you. The pain . . ."

"Yes. The pain. But you siphon it through the keeper, and the keeper is not functioning . . . up to its best levels at the moment. Nor am I. But a drunk lunatic with a sword can still do a great deal of damage."

To demonstrate, he took two lurching, staggering steps toward the Drakh. He was having trouble standing, and his hand-eye coordination was almost nonexistent. But that didn't make the blade any less deadly as it whipped through the air.

"Now then," Londo said. "You can try to stop me . . . with

the pain . . . but the question is . . . will I still be able to cut you in half . . . before you stop me completely?"

"If you kill me," Shiv'kala said quietly, "I will simply be replaced by another of the Drakh Entire. And my replacement will not be nearly so generous as I have been."

"Perhaps. But you will still be dead. Unless, of course, your own life means nothing to you, in which case your death will be . . . besides the point." He took another several steps, slicing the sword back and forth like a scythe whacking through wheat.

It was clear that he was not bluffing.

Shiv'kala did not back down, did not panic, did not even come close to doing so. Instead he said coolly, "Very well. Simply have him locked up for now. We shall settle his situation later. I give you my word that I will not call for his death . . . if you do not attempt mine."

Londo considered this, as well as his alcoholic haze would allow him. Then he tossed the sword aside, lurched to the door, and summoned the guards. They saw the emperor's condition, saw the unmoving Vir upon the floor. What they did not see was the Drakh who, to Londo's utter lack of surprise, had vanished.

"Lock him up," Londo said.

"On what charge is he being arrested, Majesty?" asked one of the guards.

Londo stared at him through bleary eyes. "For asking too many questions. Pray that you don't wind up his cell mate." Then he staggered out into the hallway, his thoughts racing.

He had been deluding himself into thinking things could go back to the way they had been. That he might actually be able to find happiness and camaraderie with loved ones. He had been fooling himself. By having people close to him, he was simply putting them in danger from the Drakh. At least Senna had a sort of dispensation, her presence in the palace was a trade-off for having to endure Durla as minister.

Say what one would about the Drakh: At least they had kept their word when a bargain was made.

But Vir . . . poor, stupid Vir, deluded Vir, Vir who had somehow stumbled across the name of Shiv'kala and, in uttering it, had drawn a huge target on his back. What was going to happen to him now? Londo had to get him out of the horrific situation that he had hurled himself blindly into.

Friends, lovers. They were liabilities to him, he understood that now. Luxuries he simply could not afford. For as long as they were around, he would continue to fool himself into thinking that he could have something vaguely approaching a normal life.

He entered his quarters and stopped dead.

Timov was in his bed.

Draped across the top of the bed, she was dressed in an alluring nightgown, with an inviting smile playing across her face. Not even on their honeymoon, the requisite consummation of their arranged marriage, had she looked so happy to see him.

"Hello, Londo," she said. "I thought you'd never get here."

"You can't be serious," he told her.

"Don't worry," she assured him. "I know you've been drinking a bit, and won't necessarily be at your best . . ."

"But . . . now? Now? After all these years? Certainly you can't be—"

"Londo," she said with a gentleness of which he would have thought her incapable. " 'All these years' is exactly the problem. So many possibilities have been sacrificed to vituperation, and to the two of us working out anger over our being forced together by our families. It's taken a lot for me to realize that it needn't be that way. What I need to find out is if you've come to that realization, too."

He had. He wanted to take her in his arms, to love her, to make up for all that wasted time. But even as he wanted it, he knew that it was impossible. Those who were close to Londo, those whom he loved, had a nasty habit of dying. The further that Timov was from him, the better, for her sake.

And besides, he had the monstrosity sitting on his shoulder. What if, in the act of love, she managed to detect it? At the very least, thanks to the keeper's presence, there would be no privacy. Everything that he and she felt and shared would become part of the awareness of the Drakh Entire. The notion was ghastly, horrific. Something as personal, as private and intimate as that, belonging to the gestalt mind of those creatures? It would be as if she were being raped without even knowing it. And he, Londo, would be the instrument through which it had occurred.

He cleared his throat and tried to give his best impression of someone seized with anticipation of an event that was eagerly awaited and long in coming. Timov actually—Great Maker help him—giggled in a faintly girlish manner. "Why, Londo. You seem positively nervous. I haven't seen you this nervous since our wedding night."

"I was not nervous on our wedding night," he said archly, stalling for time as his mind raced.

"Oh, of course not. That's why you were trembling the entire night."

"You left the windows open and there was a stiff draft."

"And is anything . . . stiff . . . this evening?" she asked.

Londo gulped. He hardly recognized the woman. She had never been an enthusiastic bedmate, even in the earliest days, and he had just written that off to a fundamental lack of interest on her part. He was beginning to perceive, however, that it wasn't lack of interest in the act, so much as it was in him.

For just a moment, he considered it. Then he felt the keeper stirring on his shoulder, as if its own interest was piqued, and immediately he dismissed the idea from his mind. However, dismissing Timov was not quite as easy.

And it had to be done with finality. There was no choice; he simply could not risk a recurrence of this night, ever.

He tugged uncomfortably at his shirt and said, "If you wouldn't mind . . . I could use a few minutes to slip into something . . ."

"Less confining?"

"Exactly, yes." He nodded. He backed out of the room, never taking his eyes off her. He allowed his breath to steady, his pulse to slow so that his heart wasn't hammering against his chest.

And then he summoned Durla. Quickly, straightforwardly, he outlined for Durla exactly what he wanted done. The minister's eyes widened as Londo explained it. Of course, this was something that was solidly within Durla's comfort zone; indeed, he would probably enjoy it, for Londo knew all too well that there was no love lost between Durla and Timov. The unjustness of it rankled at Londo; of the three of them this night, the only one who would actually have a pleasant evening was Durla, who was certainly the least entitled. Truly, the Great Maker had a perverse sense of humor some nights.

Timov was beginning to wonder if Londo would ever return. It was one of those situations where one starts to ponder how long one would stay before realizing that the person being waited for was not going to show up.

Then there was a sound at the door, and she looked up. Londo was standing there, smiling at her, dressed indeed in far more loose-fitting attire. He looked younger, more handsome, more vital than she could recall seeing him. Or perhaps it wasn't really him; perhaps it was her, or the way she was seeing him. It was as if years of resentment had been scraped away from her, like an encrustment from the hull of a ship.

She said nothing then. There didn't seem to be any requirement for words. He came to her then, lay with her, and kissed her more passionately than she could ever recall. She was stunned at the vehemence of it. In her imaginings, it was as if he was kissing her in a way that was to make up for all of the sourness of the past . . .

. . . or . . .

. . . or to last him for the entirety of their future, as if this was it, the last time they would be together.

Immediately she brushed the notion aside as ridiculous, paranoid, a residue of the antipathy they had felt for one another all these years. This was their time, and nothing was going to spoil the mo—

The doors of the bedroom burst inward. Londo immediately sat up, his head snapping around, and Timov saw that there were several soldiers standing in the door. In between them was Durla.

"Unless you truly desire to see the city from the vantage point of your head upon a pike," growled Londo, "you had best have some incredibly good explanation for your presence here."

Durla took two steps forward and said in a firm, unyielding voice, "Highness . . . I regret to inform you that we have uncovered evidence indicating that the lady Timov was plotting against the crown."

"That's preposterous!" Timov said immediately. "You can't be serious."

"Do you think, milady, I would put forward this charge if I were not positive?" asked Durla, reeking with disdain. "I am more than aware of the gravity of the charge and the stakes involved. So rest assured that I would not say this unless I knew it for a fact. She has allies, Highness. Allies who would like nothing better than to see you removed from office, your head upon that same pike that you alluded to just now. She is to search out your weaknesses, and when she has compiled them, she and her allies will strike."

"Londo, throw him out!" Timov said, rage building. "Don't listen to these calumnies! They . . . he . . ."

Londo was looking at her in a way that she couldn't even begin to decipher. It seemed to be a mixture of anger and horror and infinite loss.

"I should have known," he said quietly.

The immensity of the meaning implicit in those words stunned her at first. "You . . . you can't actually be saying that you believe these mendacities! You—"

"Why else!" he demanded. "Why else would you embark on this seduction? What was it to be, eh? Poison, perhaps? Or a simple dagger between the ribs? Or did you just want me to lower my guard sufficiently so that I would tell you something you could use against me."

"Londo!" She didn't know whether to laugh or cry. In absence of anything else, rage began to consume her. "You would actually think that of me? Of me?"

"Get out of here," he whispered.

"Londo . . . ?"

"Get out of here!" he fairly exploded. "Take her away! Lock her up! Now!"

"Are you out of your mind!" she shrieked as she got to her feet, and then the guards were upon her, dragging her out.

Londo watched her being pulled away. He felt as if his hearts were being ripped out along with her. Her voice echoed up and down the hallway, her protests, her voicing of her hurt, but there was nothing he could do. Nothing he dared do. He was still shuddering inwardly at the vomitous feeling he'd had of the Drakh watching his final, amorous moments with her in a sort of clinical manner, as if he were not a man but a laboratory specimen being put through his paces.

Durla approached Londo. He had never seemed quite so tentative before. He said in a low voice, "Sufficient, Majesty?"

Londo couldn't even stand to look at him. "Get out," he said in a voice that sounded as if it were being issued from somewhere beyond the grave.

For once in his life, Durla was wise enough to leave a room without endeavoring to have the last word.

— *chapter 22* —

The next morning, Timov was brought before him. It ached Londo just to look at her, but he kept his face impassive . . . as deadpan as Timov's own was. Guards stood on either side of Timov, watching her warily. Londo thought their caution was rather amusing in its way, as if they were concerned that somehow this small woman would overwhelm them.

He sat on his throne, with Durla standing nearby, watching with narrowed eyes.

"Timov, daughter of Algul," Londo intoned, "evidence has been uncovered that indicates treasonous activities on your part against my government."

"Yes. I'm sure it has," she said crisply.

"If you are tried . . . you will be condemned."

This comment clearly startled Durla. He turned and looked at Londo and said, " '*If*' she is tried, Majesty? But surely—"

"It is our decision," Londo continued, as if Durla had not spoken, "that such a trial is not in keeping with the more forgiving and tolerant tone of this administration. As we always have, we seek to heal rifts and build for a greater Centauri Republic. The Republic will not be served by the condemnation and execution of the wife of the emperor. If forced to take that road . . . we will walk it, of course. But we are offering you the opportunity to depart, now and forever. You will maintain your title and station, but you will never come within one hundred miles of this place. And if you persist in seditious activities, this case will be reopened and reexamined. That is the offer I am making to you, my lady." He paused, and then added, "I suggest you take it."

She regarded him for a long moment. "What was it, Londo? Was it that I reminded you too much of the man you had been . . . and could be? Or was it that I reminded you too much of the man you are. For you to believe some trumped-up charges—"

"Your decision, my lady?" he said coldly.

"Well, let me think," she replied, her voice dripping with sarcasm. "Either I can choose certain death . . . or I can choose the option of keeping away from a place that I never want to set foot in again, and refraining from activities that I never embarked upon in the first place. What a difficult choice. The latter, I should think."

"Very well. Your belongings have already been packed for you. Personnel will be provided for you to escort you to wherever you wish to go."

"I wish I could escort you to where I wish you would go," Timov shot back. "Or was that a seditious thing to say."

"No. Simply rude. Good-bye, Timov." For a moment his voice caught and then, sounding husky and forced, he said, "Enjoy . . . your life."

Not sounding the least bit conflicted, Timov shot back, "Good-bye, Londo. Rot in hell."

When she was gone, Durla turned to Londo and began, "Majesty . . . that may not have been wise. Leniency could be viewed as weakness, in some quarters."

"Durla," Londo said very softly, "if you say one more word—just one—I will demonstrate my strength of moral character by breaking your neck with my bare hands. Yes?"

Durla, wisely, said nothing.

Londo walked away from him then and out into the corridor . . . only to discover Senna running toward him, looking quite distressed. He could surmise the reason. He tried to walk past her, but she would have none of it, instead saying, "Majesty! Timov, she—I—I thought everything was going so . . ." She threw up her hands in frustration. "I don't understand!"

"With any luck, Senna," Londo said, "you never will." And he headed off down the corridor.

Vir looked up forlornly as the door to the cell opened, and he gaped in astonishment when he saw Londo standing there.

"What am I doing here, Londo?" he demanded.

Londo glanced at the manacles and then called to the guards. "Unlock him. Release him."

"Release . . . you mean it's over? I can go? I . . ."

One of the guards walked in with the key and undid his manacles. They popped open and Vir rubbed his wrists, looking in utter confusion at Londo.

"It was a misunderstanding," Londo said.

"*A what?* Londo, you knocked me cold with a bottle of wine! Just because I said a name!"

"A name," Londo replied, "that, if you are very, very wise, you will never say to anyone, anywhere, ever again."

"Londo, listen to me—"

"No, Vir. I am the emperor now. I don't have to listen. That is one of the conveniences. You will listen. I will speak. And then you will leave." He took a deep breath, glanced at his shoulder, and then said, "We have different roads to walk down, Vir, you and I. And we must watch each other from a distance. Do you understand? A distance. The thing is . . . we cannot be hurt. Not really. Death holds no terror for either of us."

"It . . . it doesn't?"

"No. For we are protected, we two. Both of us. Protected by visions, protected by prophecy. You know of what I speak."

Vir, in fact, did. He knew of Londo's prophetic dream wherein he had seen himself, an old man, dying at the hands of G'Kar.

And Vir had been present when Lady Morella had made a prediction that both of them would be emperor, with one succeeding upon the death of the other. But she had not been specific as to who would be first to wear the white. Obviously it had been Londo. That meant that Vir would succeed to the throne upon Londo's passing, which meant that—until Vir actually ascended—he was safe from harm. At least, from fatal harm.

"We can tempt our fates," continued Londo, "but ultimately, they should be on our sides. Each of us, in our way and to a degree . . . is invincible. However, it is a funny thing about the fates. It's not wise to push them too far, because they have a tendency to push back. So . . . I suggest we pursue our destinies at a comfortable distance from each other, lest our mutual fates become crossed, and the result is to the liking of neither of us. So . . . swear to me that you will not speak of these matters again. That you will return to Babylon 5, and keep your head out of the line of fire. Can you swear that to me, Vir?"

Vir gave it a long moment's thought.

"No. I'm sorry, Londo . . . I can't," he said finally. "I will never stop hoping that you retreat from the road that you're walking. I will never stop searching for a means to turn you away from it. And I will never stop being your friend . . . even if, eventually, I find that I have become your enemy."

At which point Vir firmly expected that the manacles would be reattached to his hands, and that he would be tossed back into his cell, to be forgotten by all.

Instead, Londo smiled. Then he patted Vir on the shoulder and said, "Close enough." He gestured for the guards to follow him, and moments later, Vir was alone in the cell, the door wide open.

"Londo?" Vir called cautiously.

At that point, Vir was just paranoid enough to believe that—if he chose to walk through the door—he might be shot under the guise of being an escaping prisoner. But when he stuck his head out—fully prepared for it to be blown off—he saw no one in the corridor.

He walked cautiously down the hallway, then saw a door standing open at the end. He emerged into sunlight, possibly the sunniest day that he could recall in all his life on Centauri Prime.

Sunny . . . but there was a chill, as well. Although he couldn't quite be sure whether the chill was in the air, or in him.

As soon as he had taken several steps away, the door slammed shut behind him. Vir turned and saw that he was outside the palace. There was no way back in. That was all right with him; there really wasn't any place in there for him anymore. At least, not for the time being.

Durla felt as if he was having a reasonably good day. It wasn't going exactly the way that he had hoped . . . but all in all, it wasn't bad. He settled in behind his desk, prepared for the rest of the day to be fairly productive.

At that point, Kuto showed up, all joviality and pleasantry, and brought Durla the information he had requested. Calmly and methodically, he went over each name as Durla nodded, and listened to each one, and acted as if he cared about any of them aside from the one he was waiting for.

Then Kuto got to Mariel and her activities—where she had been, what she had been up to, and, most significantly, whom she had been up to it with.

Durla managed to contain his reaction, instead simply nodding and taking in that bit of information with the same equanimity with which he had attended to the other names. He actually managed to wait until after Kuto had left and was a significant distance from his office before he let out an agonized and strangled scream.

At that point, he didn't know whom he wanted to kill more: Vir Cotto, for whom he had had no assassination plans up until that point, or Londo Mollari, for whom he had a very detailed assassination plan all worked out. Either one, however, would give him extreme satisfaction.

In his private quarters, Londo Mollari watched the slowly receding figure of Timov, walking proudly away down the main walk, head held high, dignity intact. He thought, for some reason, that he heard a distant scream, and decided that it was simply his soul giving voice to its feelings.

Vir walked the perimeter of the palace, heading toward the main street. As he did so, he saw, not far away, Timov. She and a small entourage of guards were heading in the other direction. For just a moment, he was certain she clearly spotted him out of the corner of her eye, as she cast a half glance in his direction. Then, thrusting her chin out slightly, she pointedly turned away from him and walked off in another direction.

"Hello. Are you busy?"

The voice startled him. It came from his immediate right. He turned and saw, standing at the mouth of an alleyway, a cloaked figure, who he was already coming to know quite well. On either side of the figure, however, stood two more cloaked individuals whom he didn't know at all, one male, one female.

"Actually, Merlin, I'm not busy at all. Who are your associates?"

"These?" He nodded to the female and male in turn and said, "Gwynn . . . Finian . . . this is Vir. Vir here is going to help us save the galaxy . . . provided he's not doing anything important at the moment."

"No," Vir said, glancing in the direction of the palace, which now seemed very far off. "I won't be doing anything especially important for . . . oh, I'd guess at least a decade or so."

Gwynn looked him up and down with open skepticism. "Are you sure he's going to be of use to us?"

"Oh, absolutely," Vir responded, as if she had addressed him. "You see . . . I'm invincible."

"You're very fortunate," said Finian.

And Vir thought that, far off in one of the upper palace windows, he could see the small, distant and vague outline of Londo Mollari, looking out at the city and then turning away.

"More fortunate than some," said Vir. "Far more fortunate . . . than some."